ONE STOP TO THE STARS ...

"Space vehicles are grossly inefficient, even though rockets have reached almost the absolute limits of performance. What is the alternative?"

Morgan's listeners watched incredulously as he activated the display screen.

From a point of light simulating a satellite in synchronous orbit above the equator, two lines grew on the screen—one toward Earth, one toward space —representing the rigid, capsule-carrying tubes.

Fusion-powered, the capsules would carry freight and passengers at thousands of kilometers per hour to and from Earth's true spaceport at the far end of the line, where deep-space vessels would load and discharge and begin their epic voyages, free of the need to battle Earth's gravity and atmosphere.

Man's way to the stars would be opened at last —by an elevator 50,000 kilometers high!

Arthur C. Clarke, who pioneered the concept of the communications satellite decades before it became reality, here presents an even more daring speculation.

"IN HIS LATEST NOVEL, ARTHUR C. CLARKE ONCE AGAIN SOUNDS HIS GRAND THEME . . . MAN IS MOST HIMSELF WHEN HE STRIVES GREATLY, WHEN HE CHALLENGES THE VERY LAWS OF THE UNIVERSE . . .
—THE NEW YORK TIMES BOOK REVIEW

Also by Arthur C. Clarke
Published by Ballantine Books:

ARTHUR C. CLARKE

The Fountains of Paradise

A Del Rey Book

BALLANTINE BOOKS • NEW YORK

A Del Rey Book
Published by Ballantine Books

Library of Congress Catalog Card Number: 78-14072

ISBN 0-345-25356-6

This edition published by arrangement with
Harcourt Brace Jovanovich, Inc.

Manufactured in the United States of America

First Ballantine Books Edition: February 1980

Cover painting by Terry Oakes. Used by permission of Victor
Gollancz, Ltd.

To the still-unfading memory
of
LESLIE EKANAYAKE
(13 July 1947-4 July 1977)

only perfect friend of a lifetime,
in whom were uniquely combined
Loyalty, Intelligence and Compassion.

When your radiant and living spirit
vanished from this world,
the light went out of many lives.

NIRVANA PRĀPTO BHŪYĀT

Politics and religion are obsolete; the time has come for science and spirituality.

Sri Jawaharlal Nehru
To the Ceylon Association for the
Advancement of Science
Colombo, 15 October 1962

CONTENTS

Preface xiii

I. THE PALACE

II. THE TEMPLE

III. THE BELL

IV. THE TOWER

V. ASCENSION

PREFACE

"From Paradise to Taprobane is forty leagues; there may be heard the sound of the Fountains of Paradise."

Traditional
Reported by Friar Marignolli, A.D. 1335

The country I have called Taprobane does not quite exist, but is about ninety percent congruent with the island of Ceylon (now Sri Lanka). Though the Sources and Acknowledgments will make clear what locations, events, and personalities are based on fact, the reader will not go far wrong in assuming that the more unlikely the story, the closer it is to reality.

The name "Taprobane" is now usually spoken to rhyme with "plain," but the correct classical pronunciation is "Tap-ROB-a-nee"—as Milton, of course, in "Paradise Regained," Book IV, well knew:

"From India and the golden Chersoness
And utmost Indian Isle Taprobane. . . ."

I

THE PALACE

I

KALIDASA

The crown grew heavier with each passing year. When the Venerable Bodhidharma Mahanayake Thero had —so reluctantly—first placed it upon his head, Prince Kalidasa was surprised by its lightness. Now, twenty years later, King Kalidasa gladly relinquished the jewel-encrusted band of gold whenever court etiquette allowed.

There was little of that here, upon the wind-swept summit of the rock fortress; few envoys or petitioners sought audience on its forbidding heights. Many of those who made the journey to Yakkagala turned back at the final ascent, through the very jaws of the crouching lion that seemed always about to spring from the face of the rock.

An old king could never sit upon this heaven-aspiring throne. One day, Kalidasa would be too feeble to reach his own palace. But he doubted if that day would ever come; his many enemies would spare him the humiliations of age.

Those enemies were gathering now. He glanced toward the north, as if he could already see the armies of his half-brother, returning to claim the bloodstained throne of Taprobane. But that threat was still far off, across monsoon-riven seas. Although Kalidasa put more trust in his spies than in his astrologers, it was comforting to know that they agreed on this.

Malgara, making plans and gathering the support of

foreign kings, had waited almost twenty years. A yet more patient and subtle enemy lay much nearer at hand, forever watching from the southern sky.

The perfect cone of Sri Kanda, the Sacred Mountain, looked very close today as it towered above the central plain. Since the beginning of history, it had struck awe into the heart of every man who saw it. Always, Kalidasa was aware of its brooding presence, and of the power that it symbolized.

And yet the Mahanayake Thero had no armies, no screaming war elephants tossing brazen tusks as they charged into battle. The High Priest was only an old man in an orange robe, whose sole material possessions were a begging bowl and a palm leaf to shield him from the sun. While the lesser monks and acolytes chanted the scriptures around him, he merely sat in cross-legged silence—and somehow tampered with the destinies of kings. It was very strange. . . .

The air was so clear today that Kalidasa could see the temple, dwarfed by distance to a tiny white arrowhead on the very summit of Sri Kanda. It did not look like any work of man, and it reminded the King of the still-greater mountains he had glimpsed in his youth, when he had been half guest, half hostage at the court of Mahinda the Great. All the giants that guarded Mahinda's empire bore such crowns, formed of a dazzling, crystalline substance for which there was no word in the language of Taprobane. The Hindus believed that it was a kind of water, magically transformed, but Kalidasa laughed at such superstitions.

That ivory gleam was only three days' march away —one along the royal road, through forests and paddy fields, two more up the winding stairway that he could never climb again, because at its end was the only enemy he feared, and could not conquer. Sometimes he envied the pilgrims, when he saw their torches marking a thin line of fire up the face of the mountain. The humblest beggar could greet that holy dawn and receive the blessings of the gods; the ruler of all this land could not.

But he had his consolations, if only for a little while. Guarded by moat and rampart lay the pools and fountains and pleasure gardens on which he had lavished the wealth of his kingdom. And when he was tired of these, there were the ladies of the rock—the ones of flesh and blood, whom he summoned less and less frequently, and the two hundred changeless immortals, with whom he often shared his thoughts, because there were no others he could trust.

Thunder boomed along the western sky. Kalidasa turned away from the brooding menace of the mountain, toward the distant hope of rain. The monsoon was late this season. The artificial lakes that fed the island's complex irrigation system were almost empty. By this time of year, he should have seen the glint of water in the mightiest of them all—which, as he well knew, his subjects still dared to call by his father's name: Paravana Samudra, the Sea of Paravana.

It had been completed only thirty years ago, after generations of toil. In happier days, young Prince Kalidasa had stood proudly beside his father when the great sluice gates were opened and the life-giving waters had poured out across the thirsty land. In all the kingdom, there was no lovelier sight than the gently rippling mirror of that immense, man-made lake when it reflected the domes and spires of Ranapura, City of Gold, the ancient capital which he had abandoned for his dream.

Once more the thunder rolled, but Kalidasa knew that its promise was false. Even here on the summit of Demon Rock, the air hung still and lifeless; there were none of the sudden, random gusts that heralded the onset of the monsoon. Before the rains came at last, famine might be added to his troubles.

"Majesty," said the patient voice of the Chamberlain, "the envoys are about to leave. They wish to pay their respects."

Ah yes, those two pale ambassadors from across the western ocean! He would be sorry to see them go, for they had brought news, in their abominable Taprobani, of many wonders—though none, they were willing to admit, that equaled this fortress-palace in the sky.

Kalidasa turned his back upon the white-capped mountain and the parched, shimmering landscape and began to descend the granite steps to the audience chamber. Behind him, the Chamberlain and his aides bore gifts of ivory and gems for the tall, proud men who were waiting to say farewell. Soon they would carry the treasures of Taprobane across the sea, to a city younger by centuries than Ranapura; and perhaps, for a little while, divert the brooding thoughts of the Emperor Hadrian.

His robes a flare of orange against the white plaster of the temple walls, the Mahanayake Thero walked slowly to the northern parapet. Far below lay the checkerboard of paddy fields stretching from horizon to horizon, the dark lines of irrigation channels, the blue gleam of the Paravana Samudra—and, beyond that inland sea, the sacred domes of Ranapura floating like ghostly bubbles, impossibly huge when one realized their true distance. For thirty years he had watched that ever-changing panorama, but he knew that he would never grasp all the details of its fleeting complexity. Colors, boundaries altered with every season—indeed, with every passing cloud. On the day that he, too, passed, thought Bodhidharma, he would still see something new.

Only one thing jarred in all this exquisitely patterned landscape. Tiny though it appeared from this altitude, the gray boulder of Demon Rock seemed an alien intruder. Legend had it that Yakkagala was a fragment of the herb-bearing Himalayan peak that the monkey god Hanuman had dropped as he hastily carried both medicine and mountain to his injured comrades when the battles of the *Ramayana* were over.

From this distance, it was impossible, of course, to see any details of Kalidasa's folly, except for a faint line that hinted at the outer rampart of the pleasure gardens. Yet once it had been experienced, such was the impact of Demon Rock that it was impossible to forget it. The Mahanayake Thero could see in imagination, as clearly as if he stood between them, the immense lion's claws protruding from the sheer face of the cliff, while overhead loomed the battlements upon which, it was easy to believe, the accursed King still walked. . . .

Thunder crashed down from above, rising swiftly to such a crescendo of power that it seemed to shake the mountain itself. In a continuous, sustained concussion it raced across the sky, dwindling away into the east. For long seconds, echoes rolled around the rim of the horizon.

No one could mistake *this* as any herald of the coming rains. They were not scheduled for another three weeks, and Monsoon Control was never in error by more than twenty-four hours. When the reverberations had died away, the High Priest turned to his companion.

"So much for designated re-entry corridors," he said, with slightly more annoyance than an exponent of the Dharma should permit himself. "Did we get a meter reading?"

The younger monk spoke briefly into his wrist microphone, and waited for a reply.

"Yes—it peaked at a hundred and twenty. That's five db above the previous record."

"Send the usual protest to Kennedy or Gagarin Control, whichever it is. On second thought, complain to them *both*. Not that it will make any difference, of course."

As his eye traced the slowly dissolving vapor trail across the sky, the Venerable Bodhidharma Mahanayake Thero—eighty-fifth of his name—had a sudden and most unmonkish fantasy: Kalidasa would have had a suitable treatment for space-line operators who thought only of dollars per kilo to orbit—something that probably involved impalement, or metal-shod elephants, or boiling oil.

But life, of course, had been so much simpler, two thousand years ago.

2

THE ENGINEER

His friends, whose numbers sadly dwindled every year, called him Johan. The world, when it remembered him, called him Raja. His full name epitomized five hundred years of history: Johan Oliver de Alwis Sri Rajasinghe.

There had been a time when the tourists visiting Demon Rock had sought him out with cameras and recorders, but now a whole generation knew nothing of the days when his was the most familiar face in the solar system. He did not regret his past glory, for it had brought him the gratitude of all mankind. But it had also brought vain regrets for the mistakes he had made, and sorrow for the lives he had squandered, when a little more foresight or patience might have saved them.

It was easy now, with the perspective of history, to see what *should* have been done to avert the Auckland Crisis, or to assemble the unwilling signatories of the Treaty of Samarkand. To blame himself for the unavoidable errors of the past was folly; yet there were times when his conscience hurt him more than the fading twinges of that old Patagonian bullet. . . .

No one had believed that his retirement would last so long. "You'll be back within six months," World President Chu had told him. "Power is addictive."

"Not to *me*," he had answered, truthfully enough.

For power had come to him; he had never sought it.

8

And it had always been a special, limited kind of power—advisory, not executive. He was only Special Assistant (Acting Ambassador) for Political Affairs, directly responsible to President and Council, with a staff that never exceeded ten—eleven, if one included ARISTOTLE. (His own console still had direct access to Ari's memory and processing banks, and they talked to each other several times a year.) But toward the end, the Council had invariably accepted his advice, and the world had given him much of the credit that should have gone to the unsung, unhonored bureaucrats of the Peace Division.

And so it was Ambassador-at-Large Rajasinghe who got all the publicity, as he moved from one trouble spot to another, massaging egos here, defusing crises there, and manipulating the truth with consummate skill. Never actually lying, of course; that would have been fatal. Without Ari's infallible memory, he could never have kept control of the intricate webs he was sometimes compelled to spin, in order that mankind might live in peace. When he had begun to enjoy the game for its own sake, he knew it was time to quit.

That had been twenty years ago, and he had never regretted his decision. Those who predicted that boredom would succeed where the temptations of power had failed did not know their man or understand his origins. He had gone back to the fields and forests of his youth, and was living only a kilometer from the great, brooding rock that had dominated his childhood. Indeed, his villa was actually inside the wide moat that surrounded the pleasure gardens, and the fountains that Kalidasa's architect had designed now splashed in Johan's own courtyard, after a silence of two thousand years. The water flowed in the original stone conduits; nothing had been changed, except that the cisterns high up on the rock were now filled by electric pumps, not relays of sweating slaves.

Securing this history-drenched piece of land for his retirement had given Johan more satisfaction than anything in his whole career, fulfilling a dream that he had never really believed could come true. The achievement had required all his diplomatic skills, plus some delicate blackmail in the Department of Archaeology. Later, questions had been asked in the State Assembly; but fortunately not answered.

He was insulated from all but the most determined tourists and students by an extension of the moat, and screened from their gaze by a thick wall of mutated Ashoka trees, blazing with flowers throughout the year. The trees also supported several families of monkeys, who were amusing to watch but occasionally invaded the villa and made off with any portable objects that took their fancy. Then there would be a brief interspecies war, with firecrackers and recorded danger cries that distressed the humans at least as much as the simians—who would be back quickly enough, since they had long ago learned that no one would really harm them.

One of Taprobane's more outrageous sunsets was transfiguring the western sky when a small electrotricycle came silently through the trees and drew up beside the granite columns of the portico. (Genuine Chola, from the late Ranapura period, and therefore a complete anachronism here. But only Professor Paul Sarath had ever commented on it; and of course he invariably did so.)

Through long and bitter experience, Rajasinghe had learned never to trust first impressions, but also never to ignore them. He had half expected that Vannevar Morgan would, like his achievements, be a large, imposing man. Instead, the engineer was well below average height, and at first glance might have been called frail. That slender body was all sinew, however, and the raven-black hair framed a face that looked considerably younger than its fifty-one years.

The video display from Ari's Biog file had not done him justice. He should have been a romantic poet, or a concert pianist—or, perhaps, a great actor, holding thousands spellbound by his skill. Rajasinghe knew power when he saw it, since power had been his business; and it was power that he was facing now. Beware of small men, he had often told himself, because they are the movers and shakers of the world.

And with this thought, there came the first flicker of apprehension. Almost every week, old friends and old enemies came to this remote spot, to exchange news and to reminisce about the past. He welcomed such visits; they gave a continuing pattern to his life. Yet he always knew, to a high degree of accuracy, the purpose of the meeting, and the ground that would be covered.

But as far as Rajasinghe was aware, he and Morgan had no interests in common beyond those of any men in this day and age. They had never met or had any prior communication. Indeed, he had barely recognized Morgan's name. Still more unusual was the fact that the engineer had asked him to keep this meeting confidential.

Though Rajasinghe had complied, he had done so with a feeling of resentment. There was no need, any more, for secrecy in his peaceful life. The very last thing he wanted now was for some important mystery to impinge upon his well-ordered existence. He had finished with Security forever. Ten years ago—or was it even longer?—his personal guards had been removed, at his own request.

What upset him most was not the mild secrecy, but his own total bewilderment. The Chief Engineer (Land) of the Terran Construction Corporation was not going to travel thousands of kilometers merely to ask for his autograph, or to express the usual tourist platitudes. He must have come here for some specific purpose—and, try as he might, Rajasinghe was unable to imagine it.

Even in his days as a public servant, Rajasinghe had never had occasion to deal with TCC. Its three divisions—Land, Sea, Space—huge though they were, made perhaps the least news of all the World Federation's specialized bodies. Only when there was some resounding technical failure, or a head-on collision with an environmental or historical group, did TCC emerge from the shadows. The last confrontation of this kind had involved the Antarctic Pipeline, that miracle of twenty-first-century engineering, built to pump fluidized coal from the vast polar deposits to the power plants and factories of the world. In a mood of ecological euphoria, TCC had proposed demolishing the last remaining section of the pipeline and restoring the land to the penguins.

Instantly, there had been cries of protest from the industrial archaeologists, outraged at such vandalism, and from the naturalists, who pointed out that the penguins simply loved the abandoned pipeline. It had provided housing of a standard they had never before enjoyed, and thus contributed to a population explosion that the killer whales could barely handle. So TCC had surrendered without a fight.

Rajasinghe did not know if Morgan had been associated with this minor debacle. It hardly mattered, since his name was now linked with TCC's greatest triumph. . . .

The Ultimate Bridge, it had been christened; and perhaps with justice. Rajasinghe had watched, with half the world, when the final section was lifted gently skyward by the *Graf Zeppelin II*—itself one of the marvels of the age. All the airship's luxurious fittings had been removed to save weight, the famous swimming pool had been drained, and the reactors pumped their excess heat into the gasbags to give extra lift. It was the first time that a dead weight of more than a thousand tons had ever been hoisted three kilometers straight up into the sky, and everything—doubtless to the disappointment of millions—had gone without a hitch.

No ship would ever again pass the Pillars of Hercules without saluting the mightiest bridge that man had ever built—or, in all probability, would ever build. The twin towers at the junction of Mediterranean and Atlantic were themselves the tallest structures in the world, and faced each other across fifteen kilometers of space—empty except for the incredible, delicate arch of the Gibraltar Bridge. It would be a privilege to meet the man who had conceived it; even though he was an hour late. . . .

"My apologies, Ambassador," said Morgan as he climbed out of the electrotricycle. "I hope the delay hasn't inconvenienced you."

"Not at all. My time is my own. You've eaten, I hope?"

"Yes. When they canceled my Rome connection, at least they gave me an excellent lunch."

"Probably better than you'd get at the Hotel Yakkagala. I've arranged a room for the night—it's only a kilometer from here. I'm afraid we'll have to postpone our discussion until breakfast."

Morgan looked disappointed, but gave a shrug of acquiescence.

"Well, I've plenty of work to keep me busy. I assume that the hotel has full executive facilities—or at least a standard terminal."

Rajasinghe laughed.

"I wouldn't guarantee anything much more sophisticated than a telephone. But I have a better suggestion. In just over half an hour, I'm taking some friends to the Rock. There's a *son-et-lumière* performance that I strongly recommend, and you're welcome to join us."

He could tell that Morgan was hesitating, as he tried to think of a polite excuse.

"That's very kind of you, but I really must get in touch with my office."

"You can use my console. I can promise you—you'll find the show fascinating, and it lasts only an hour. . . . Oh, I forgot—you don't want anyone to know you're here. Well, I'll introduce you as Dr. Smith from the University of Tasmania. I'm sure my friends won't recognize you."

Rajasinghe had no intention of offending his visitor, but there was no mistaking Morgan's brief flash of irritation. The former diplomat's instincts automatically came into play; he filed the reaction for future reference.

"I'm sure they won't," Morgan said, and Rajasinghe noted the unmistakable tone of bitterness in his voice. "Dr. Smith will be fine. And now—if I could use your console."

Interesting, thought Rajasinghe as he led his guest into the villa, but probably not important. Provisional hypothesis: Morgan is a frustrated, perhaps even a disappointed, man. It was hard to see why, since he was one of the leaders of his profession. What *more* could he want?

There was one obvious answer. Rajasinghe knew the symptoms well, if only because in his case the disease had long since burned itself out.

"Fame is the spur . . ." he recited in the silence of his thoughts. How did the rest of it go? "(That last infirmity of noble mind) / To scorn delights, and live laborious days."

Yes, that might explain the discontent his still-sensitive antennae had detected. And he suddenly recalled that the immense rainbow linking Europe and

Africa was almost invariably called *the* Bridge, sometimes the Ultimate Bridge or the Gibraltar Bridge—but never Morgan's Bridge.

Well, Rajasinghe thought, if you're looking for fame, Dr. Morgan, you won't find it here. So why in the name of a thousand *yakkas* have you come to quiet little Taprobane?

3

THE FOUNTAINS

For days, elephants and slaves had toiled in the cruel sun, hauling the endless chains of buckets up the face of the cliff. "Is it ready?" the King had asked, time and again. "No, Majesty," the master craftsman had answered. "The tank is not yet full. But tomorrow, perhaps . . ."

Tomorrow had come at last, and now the whole court was gathered in the pleasure gardens, beneath awnings of brightly colored cloth. The King himself was cooled by large fans, waved by supplicants who had bribed the Chamberlain for this risky privilege. It was an honor that might lead to riches, or to death.

All eyes were on the face of the Rock, and the tiny figures moving upon its summit. A flag fluttered; far below, a horn sounded briefly. At the base of the cliff, workmen frantically manipulated levers, hauled on ropes. For a long time, nothing happened.

A frown began to spread across the face of the King, and the whole court trembled. Even the waving fans lost momentum for a few seconds, only to speed up again as the wielders recalled the hazards of their task.

Then a great shout came from the workers at the foot of Yakkagala—a cry of joy and triumph that swept steadily closer and closer as it was taken up all along the flower-lined paths. And with it came another sound, one not so loud, yet giving the impression

16

of irresistible, pent-up forces, rushing toward their goal.

One after the other, springing from the earth as if by magic, the slim columns of water leaped toward the cloudless sky. At four times the height of a man, they burst into flowers of spray. The sunlight, breaking through them, created a rainbow-hued mist that added to the strangeness and beauty of the scene. Never, in the whole history of Taprobane, had the eyes of men witnessed such a wonder.

The King smiled, and the courtiers dared to breathe again. This time, the buried pipes had not burst beneath the weight of water; unlike their luckless predecessors, the masons who had laid them had as good a chance of reaching old age as anyone who labored for Kalidasa.

Almost as imperceptibly as the westering sun, the jets were losing altitude. Presently they were no taller than a man; the painfully filled reservoirs were nearly drained. But the King was well satisfied; he lifted his hand, and the fountains dipped and rose again as if in one last curtsy before the throne, then silently collapsed. For a little while, ripples raced back and forth across the surface of the reflecting pools, before they once again became still mirrors, framing the image of the eternal Rock.

"The workmen have done well," said Kalidasa. "Give them their freedom."

How well, of course, they would never understand, for none could share the lonely visions of an artist-king. As Kalidasa surveyed the exquisitely tended gardens that surrounded Yakkagala, he felt as much contentment as he would ever know.

Here, at the foot of Demon Rock, he had conceived and created Paradise. There only remained, upon its summit, to build Heaven.

4

DEMON ROCK

The cunningly contrived pageant of light and sound still had power to move Rajasinghe, though he had seen it a dozen times and knew every trick of the programing. To see it was, of course, obligatory for every visitor to the Rock, though critics like Paul Sarath complained that it was merely instant history for tourists. Yet instant history was better than no history at all, and it would have to serve while Sarath and his colleagues continued vociferously to disagree about the precise sequence of events here two thousand years ago.

The little amphitheater faced the western wall of Yakkagala, its two hundred seats all carefully orientated so that each spectator looked up into the laser projectors at the correct angle. The performance always began at exactly the same time throughout the year—1900 hours—as the last glow of the invariant equatorial sunset faded from the sky.

Already, it was so dark that the Rock was invisible, revealing its presence only as a huge black shadow eclipsing the early stars. Out of that darkness, there came the slow beating of a muffled drum, and presently a calm, dispassionate voice:

"This is the story of a king who murdered his father and was killed by his brother. In the bloodstained history of mankind, that is nothing new. But *this* king

18

left an abiding monument; and a legend that has endured for centuries."

Rajasinghe stole a glance at Vannevar Morgan, sitting there in the darkness on his right. Though he could see the engineer's features only in silhouette, he could tell that his visitor was already caught in the spell of the narration. On his left, his other two guests, old friends from his diplomatic days, were equally entranced. As he had assured Morgan, they had not recognized Dr. Smith; or, if they had, they had politely accepted the fiction.

"His name was Kalidasa, and he was born a hundred years after Christ, in Ranapura, City of Gold —for centuries the capital of the Taprobanean kings. But there was a shadow across his birth. . . ."

The music became louder as flutes and strings joined the throbbing drum to trace a haunting, regal melody in the night air. A point of light began to burn on the face of the Rock; abruptly, it expanded, and suddenly it seemed that a magic window had opened into the past, to reveal a world more vivid and colorful than life itself.

The dramatization, thought Morgan, was excellent. He was glad that, for once, he had let courtesy override his impulse to work. He saw the joy of King Paravana when his favorite concubine presented him with his first-born son—and understood how that joy was both augmented and diminished when, only twenty-four hours later, the Queen herself produced a better claimant to the throne. Though first in time, Kalidasa would not be first in precedence; and so the stage was set for tragedy.

"Yet in the early years of their boyhood, Kalidasa and his half-brother, Malgara, were the closest of friends. They grew up together quite unconscious of their rival destinies, and the intrigues that festered around them. The first cause of trouble had nothing to do with the accident of birth; it was only a well-intentioned, innocent gift. . . .

"To the court of King Paravana came envoys bearing tribute from many lands—silk from Cathay, gold from Hindustan, burnished armor from Imperial Rome. And one day a simple hunter from the jungle ventured into the great city bearing a gift that he hoped would please the royal family. . . ."

Morgan heard, all around him, a chorus of involuntary "oooh"'s and "aah"'s from his unseen companions. Although he had never been fond of animals, he had to admit that the tiny snow-white monkey that nestled so trustingly in the arms of young Prince Kalidasa was most endearing. Out of the wrinkled little face two huge eyes stared across the centuries —and across the mysterious, yet not wholly unbridgeable, gulf between man and beast.

"According to the chronicles, nothing like it had ever been seen before. Its hair was white as milk, its eyes pink as rubies. Some thought it a good omen; others, an evil one, because white is the color of death and of mourning. And their fears, alas, were well founded. . . .

"Prince Kalidasa loved his little pet, and called it Hanuman, after the valiant monkey god of the *Ramayana*. The King's jeweler constructed a small golden cart, in which Hanuman would sit solemnly while he was drawn through the court, to the amusement and delight of all who watched.

"For his part, Hanuman loved Kalidasa, and would allow no one else to handle him. He was especially jealous of Prince Malgara—almost as if he sensed the rivalry to come. And then, one unlucky day, he bit the heir to the throne. . . .

"The bite was trifling; its consequences, immense. A few days later, Hanuman was poisoned—doubtless by order of the Queen. That was the end of Kalidasa's childhood. Thereafter, it is said, he never loved or trusted another human being. And his friendship with Malgara turned to bitter enmity.

"Nor was this the only trouble that stemmed from the death of one small monkey. By command of the King, a special tomb was built for Hanuman, in the shape of the traditional bell-shaped shrine, or dagoba.

"Now this was an extraordinary thing to do, for it aroused the instant hostility of the monks. Dagobas were reserved for relics of the Buddha, and this act appeared to be one of deliberate sacrilege.

"Indeed, that may well have been its intention, because King Paravana had come under the sway of a Hindu swami and was turning against the Buddhist faith. Although Prince Kalidasa was too young to be involved in this conflict, much of the monks' hatred was now directed against him. So began a feud that in the years to come was to tear the kingdom apart. . . .

"Like many of the other tales recorded in the ancient chronicles of Taprobane, for almost two thousand years there was no proof that the story of Hanuman and young Prince Kalidasa was anything but a charming legend. Then, in 2015, a team of Harvard archaeologists discovered the foundations of a small shrine in the grounds of the old Ranapura Palace. The shrine appeared to have been deliberately destroyed. All the brickwork of the superstructure had vanished.

"The usual relic chamber set in the foundations was empty, apparently robbed of its contents centuries ago. But the students had tools of which the old-time treasure hunters never dreamed. Their neutrino survey disclosed a second relic chamber, much deeper. The upper one was only a decoy, and it had served its purpose well. The lower chamber still held the burden of love and hate it had carried down the centuries—to its resting place today, in the Ranapura Museum."

Morgan had always considered himself, with justification, reasonably hardheaded and unsentimental, not prone to gusts of emotion. Yet now, to his considerable embarrassment—he hoped that his companions wouldn't notice—he felt his eyes brim with sudden tears. How ridiculous, he told himself angrily, that some saccharine music and maudlin narration could have such an impact on a sensible man! He would never have believed that the sight of a child's toy could have set him weeping.

And then he knew, in a lightning flash of memory that brought back a moment more than forty years in the past, why he had been so deeply moved. He saw again his beloved kite, dipping and weaving above the Sydney park where he had spent much of his childhood. He could feel the warmth of the sun, the gentle wind on his bare back—the treacherous wind that suddenly failed, so that the kite plunged earthward. It became snagged in the branches of the giant oak that was supposed to be older than the country itself, and, foolishly, he tugged at the string, trying to pull it free. It was his first lesson in the strength of materials, and one that he was never to forget.

The string had broken, just at the point of capture, and the kite had rolled crazily away in the summer sky, slowly losing altitude. He had rushed down to the water's edge, hoping that it would fall on land; but the wind would not listen to the prayers of a little boy.

For a long time he had stood weeping as he watched the shattered fragments, like some dismasted sailboat, drift across the great harbor and out toward the open sea, until they were lost from sight. That had been the first of those trivial tragedies that shape a man's childhood, whether he remembers them or not.

Yet what Morgan had lost then was only an inanimate toy; his tears were of frustration rather than grief. Prince Kalidasa had much deeper cause for anguish. Inside the little golden cart, which still looked as if it had come straight from the craftman's workshop, was a bundle of tiny white bones.

Morgan missed some of the history that followed. When he had cleared his eyes, a dozen years had passed, a complex family quarrel was in progress, and he was not quite sure who was murdering whom. After the armies had ceased to clash and the last dagger had fallen, Prince Malgara and the Queen Mother had fled to India, and Kalidasa had seized the throne, imprisoning his father in the process.

That the usurper had refrained from executing Paravana was not due to any filial devotion, but to his belief that the old King possessed some secret treasure, which he was saving for Malgara. As long as Kalidasa believed this, Paravana knew that he was safe. At last, however, he grew tired of the deception.

"I will show you my real wealth," he told his son. "Give me a chariot, and I will take you to it."

But on his last journey, unlike little Hanuman, Paravana rode in a decrepit oxcart. The chronicles record that it had a damaged wheel, which squeaked all the way—the sort of detail that must be true, because no historian would have bothered to invent it.

To Kalidasa's surprise, his father ordered the cart to carry him to the great artificial lake that irrigated the central kingdom, the completion of which had occupied most of his reign. He walked along the edge of the huge bund and gazed at his own statue, twice life-size, which looked out across the waters.

"Farewell, old friend," he said, addressing the towering stone figure that symbolized his lost power and glory and that held forever in its hands the stone map of this inland sea. "Protect my heritage."

Then, closely watched by Kalidasa and his guards, he descended the spillway steps, not pausing at the edge of the lake. When he was waist-deep, he scooped up the water and threw it over his head, then turned toward Kalidasa with pride and triumph.

"*Here,* my son," he cried, waving toward the leagues of pure life-giving water, "here—*here* is all my wealth!"

"Kill him!" screamed Kalidasa, mad with rage and disappointment.

And the soldiers obeyed.

So Kalidasa became the master of Taprobane, but at a price that few men would be willing to pay: as the chronicles recorded, always he lived "in fear of the next world, and of his brother." Sooner or later, Malgara would return to seek his rightful throne.

For a few years, like the long line of kings before him, Kalidasa held court in Ranapura. Then, for reasons of which history is silent, he abandoned the royal capital for the isolated rock monolith of Yakkagala, forty kilometers away in the jungle.

There were some who argued that he sought an impregnable fortress, safe from the vengeance of his brother. Yet in the end he spurned its protection. If it was merely a citadel, why was Yakkagala surrounded by immense pleasure gardens whose construction must have demanded as much labor as the walls and moat themselves? Above all, *why the frescoes?*

As the narrator posed this question, the entire western face of the rock materialized out of the darkness—not as it was now, but as it must have been two thousand years ago. A band, starting a hundred meters from the ground and running the full width of the rock, had been smoothed and covered with plaster, upon which were portrayed scores of beautiful women, life-size and from the waist upward. Some were in profile, others full-face, and all followed the same basic pattern.

Ocher-skinned, voluptuously bosomed, they were clad either in jewels alone or in the most transparent of upper garments. Some wore towering and elaborate headdresses; others, apparently, crowns. Many carried bowls of flowers, or held single blossoms nipped delicately between thumb and forefinger. Though about half were darker-skinned than their companions, and appeared to be handmaidens, they were no less elaborately coiffured and bejeweled.

"Once, there were more than two hundred figures. But the rains and winds of centuries have destroyed all except twenty, which were protected by an overhanging ledge of rock. . . ."

The image zoomed forward. One by one, the last survivors of Kalidasa's dream came floating out of the darkness, to the hackneyed yet singularly appropriate music of "Anitra's Dance." Defaced though they were by weather, decay, and vandals, they had lost none of their beauty down the ages. The colors were fresh, unfaded by the light of more than half a million westering suns. Goddesses or women, they had kept alive the legend of Demon Rock.

"No one knows who they were, what they represented, and *why* they were created with such labor, in so inaccessible a spot. The favorite theory is that they were celestial beings, and that all Kalidasa's efforts here were devoted to creating a heaven on earth, with its attendant goddesses. Perhaps he believed himself a god-king, as the Pharaohs of Egypt had; perhaps that is why he borrowed from them the image of the Sphinx, guarding the entrance to his palace."

Now the scene shifted to a distant view of the Rock, seen reflected in the small lake at its base. The water trembled; the outlines of Yakkagala wavered and dissolved. When they had reformed, the Rock was crowned by walls and battlements and spires, clinging to its entire upper surface. It was impossible to see them clearly; they remained tantalizingly out of focus, like the images in a dream. No man would ever know what Kalidasa's aerial palace had really looked like, before it was destroyed by those who sought to extirpate his very name.

"And here he lived, for twenty years, awaiting the doom that he knew would come. His spies must have told him that, with the help of the kings of southern Hindustan, Malgara was patiently gathering his armies.

"And at last Malgara came. From the summit of the Rock, Kalidasa saw the invaders marching from the north. Perhaps he believed himself impregnable; but he did not put that belief to the test.

"He left the safety of his great fortress and rode out to meet his brother on the neutral ground between the two armies. One would give much to know what words they spoke, at that last encounter. Some say they embraced before they parted. It may be true.

"Then the armies met, like the waves of the sea. Kalidasa was fighting on his own territory, with men who knew the land, and at first it seemed certain that victory would go to him. But then occurred another of those accidents that determine the fate of nations.

"Kalidasa's great war elephant, caparisoned with the royal banners, turned aside to avoid a patch of marshy ground. The defenders thought that the King was retreating. Their morale broke. They scattered, as the chronicles record, like chaff from the winnowing fan.

"Kalidasa was found on the battlefield, dead by his own hand. Malgara became king. And Yakkagala was abandoned to the jungle, not to be discovered again for seventeen hundred years."

5

THROUGH THE TELESCOPE

"My secret vice," Rajasinghe called it, with wry amusement but also with regret. It had been years since he had climbed to the summit of Yakkagala, and though he could fly there whenever he wished, that did not give the same feeling of achievement. To do it the easy way bypassed the most fascinating architectural details of the ascent. No one could hope to understand the mind of Kalidasa without following his footsteps all the way from pleasure gardens to aerial palace.

But there was a substitute, which could give an aging man considerable satisfaction. Years ago, he had acquired a compact and powerful twenty-centimeter telescope. Through it he could roam the entire western wall of the Rock, retracing the path he had followed to the summit so many times in the past. When he peered through the binocular eyepiece, he could easily imagine that he was hanging in mid-air, close enough to the sheer granite wall to reach out and touch it.

In the late afternoon, as the rays of the westering sun reached beneath the rock overhang that protected them, Rajasinghe would visit the frescoes, and pay tribute to the ladies of the court. Though he loved them all, he had his favorites. Sometimes he would talk silently to them, using the most archaic words and phrases he knew, well aware of the fact that his oldest Taprobani lay a thousand years in *their* future.

It also amused him to watch the living, and to study their reactions as they scrambled up the Rock, took photographs of each other on the summit, or admired the frescoes. They could have no idea that they were accompanied by an invisible—and envious—spectator, moving effortlessly beside them like a silent ghost, and so close that he could see every expression and every detail of their clothing. Such was the power of the telescope that if Rajasinghe had been able to lip-read, he could have eavesdropped on the tourists' conversations.

If this was voyeurism, it was harmless enough, and his little "vice" was hardly a secret, since he was delighted to share it with visitors. The telescope provided one of the best introductions to Yakkagala, and it had often served other useful purposes. Rajasinghe had several times alerted the guards to attempted souvenir hunting, and more than one astonished tourist had been caught carving his initials on the face of the Rock.

Rajasinghe seldom used the telescope in the morning, because the sun was then on the far side of Yakkagala and little could be seen on the shadowed western face. And as far as he could recall, he had *never* used it so soon after dawn, while he was still enjoying the delightful local custom of "bed-tea," introduced by the European planters three centuries ago.

Yet now, as he glanced out the wide picture window that gave him an almost complete view of Yakkagala, he was surprised to see a tiny figure moving along the crest of the Rock, partly silhouetted against the sky. Visitors never climbed to the top so soon after dawn; the guard wouldn't even unlock the elevator to the frescoes for another hour. Idly, Rajasinghe wondered who the early bird could be.

He rolled out of bed, slipped into a bright batik sarong, and made his way out to the veranda and

thence to the stout concrete pillar supporting the telescope. Making a mental note, for about the fiftieth
time, that he really should get the instrument a new
dust cover, he swung the stubby barrel toward the
Rock.

I might have guessed it! he said to himself, with
considerable pleasure, as he switched to high power.
So last night's show had impressed Morgan, as well it
should have done. The engineer was seeing for himself, in the short time available, how Kalidasa's archi-
tects had met the challenge imposed upon them.

Then Rajasinghe noticed something quite alarming.
Morgan was walking briskly around at the very edge
of the plateau, just centimeters away from the sheer
drop that few tourists ever dared to approach. Not
many had the courage even to sit in the Elephant
Throne, with their feet dangling over the abyss; but
now the engineer was actually kneeling beside it,
holding on to the carved stonework with one casual
arm, and leaning right out into nothingness as he surveyed the rock face below. Rajasinghe, who had never
been happy with even such familiar heights as Yakkagala's, could scarcely bear to watch.

After a few minutes of incredulous observation, he
decided that Morgan must be one of those rare people
who are completely unaffected by heights. Rajasinghe's memory, which was still excellent but delighted in playing tricks on him, was trying to bring
something to his notice. Hadn't there once been a
Frenchman who had tightroped across Niagara Falls,
and even stopped in the middle to cook a meal? If the
documentary evidence had not been overwhelming,
Rajasinghe would never have believed such a story.

And there was something else that was relevant
here—an incident that concerned Morgan himself.
What could it possibly be? Morgan . . . Morgan . . .
He had known virtually nothing about him until a
week ago. . . .

Yes, *that* was it. There had been a brief controversy that had amused the news media for a day or so, and that must have been the first time he had ever heard Morgan's name.

The Chief Engineer of the proposed Gibraltar Bridge had announced a startling innovation. Because all vehicles would be on automatic guidance, there was absolutely no point in having parapets or guardrails at the edge of the roadway. Eliminating them would save thousands of tons.

Of course, everyone thought that this was a perfectly horrible idea. What would happen, the public demanded, if some car's guidance failed and the vehicle headed toward the edge?

The Chief Engineer had the answers. Unfortunately, he had rather too many.

If the guidance failed, the brakes would go on automatically, as everyone knew, and the vehicle would stop in less than a hundred meters. Only in the outermost lanes was there any possibility that a car could go over the edge, and that would require a total failure of guidance, sensors, *and* brakes, and might happen once in twenty years.

So far, so good. But then the Chief Engineer added a caveat. Perhaps he did not intend it for publication; possibly he was half joking. He went on to say that if such an accident did occur, the quicker the car went over the edge, without damaging his beautiful bridge, the happier he would be. . . .

Needless to say, the Bridge was eventually built with wire deflector cables along the outer lanes, and, as far as Rajasinghe knew, no one had yet taken a high dive into the Mediterranean. Morgan, however, appeared suicidally determined to sacrifice himself to gravity here on Yakkagala. Otherwise, it was hard to account for his actions.

Now what was he doing? He was on his· knees at the side of the Elephant Throne, and was holding a small rectangular box, about the shape and size of an old-fashioned book. Rajasinghe could catch only glimpses of it, and the manner in which the engineer was using it made no sense at all. Possibly it was some kind of analysis device, though he did not see why Morgan should be interested in the composition of Yakkagala.

Was he planning to build something here? Not that it would be allowed, of course, and Rajasinghe could imagine no conceivable attractions for such a site; megalomaniac kings were fortunately now in short supply. In any event, he was quite certain, from the engineer's reactions on the previous evening, that Morgan had never heard of Yakkagala before coming to Taprobane.

And then Rajasinghe, who had always prided himself on his self-control even in the most dramatic and unexpected situations, gave an involuntary cry of horror. Vannevar Morgan had stepped casually backward off the face of the cliff, out into empty space.

6

THE ARTIST

"Bring the Persian to me," said Kalidasa, as soon as he had recovered his breath. The climb from the frescoes back to the Elephant Throne was not difficult, and it was perfectly safe now that the stairway down the sheer rock face had been enclosed by walls. But it was tiring; for how many more years, Kalidasa wondered, would he be able to make this journey unaided? Though slaves could carry him, that did not befit the dignity of a king. And it was intolerable that any eyes but his should look upon the hundred goddesses and their hundred equally beautiful attendants, who formed the retinue of his celestial court.

So from now on, night and day, there would always be a guard standing at the entrance to the stairs, the only way down from the palace to the private heaven that Kalidasa had created. After ten years of toil, his dream was now complete. Whatever the jealous monks on their mountaintop might claim to the contrary, he was a god at last.

Despite his years in the Taprobanean sun, Firdaz was as light-skinned as a Roman. Today, as he bowed before the King, he looked even paler, and ill at ease. Kalidasa regarded him thoughtfully, then gave one of his rare smiles of approval.

"You have done well, Persian," he said. "Is there any artist in the world who could do better?"

Pride obviously strove with caution before Firdaz gave his hesitant reply.

"None that I know of, Majesty."

"And have I paid you well?"

"I am quite satisfied."

That reply, thought Kalidasa, was hardly accurate. There had been continuous pleas for more money, more assistants, expensive materials that could be obtained only from distant lands. But artists could not be expected to understand economics, or to know how the royal treasury had been drained by the awesome cost of the palace and its surroundings.

"And now that your work here is finished, what do you wish?"

"I would like Your Majesty's permission to return to Isfahan, so that I may see my own people once again."

It was the answer that Kalidasa had expected, and he sincerely regretted the decision he must make. But there were too many other rulers on the long road to Persia, who would not let the master artist of Yakkagala slip through their greedy fingers. And the painted goddesses of the western wall must remain forever unchallenged.

"There is a problem," he said flatly, and Firdaz turned yet paler, his shoulders slumping at the words. A king did not have to explain anything, but this was one artist speaking to another.

"You have helped me to become a god. That news has already reached many lands. If you leave my protection, there are others who will make similar requests of you."

For a moment, the artist was silent. The only sound was the moaning of the wind, which seldom ceased to complain when it met this unexpected obstacle upon its journey. Then Firdaz said, so quietly that Kalidasa could hardly hear him: "Am I then forbidden to leave?"

"You may go, and with enough wealth for the rest of your life. But only on condition that you never work for any other prince."

"I am willing to give that promise," replied Firdaz, with almost unseemly haste.

Sadly, Kalidasa shook his head.

"I have learned not to trust the word of artists," he said. "Especially when they are no longer within my power. So I will have to enforce that promise."

To Kalidasa's surprise, Firdaz no longer looked so uncertain. It was almost as if he had made some great decision, and was finally at ease.

"I understand," he said, drawing himself up to his full height. Then he deliberately turned his back upon the King, as though his royal master no longer existed, and stared straight into the blazing sun.

The sun, Kalidasa knew, was the god of the Persians, and those words Firdaz was murmuring must be a prayer in his language. There were worse gods to worship, and the artist was staring into that blinding disk as if he knew it was the last thing he would ever see.

"Hold him!" cried the King.

The guards rushed swiftly forward, but they were too late. Blind though he must now have been, Firdaz moved with precision. In three steps he had reached the parapet, and vaulted over it. He made no sound in his long arc down to the gardens he had planned over so many years, nor was there any echo when the architect of Yakkagala reached the foundations of his masterwork.

Kalidasa grieved for many days, but his grief turned to rage when the Persian's last letter to Isfahan was intercepted. Someone had warned Firdaz that he would be blinded when his work was done; and that was a damnable falsehood.

He never discovered the source of the rumor, though not a few men died slowly before they proved their innocence. It saddened him that the Persian had believed such a lie; surely he should have known that a fellow artist would never have robbed him of the gift of sight.

Kalidasa was not a cruel man, or an ungrateful one. He would have laden Firdaz with gold—or at least silver—and sent him on his way with servants to take care of him for the remainder of his life.

He would never have needed to use his hands again; and after a while, he would not have missed them.

7

THE GOD-KING'S PALACE

Vannevar Morgan had not slept well, and that was most unusual. He had always taken pride in his self-awareness and his insight into his own drives and emotions. If he could not sleep, he wanted to know why.

Slowly, as he watched the first predawn light glimmer on the ceiling of his hotel bedroom, and heard the bell-like cries of alien birds, he began to marshal his thoughts. He would never have become a senior engineer of Terran Construction if he had not planned his life to avoid surprises. Although no man could be immune to the accidents of chance and fate, he had taken all reasonable steps to safeguard his career and, above all, his reputation. His future was as fail-safe as he could make it; even if he died suddenly, the programs stored in his computer bank would protect his cherished dream beyond the grave.

Until yesterday, he had never heard of Yakkagala; indeed, until a few weeks ago, he was only vaguely aware of Taprobane itself, until the logic of his quest directed him inexorably toward the island. By now, he should already have left, whereas in fact his mission had not yet begun. He did not mind the slight disruption of his schedule; what *did* perturb him was the feeling that he was being moved by forces beyond his understanding.

Yet the sense of awe had a familiar resonance. He had experienced it before, when, as a child, he had flown his kite in Kiribilli Park, beside the granite monoliths that had once been the piers of the long-demolished Sydney Harbour Bridge.

Those twin mountains had dominated his boyhood, and had controlled his destiny. Perhaps, in any event, he would have been an engineer; but the accident of his birthplace had determined that he would be a builder of bridges. And so he had been the first man to step from Morocco to Spain, with the angry waters of the Mediterranean three kilometers below—never dreaming, in that moment of triumph, of the far more stupendous challenge that lay ahead.

If he succeeded in the task that confronted him, he would be famous for centuries to come. Already, his mind, strength, and will were being taxed to the utmost; he had no time for idle distractions. Yet he had become fascinated by the achievements of an engineer-architect two thousands years dead, belonging to a totally alien culture. And there was the mystery of Kalidasa himself. What was his purpose in building Yakkagala? The King might have been a monster, but there was something about his character that struck a chord in the secret places of Morgan's own heart.

Sunrise would be in thirty minutes. It was two hours before his breakfast with Ambassador Rajasinghe. That would be long enough—and he might have no other opportunity.

Morgan was never one to waste time. Slacks and sweater were on in less than a minute, but the careful checking of his footwear took considerably longer. Though he had done no serious climbing for years, he always carried a pair of strong light-weight boots; in his profession, he often found them essential.

He had already closed the door of his room when he had a sudden afterthought. For a moment he stood hesitantly in the corridor; then he smiled and shrugged his shoulders. It wouldn't do any harm, and one never knew. . . .

Back in the room, Morgan unlocked his suitcase and took out a small flat box, about the size and shape of a pocket calculator. He checked the battery charge, tested the manual override, and clipped it to the steel buckle of his waist belt. Now he was ready to enter Kalidasa's haunted kingdom, and to face whatever demons it held.

The sun rose, pouring welcome warmth upon his back as Morgan passed through the gap in the massive rampart that formed the outer defenses of the fortress. Before him, spanned by a narrow stone bridge, were the still waters of the great moat, stretching in a perfectly straight line for half a kilometer on either side. A small flotilla of swans sailed hopefully toward him through the lilies, then dispersed with ruffled feathers when it was clear that he had no food to offer. On the far side of the bridge, he came to a second, smaller, wall and climbed the narrow flight of stairs cut through it. There before him were the pleasure gardens, with the sheer face of the Rock looming beyond them.

The fountains along the axis of the gardens rose and fell together with a languid rhythm, as if they were breathing slowly in unison. There was not another human being in sight; he had the whole expanse of Yakkagala to himself. The fortress-city could hardly have been lonelier, even during the seventeen hundred years when the jungle had overwhelmed it, between the death of Kalidasa and its rediscovery by nineteenth-century archaeologists.

Morgan walked past the line of fountains, feeling their spray against his skin, and stopped once to admire the beautifully carved stone guttering, obviously original, that carried the overflow. He wondered how the old-time hydraulic engineers lifted the water to drive the fountains, and what pressure differences they could handle. These soaring vertical jets must have been truly astonishing to those who first witnessed them.

Now ahead was a steep flight of granite steps, their treads so uncomfortably narrow that they could barely accommodate Morgan's boots. Did the people who built this extraordinary place really have such tiny feet? he wondered. Or was it a clever ruse of the architect, to discourage unfriendly visitors? It would certainly be difficult for soldiers to charge up this sixty-degree slope on steps that seemed to have been made for midgets.

A small platform, then an identical flight of steps, and Morgan found himself on a long, slowly ascending gallery cut into the lower flanks of the Rock. He was now more than fifty meters above the surrounding plain, but the view was completely blocked by a high wall coated with smooth yellow plaster. The rock above him overhung so much that he might almost have been walking along a tunnel, for only a narrow band of sky was visible.

The plaster of the wall looked completely new and unworn; it was almost impossible to believe that the masons had left their work two thousand years ago. Here and there, however, the gleaming, mirror-flat surface was scarred with scratched messages, where visitors had made their usual bids for immortality. Few of the inscriptions were in alphabets that Morgan could recognize, and the latest date he noticed was 1931. Thereafter, presumably, the Department of Archaeology had intervened to prevent such vandalism. Most of the graffiti were in flowing, rounded Taprobani. Morgan recalled from the previous night's entertainment that many were poems, dating back to the second and third centuries. For a little while after the death of Kalidasa, Yakkagala had known its first brief spell as a tourist attraction, thanks to the still-lingering legends of the accursed King.

Halfway along the stone gallery, Morgan came to the now locked door of the little elevator leading to the famous frescoes, twenty meters directly above. He craned his head to see them, but they were obscured by the platform of the visitors' viewing cage, clinging like a metal bird's nest to the outward-leaning face of the rock. Some tourists, Rajasinghe had told him, took one look at the dizzy location of the frescoes and decided to satisfy themselves with photographs.

For the first time, Morgan could appreciate one of the chief mysteries of Yakkagala. It was not *how* the frescoes were painted—a scaffolding of bamboo could have taken care of that problem—but *why*. Once they were completed, no one could ever have seen them properly. From the gallery immediately beneath, they were hopelessly foreshortened, and from the base of the Rock, they were no more than tiny, unrecognizable patches of color. Perhaps, as some had suggested, they were of purely religious or magical significance, like those Stone Age paintings found in the depths of almost inaccessible caves.

The frescoes would have to wait until the attendants arrived and unlocked the elevator. There were plenty of other things to see. He was only a third of the way to the summit, and the gallery was still slowly ascending, as it clung to the face of the Rock.

The high yellow-plastered wall gave way to a low parapet, and Morgan could once more see the surrounding countryside. There below him lay the whole expanse of the pleasure gardens, and he could now appreciate not only their huge scale (was Versailles larger?), but also their skillful plan, and the way in which the moat and outer ramparts protected them from the forest beyond.

No one knew what trees and shrubs and flowers had grown here in Kalidasa's day, but the pattern of artificial lakes, canals, pathways, and fountains was exactly as he had left it. As Morgan looked down on those dancing jets of water, he suddenly remembered a quotation from the previous night's commentary:

"From Taprobane to Paradise in forty leagues; there

may be heard the sound of the Fountains of Paradise."

He savored the phrase in his mind: the Fountains of Paradise. Was Kalidasa trying to create, here on earth, a garden fit for the gods, in order to establish his claim to divinity? If so, it was no wonder that the priests had accused him of blasphemy, and placed a curse upon all his work.

At last, the long gallery, which had skirted the entire western face of the Rock, ended in another steeply rising stairway, though this time the steps were much more generous in size. But the palace was still far above. The stairs ended on a large plateau, obviously artificial. Here was all that was left of the gigantic, leonine monster which had once dominated the landscape and struck terror into the hearts of everyone who looked upon it. Springing from the face of the rock were the paws of the gigantic crouching beast; the claws alone were half the height of a man.

Nothing else remained except another granite stairway, rising up through the piles of rubble that must once have formed the head of the creature. Even in ruin, the concept was awe-inspiring. Anyone who dared to approach the King's ultimate stronghold had first to walk through gaping jaws.

The final ascent up the sheer—indeed, slightly overhanging—face of the cliff was by a series of iron ladders, with guard-rails to reassure nervous climbers. But the real danger here, Morgan had been warned, was not vertigo. Swarms of normally placid hornets occupied small caves in the rock, and visitors who made too much noise had sometimes disturbed them, with fatal results.

Two thousand years ago, this northern face of Yakkagala had been covered with walls and battlements to provide a fitting background to the Taprobanean sphinx, and behind those walls there must have been stairways that gave easy access to the summit. Now, time, weather, and the vengeful hand of man had swept everything away. There was only the bare rock, grooved with myriads of horizontal slots and narrow ledges that had once supported the foundations of vanished masonry.

Abruptly, the climb was over. Morgan found himself standing on a small island floating two hundred meters above a landscape of trees and fields that was flat in all directions except southward, where the central mountains broke up the horizon. He was completely isolated from the rest of the world, yet felt master of all he surveyed. Not since he had stood among the clouds on the bridge straddling Europe and Africa had he known such a moment of aerial ecstasy. This was indeed the residence of a god-king, and the ruins of his palace were all around.

A baffling maze of broken walls—none more than waist-high—piles of weathered brick, and granite-paved pathways covered the entire surface of the plateau, right to the precipitous edge. Morgan could also see a large cistern cut deeply into the solid rock, presumably a water-storage tank. As long as supplies were available, a handful of determined men could have held this place forever; but if Yakkagala had been intended as a fortress, its defenses had never been put to the test. Kalidasa's fateful last meeting with his brother had taken place far beyond the outer ramparts.

Almost forgetting time, Morgan roamed among the foundations of the palace that had once crowned the Rock. He tried to enter the mind of the architect, from what he could see of his surviving handiwork. Why was there a pathway *here*? Did this truncated flight of steps lead to an upper floor? If this coffin-shaped recess in the stone was a bath, how was the water supplied and how did it drain away? His research was so fascinating that he was quite oblivious of the increasing heat of the sun, striking down from a cloudless sky.

Far below, the emerald-green landscape was waking into life. Like brightly colored beetles, a swarm of robot tractors was heading toward the rice fields. Improbable though it seemed, a helpful elephant was pushing an overturned bus back onto the road, which it had obviously left while taking a bend at too high a speed. Morgan could even hear the shrill voice of the rider, perched just behind the enormous ears. And a stream of tourists was pouring like army ants through the pleasure gardens from the general direction of the Hotel Yakkagala. He would not enjoy his solitude much longer.

However, he had virtually completed his exploration of the ruins—though one could, of course, spend a lifetime investigating them in detail. He was happy to rest for a while, on a beautifully carved granite bench at the very edge of the two-hundred-meter drop, overlooking the entire southern sky.

Morgan let his eyes scan the distant line of mountains, partly concealed by a blue haze which the morning sun had not yet dispersed. As he examined it idly, he realized that what he had assumed to be a part of the cloudscape was nothing of the sort. That misty cone was no ephemeral construct of wind and vapor. There was no mistaking its perfect symmetry, as it towered above its lesser brethren.

For a moment, the shock of recognition emptied his mind of everything except wonder, and an almost superstitious awe. He had not known that one could see the Sacred Mountain so clearly from Yakkagala. But there it was, slowly emerging from the shadow of night, preparing to face a new day; and, if he succeeded, a new future.

He knew all its dimensions, all its geology. He had mapped it through stereophotographs and had scanned it from satellites. But to see it for the first time with his own eyes made it real; until now, everything had been theory. And sometimes not even that. More than once, in the small gray hours before dawn, Morgan had awakened from nightmares in which his whole project had appeared as some preposterous fantasy, which, far from bringing him fame, would make him the laughingstock of the world. Morgan's Folly, some of his peers had once dubbed the bridge. What would they call his latest dream?

But man-made obstacles had never stopped him before. Nature was his real antagonist—the friendly enemy who never cheated, always played fair, but never failed to take advantage of the tiniest oversight or omission. And all the forces of Nature were epitomized for him now in that distant blue cone, which he knew so well but had yet to feel beneath his feet.

As Kalidasa had done so often from this very spot, Morgan stared across the fertile green plain, measuring the challenge and considering his strategy. To Kalidasa, Sri Kanda represented both the power of the priesthood and the power of the gods, conspiring together against him. Now the gods were gone; but the priests remained. They represented something that Morgan did not understand, and would therefore treat with wary respect.

It was time to descend. He must not be late again, especially through his own miscalculation. As he rose from the stone slab on which he had been sitting, a thought that had been worrying him for several minutes finally rose to consciousness. It was strange to have placed so ornate a seat, with its beautifully carved supporting elephants, at the very edge of a precipice. . . .

Morgan could never resist such an intellectual challenge. Leaning out over the abyss, he once again tried to attune his engineer's mind to that of a colleague two thousand years dead.

8

MALGARA

Not even his closest comrades could read the expression on Prince Malgara's face when, for the last time, he gazed upon the brother who had shared his boyhood. The battlefield was quiet; even the cries of the injured had been silenced by healing herb or yet more potent sword.

After a long while, the Prince turned to the yellow-robed figure standing by his side.

"*You* crowned him, Venerable Bodhidharma. Now you can do him one more service. See that he receives the honors of a king."

For a moment, the High Priest did not reply. Then he answered softly:

"He destroyed our temples and scattered the priests. If he worshipped any god, it was Siva."

Malgara bared his teeth in the fierce smile that the Mahanayake Thero was to know all too well in the years that were left to him.

"Revered sire," said the Prince, in a voice that dripped venom, "he was the first-born of Paravana the Great, he sat on the throne of Taprobane, and the evil that he did dies with him. When the body is burned, you will see that the relics are properly entombed before you dare set foot upon Sri Kanda again."

The Mahanayake Thero bowed, ever so slightly.

"It shall be done—according to your wishes."

"And there is another thing," said Malgara, speaking now to his aides. "The fame of Kalidasa's fountains reached us even in Hindustan. We would see them once, before we march on Ranapura. . . ."

From the heart of the pleasure gardens, which had given him such delight, the smoke of Kalidasa's funeral pyre rose into the cloudless sky, disturbing the birds of prey that had gathered from far and wide. Grimly content, though sometimes haunted by sudden memories, Malgara watched the symbol of his triumph spiraling upward, announcing to all the land that the new reign had begun.

As if in continuation of their ancient rivalry, the water of the fountains challenged the fire, leaping skyward before it fell back to shatter the surface of the reflecting pool. But presently, long before the flames had finished their work, the reservoirs began to fail, and the jets collapsed in liquid ruin. Before they rose again in the gardens of Kalidasa, Imperial Rome would have passed away, the armies of Islam would have marched across Africa, Copernicus would have dethroned the earth from the center of the universe, the American Declaration of Independence would have been signed, and men would have walked upon the moon. . . .

Malgara waited until the pyre had disintegrated in a final brief flurry of sparks. As the last smoke drifted against the towering face of Yakkagala, he raised his eyes toward the palace on its summit, and stared for a long time in silent appraisal.

"No man should challenge the gods," he said at last. "Let it be destroyed."

9

FILAMENT

"You nearly gave me a heart attack," said Rajasinghe accusingly, as he poured the morning coffee. "At first, I thought you had some antigravity device—but even I know that's impossible. How *did* you do it?"

"My apologies," Morgan answered with a smile. "If I'd known you were watching, I'd have warned you—though the whole exercise was entirely unplanned. I'd merely intended to take a scramble over the Rock, but then I got intrigued by that stone bench. I wondered why it was on the very edge of the cliff, and started to explore."

"There's no mystery about it. At one time, there was a floor, probably wood, extending outward, and a flight of steps leading down to the frescoes from the summit. You can still see the grooves where it was keyed into the rock face."

"So I discovered," said Morgan a little ruefully. "I might have guessed that someone would have found that out already."

Two hundred and fifty years ago, thought Rajasinghe. That crazy and energetic Englishman Arnold Lethbridge, Taprobane's first Director of Archaeology. He had himself lowered down the face of the Rock, exactly as you did. Well, not *exactly* . . .

Morgan had now produced the metal box that had allowed him to perform his miracle. Its only features were a few buttons, and a small read-out panel. It

47

looked for all the world like some form of simple communications device.

"This is it," he said proudly. "Since you saw me make a hundred-meter vertical walk, you must have a very good idea how it operates."

"Common sense gave me one answer, but even my excellent telescope didn't confirm it. I could have sworn there was absolutely nothing supporting you."

"That wasn't the demonstration I'd intended, but it must have been effective. Now for my standard sales pitch. Please hook your finger through this ring."

Rajasinghe hesitated. Morgan was holding the small metal torus—about twice the size of an ordinary wedding ring—almost as if it were electrified.

"Will it give me a shock?" he asked.

"Not a shock—but perhaps a surprise. Try to pull it away from me."

Rather gingerly, Rajasinghe took hold of the ring— then almost dropped it. It seemed alive; it was straining toward Morgan—or, rather, toward the box that the engineer was holding in his hand. Then the box gave a slight whirring noise, and Rajasinghe felt his finger being dragged forward by some mysterious force. Magnetism? he asked himself. Of course not; no magnets could behave in this fashion. His tentative but improbable theory was correct; indeed, there was really no alternative explanation. They were engaged in a perfectly straightforward tug-of-war—*but with an invisible rope.*

Though Rajasinghe strained his eyes, he could see no trace of any thread or wire connecting the ring through which his finger was hooked and the box that Morgan was operating much like a fisberman reeling in his catch. He reached out his free hand to explore the apparently empty space, but the engineer quickly knocked it away.

"Sorry!" he said. "Everyone tries that, when they

realize what's happening. You could cut yourself very badly."

"So you *do* have an invisible wire. Clever—but what use is it, except for parlor tricks?"

Morgan gave a broad smile.

"I can't blame you for jumping to that conclusion; it's the usual reaction. But it's quite wrong. The reason you can't see this sample is that it's only a few microns thick. Much thinner than a spider's web."

For once, thought Rajasinghe, an overworked adjective was fully justified.

"That's—incredible. What *is* it?"

"The result of about two hundred years of solid-state physics. For whatever good that does, it's a continuous pseudo-one-dimensional diamond crystal —though it's not actually pure carbon. There are several trace elements in carefully controlled amounts. It can be mass-produced only in the orbiting factories, where there's no gravity to interfere with the growth process."

"Fascinating," whispered Rajasinghe, almost to himself. He gave little tugs on the ring hooked around his finger, to test that the tension was still there and that he was not hallucinating. "I can appreciate that this may have all sorts of technical applications. It would make a splendid cheese cutter."

Morgan laughed.

"One man can bring a tree down with it, in a couple of minutes. But it's tricky to handle—even dangerous. We've had to design special dispensers to spool and unspool it. We call them 'spinnerettes.' This is a power-operated one, made for demonstration purposes. The motor can lift a couple of hundred kilos, and I'm always finding new uses for it. Today's little exploit wasn't the first by any means."

Almost reluctantly, Rajasinghe unhooked his finger from the ring. It started to fall, then swung back and forth like a pendulum without visible means of support until Morgan pressed a button and the spinner-ette reeled it in with a gentle whirr.

"You haven't come all this way, Dr. Morgan, just to impress me with this latest marvel of science—though I *am* impressed. I want to know what all this has to do with me."

"A great deal, Mr. Ambassador," answered the engineer, equally serious and formal. "You are quite correct in thinking that this material will have many applications, some of which we are only now beginning to foresee.

"And one of them, for better or for worse, is going to make your quiet little island the center of the world. No—not merely the world. The whole solar system.

"Thanks to this filament, Taprobane will be the stepping-stone to all the planets. And one day, perhaps, the stars."

10

THE ULTIMATE BRIDGE

Paul and Maxine were two of his best and oldest friends, yet until this moment they had never met, or, as far as Rajasinghe knew, even communicated. There was little reason why they should; no one outside Taprobane had ever heard of Professor Sarath, but the whole solar system would instantly recognize Maxine Duval, either by sight or by sound.

His two guests were reclining in the library's comfortable lounge chairs, while Rajasinghe sat at the villa's main console. They were all staring at the fourth figure, who was standing motionless.

Too motionless. A visitor from the past, knowing nothing of the everyday electronic miracles of this age, might have decided after a few seconds that he was looking at a superbly detailed wax dummy. However, more careful examination would have revealed two disconcerting facts. The "dummy" was transparent enough for highlights to be clearly visible through it; and its feet blurred out of focus a few centimeters above the carpet.

"Do you recognize this man?" Rajasinghe asked.

"I've never seen him in my life," Sarath replied instantly. "He'd better be important, since you dragged me back from Maharamba. We were just about to open the relic chamber."

"*I* had to leave my trimaran at the beginning of the Lake Saladin races," said Duval, her famous contralto voice containing just enough annoyance to put anyone less thick-skinned than Professor Sarath neatly in his place. "And I know him, of course. Does he want to build a bridge from Taprobane to Hindustan?"

Rajasinghe laughed.

"No. We've had a perfectly serviceable causeway for two centuries. And I'm sorry to have dragged you both here—though *you,* Maxine, have been promising to come for twenty years."

"True." She sighed. "But I have to spend so much time in my studio that I sometimes forget there's a *real* world out there, occupied by about five thousand dear friends and fifty million intimate acquaintances."

"In which category would you put Dr. Morgan?"

"I've met him—oh, three or four times. We did a special interview when the Gibraltar Bridge was completed. He's a very impressive character."

Coming from Maxine Duval, thought Rajasinghe, that was a fine tribute. For more than thirty years, she had been perhaps the most respected member of her exacting profession, and had won every honor that it could offer. A Pulitzer Prize, the *Global Times* Trophy, the David Snow Award—these were merely the tip of the iceberg. And she had only recently returned to active work after two years as Walter Cronkite Professor of Electronic Journalism at Columbia University.

All this had mellowed her, though it had not slowed her down. She was no longer the sometimes fiery chauvinist who had once remarked: "Since women are better at producing babies, presumably Nature has given men some talent to compensate. But for the moment I can't think of it." However, she had only recently embarrassed a hapless panel chairman with the loud aside: "I'm a news*woman,* dammit—not a news*person.*"

Of her femininity, there had never been any doubt. She had been married four times, and her choice of

Rems was famous. Whatever their sex, remotes were always young and athletic, so that they could move swiftly despite the encumbrance of up to twenty kilos of communications gear. Duval's were invariably very male and very handsome; it was an old joke in the trade that all her Rems were also rams. The jest was completely without rancor, since even her fiercest professional rivals liked her almost as much as they envied her.

"I'm sorry about the race," said Rajasinghe, "but I note that *Marlin III* won handily without you. I think you'll admit that this is rather more important. . . . But let Morgan speak for himself. . . ."

He released the PAUSE button on the projector, and the frozen statue came instantly to life.

"My name is Vannevar Morgan. I am Chief Engineer of Terran Construction's Land Division. My last project was the Gibraltar Bridge. Now I want to talk about something incomparably more ambitious."

Rajasinghe glanced around the room. Morgan had hooked them, just as he had expected.

He leaned back in his chair and waited for the now familiar, yet still almost unbelievable, prospectus to unfold. Odd, he thought, how quickly one accepted the conventions of the display, and ignored quite large errors of the TILT and LEVEL controls. Even the fact that Morgan "moved" while staying in the same place, and the totally false perspective of exterior scenes, failed to destroy the sense of reality.

"The Space Age is almost two hundred years old. For more than half that time, our civilization has been utterly dependent upon the host of satellites that now orbit the earth.

"Global communications, weather forecasting and control, land and ocean resources, banks, postal and information services—if anything happened to their spaceborne systems, we would sink back into a dark age. During the resultant chaos, disease and starvation would destroy much of the human race.

"And looking beyond the earth, now that we have self-sustaining colonies on Mars, Mercury, and the moon, and are mining the incalculable wealth of the asteroids, we see the beginnings of true interplanetary commerce. Though it took a little longer than the optimists predicted, it is now obvious that the conquest of the air was only a modest prelude to the conquest of space.

"But now we are faced with a fundamental problem, an obstacle that stands in the way of all future progress. Although the research work of generations has made the rocket the most reliable form of propulsion ever invented . . ."

"Has he considered bicycles?" muttered Sarath.

". . . space vehicles are still grossly inefficient. Even worse, their effect on the environment is appalling. Despite all attempts to control approach corridors, the noise of take-off and re-entry disturbs millions of people. Exhaust products dumped in the upper atmosphere have triggered climatic changes, which may have very serious results. Everyone remembers the skin-cancer crisis of the twenties, caused by ultraviolet breakthrough—and the astronomical cost of the chemicals needed to restore the ozonosphere.

"Yet if we project traffic growth to the end of the century, we find that earth-to-orbit tonnage must be increased almost fifty percent. This cannot be achieved without intolerable costs to our way of life—perhaps to our very existence. And there is nothing that the rocket engineers can do. They have almost reached the absolute limits of performance, set by the laws of physics.

"What is the alternative? For centuries, men have dreamed of antigravity and of 'spacedrives.' No one has ever found the slightest hint that such things are possible; today we believe that they are only fantasy.

"In the very decade that the first satellite was launched, however, one daring Russian engineer conceived a system that would make the rocket obsolete. It was years before anyone took Yuri Artsutanov seriously. It has taken two centuries for our technology to match his vision."

Each time he played the recording, it seemed to Rajasinghe that Morgan really came alive at this point. It was easy to see why; now he was on his own territory, no longer relaying information from an alien field of expertise. And despite all his reservations and fears, Rajasinghe could not help sharing some of that enthusiasm. It was a quality that, nowadays, seldom impinged upon his life.

"Go out of doors any clear night," continued Morgan, "and you will see that commonplace wonder of our age—the stars that never rise or set, but are fixed motionless in the sky. We, and our parents, and *their* parents have long taken for granted the synchronous satellites and space stations, which move above the equator at the same speed as the turning earth, and so hang forever above the same spot.

"The question Artsutanov asked himself had the childlike brilliance of true genius. A merely clever man could never have thought of it—or would have dismissed it instantly as absurd.

"*If* the laws of celestial mechanics make it possible for an object to stay fixed in the sky, might it not be possible to lower a cable down to the surface, and *so to establish an elevator system linking earth to space?*

"There was nothing wrong with the theory, but the practical problems were enormous. Calculations showed that no existing materials would be strong enough. The finest steel would snap under its own weight long before it could span the thirty-six thousand kilometers between earth and synchronous orbit.

"However, even the best steels were nowhere near the theoretical limits of strength. On a microscopic scale, materials had been created in the laboratory with far greater breaking strength. If they could be mass-produced, Artsutanov's dream could become reality—and the economics of space transportation would be utterly transformed.

"Before the end of the twentieth century, superstrength materials—hyperfilaments—had begun to emerge from the laboratory. But they were extremely expensive, costing many times their weight in gold. Millions of tons would be needed to build a system that could carry all earth's outbound traffic. So the dream remained a dream—until a few months ago.

"Now the deep-space factories can manufacture virtually unlimited quantities of hyperfilament. At last we can build the Space Elevator—or the Orbital Tower, as I prefer to call it. In a sense it *is* a tower, rising clear through the atmosphere, and far, far beyond. . . ."

Morgan faded out, like a ghost that had been suddenly exorcised. He was replaced by a football-sized earth, slowly revolving. Moving an arm's breadth above it, and keeping always poised above the same spot on the equator, a flashing star marked the location of a synchronous satellite.

From the star, two thin lines of light started to extend—one directly down toward the earth, the other in exactly the opposite direction, out into space.

"When you build a bridge," continued Morgan's disembodied voice, "you start from the two ends and meet in the middle. With the Orbital Tower, it would be the exact opposite. You have to build upward *and* downward simultaneously from the synchronous satellite, according to a careful program. The trick is to keep the structure's center of gravity always balanced at the stationary point. If you don't, it will move into the wrong orbit, and start drifting slowly around the earth."

The descending line of light reached the equator; at the same moment, the outward extension also ceased.

"The total height must be at least forty thousand kilometers, and the lowest hundred, going down through the atmosphere, may be the most critical part, because there the Tower may be subject to hurricanes. It won't be stable until it's securely anchored to the ground.

"And then, for the first time in history, we will have a stairway to heaven—a bridge to the stars. A simple elevator system, driven by cheap electricity, will replace the noisy and expensive rocket, which will then be used only for its proper job of deep-space transport. Here's one possible design for the Orbital Tower."

The image of the turning earth vanished as the camera swooped down toward the Tower, and passed through the walls to reveal the structure's cross-section.

"You'll see that it consists of four identical tubes—two for up traffic, two for down. Think of it as a four-track *vertical* subway or railroad, from earth to synchronous orbit.

"Capsules for passengers, freight, fuel would ride up and down the tubes, at several thousand kilometers an hour. Fusion power stations at intervals would provide all the energy needed; since ninety percent of it would be recovered, the net cost per passenger would be only a few dollars. As the capsules fall earthward again, their motors will act as magnetic brakes, generating electricity. Unlike re-entering spacecraft, they won't waste all their energy heating up the atmosphere and making sonic booms; it will be pumped back into the system. You could say that the down trains will power the up ones. So even at the most conservative estimate, the Space Elevator will be a hundred times more efficient than any rocket.

"And there's virtually no limit to the traffic it could handle, for additional tubes could be added as required. If the time ever comes when a million people a day wish to visit earth—or to leave it—the Orbital

Tower could cope with them. After all, the subways of our great cities once did as much. . . ."

Rajasinghe touched a button, silencing Morgan.

"The rest is rather technical. He goes on to explain how the Tower can act as a cosmic sling, and send payloads whipping off to the moon and planets without the use of any rocket power at all. But I think you've seen enough to get the general idea."

"My mind is suitably boggled," said Sarath. "But what on earth—or off it—has all this to do with me? Or with you, for that matter?"

"Everything in due time, Paul. Any comments, Maxine?"

"Perhaps I may yet forgive you. This *could* be one of the stories of the decade—or the century. But why the hurry—not to mention the secrecy?"

"There's a lot going on that I don't understand, which is where you can help me. I suspect that Morgan's fighting a battle on several fronts; he's planning an announcement in the very near future, but doesn't want to act until he's quite sure of his ground. He gave me that presentation on the understanding that it wouldn't be sent over public circuits. That's why I had to ask you here."

"Does he know about this meeting?"

"Of course. He was actually quite happy when I said I wanted to talk to you, Maxine. Obviously, he trusts you and would like you as an ally. And as for *you,* Paul, I assured him that you could keep a secret for up to six days without apoplexy."

"Only if there's a very good reason for it."

"I begin to see light," said Duval. "Several things have been puzzling me, and now they're starting to make sense. First of all, this is a *space* project; Morgan is Chief Engineer, *Land.*"

"So?"

"*You* should ask, Johan! Think of the bureaucratic infighting when the rocket designers and the aerospace industry get to hear about this! Trillion-dollar empires will be at stake, just to start with. If he's not very careful, Morgan will be told 'Thank you very much—now we'll take over. Nice knowing you.' "

"I can appreciate that, but he has a good case. After all, the Orbital Tower *is* a building—not a vehicle."

"Not when the lawyers get hold of it, it won't be. There aren't many buildings whose upper floors are moving at ten kilometers a second, or whatever it is, faster than the basement."

"You may have a point. Incidentally, when I showed signs of vertigo at the idea of a tower going a good part of the way to the moon, Morgan said, 'Then don't think of it as a tower going *up;* think of it as a bridge going *out.*' I'm still trying, without much success."

"Oh!" said Duval suddenly. "That's another piece of your jigsaw puzzle. The Bridge."

"What do you mean?"

"Did you know that Terran Construction's Chairman, that pompous ass Senator Collins, wanted to get the Gibraltar Bridge named after himself?"

"I didn't. That explains several things. But I rather like Collins. The few times we've met, I found him very pleasant, and very bright. Didn't he do some first-rate geothermal engineering in his time?"

"That was a thousand years ago. And *you* aren't any threat to his reputation; he can be nice to you."

"How was the Bridge saved from its fate?"

"There was a small palace revolution among Terran's senior engineering staff. Morgan, of course, was in no way involved."

"So that's why he's keeping his cards close to his chest! I'm beginning to admire him more and more. But now he's come up against an obstacle he doesn't know how to handle. He discovered it only a few days ago, and it's stopped him dead in his tracks."

"Let me go on guessing," said Duval. "It's good practice—helps me to keep ahead of the pack. I can see why he's here. The earth end of the system has to be on the equator; otherwise it can't be vertical. It would be like that tower they used to have in Pisa, before it fell over."

"I don't *see* . . ." said Sarath, waving his arms vaguely up and down. "Oh, of course . . ." His voice trailed away into thoughtful silence.

"Now," continued Duval, "there are only a limited number of possible sites on the equator. It's mostly ocean, isn't it? And Taprobane's obviously one of them. Though I don't see what particular advantages it has over Africa or South America. Or is Morgan covering all his bets?"

"As usual, my dear Maxine, your powers of deduction are phenomenal. You're on the right line—but you won't get any further. Though Morgan's done his best to explain the problem to me, I don't pretend to understand all the scientific details.

"Anyway, it turns out that Africa and South America are *not* suitable for the Space Elevator. It's something to do with unstable points in the earth's gravitational field. Only Taprobane will do. Worse still, only one spot in Taprobane. And that, Paul, is where *you* come into the picture."

"Mamada?" yelped Sarath, indignantly reverting to Taprobani in his surprise.

"Yes, you. To his great annoyance, Morgan has just discovered that the one site he *must* have is already occupied—to put it mildly. He wants my advice on dislodging your good friend Buddy."

Now it was Duval's turn to be baffled.

"Who?" she queried.

Sarath answered at once. "The Venerable Anandatissa Bodhidharma Mahanayake Thero, incumbent of the Sri Kanda temple," he intoned, almost as if chanting a litany. "So *that's* what it's all about."

There was silence for a moment. Then a look of pure mischievous delight appeared on the face of Paul Sarath, Emeritus Professor of Archaeology of the University of Taprobane.

"I've always wanted," he said dreamily, "to know exactly what would happen when an irresistible force meets an immovable object."

11

THE SILENT PRINCESS

When his visitors had left, in a very thoughtful mood, Rajasinghe depolarized the library windows and sat for a long time staring out at the trees around the villa, and the rock walls of Yakkagala looming beyond. He had not moved when, precisely on the stroke of four, the arrival of his afternoon tea jolted him out of his reverie.

"Rani," he said, "ask Dravindra to get out my heavy shoes, if he can find them. I'm going up the Rock."

Rani pretended to drop the tray in astonishment. *"Aiyo,* Mahathaya!" she keened in mock distress. "You must be mad! Remember what Dr. McPherson told you."

"That Scots quack always reads my cardiogram backward. Anyway, my dear, what have I got to live for, when you and Dravindra leave me?"

He spoke not entirely in jest, and was instantly ashamed of his self-pity. For Rani detected it, and the tears started in her eyes.

She turned away so that he could not see her emotion, and said in English:

"I *did* offer to stay—at least for Dravindra's first year. . . ."

"I know you did, and I wouldn't dream of it. Unless Berkeley's changed since I last saw it, he'll need you there." (Yet no more than I, though in different ways, he added silently to himself.) "And whether you take your own degree or not, you can't start training *too* early to be a college president's wife."

Rani smiled.

"I'm not sure that's a fate I'd welcome, from some of the horrid examples I've seen." She switched back to Taprobani. "You aren't *really* serious, are you?"

"Quite serious. Not to the top, of course—only to the frescoes. It's five years since I visited them. If I leave it much longer . . ." There was no need to complete the sentence.

Rani studied him in silence for a few moments, and decided that argument was futile.

"I'll tell Dravindra," she said. *"And* Jaya—in case they have to carry you back."

"Very well—though I'm sure Dravindra could manage that by himself."

Rani gave him a delighted smile, mingling pride and pleasure. This couple, he thought fondly, had been his luckiest draw in the state lottery, and he hoped that their two years of social service had been as enjoyable to them as it had been to him. In this age, personal servants were the rarest of luxuries, awarded only to men of outstanding merit. Rajasinghe knew of no other private citizen who had three.

To conserve his strength, he rode a sun-powered tricycle through the pleasure gardens. Dravindra and Jaya preferred to walk, claiming that it was quicker. They were right; but they were able to take short cuts. He climbed very slowly, pausing several times for breath, until he had reached the long corridor of the Lower Gallery, where the Mirror Wall ran parallel to the face of the Rock.

Watched by the usual inquisitive tourists, a young archaeologist from one of the African countries was searching the wall for inscriptions, with the aid of a powerful oblique light. Rajasinghe felt like warning her that the chance of making a new discovery was virtually zero. Paul Sarath had spent twenty years going over every square millimeter of the surface, and the three-volume *Yakkagala Graffiti* was a monumental work of scholarship that would never be superseded—if only because no other man would ever again be so skilled at reading archaic Taprobani inscriptions.

They had both been young men when Paul had begun his life's work. Rajasinghe could remember standing at this very spot while the then Deputy Assistant Epigrapher of the Department of Archaeology had traced out the almost indecipherable marks on the yellow plaster, and translated the poems addressed to the beauties on the rock above. After all these centuries, the lines could still strike echoes in the human heart:

> I am Tissa, Captain of the Guard.
> I came fifty leagues to see the doe-eyed ones,
> but they would not speak to me.
> Is this kind?

> May you remain here for a thousand years,
> like the hare which the King of the Gods
> painted on the moon. I am the priest Mahinda
> from the vihara of Tuparama.

That hope had been partly fulfilled, partly denied. The ladies of the Rock had been standing here for twice the time that the cleric had imagined, and had survived into an age beyond his uttermost dreams. But how few of them were left! Some of the inscriptions referred to "five hundred golden-skinned maidens"; even allowing for considerable poetic license, it was clear that not one tenth of the original frescoes had escaped the ravages of time or the malevolence of men. But the twenty that remained were now safe forever, their beauty stored on countless films and tapes and crystals.

Certainly they had outlasted one proud scribe, who had thought it quite unnecessary to give his name.

I ordered the road to be cleared, so that pilgrims could see the fair maidens standing on the mountainside. I am the King.

Over the years, Rajasinghe—himself the bearer of a royal name, and doubtless host to many regal genes —had often thought of those words. They demonstrated so perfectly the ephemeral nature of power, and the futility of ambition. "I am the King." Ah, but *which* king? The monarch who had stood on these granite flagstones—scarcely worn then, eighteen hundred years ago—was probably an able and intelligent man; but he failed to conceive that the time could ever come when he would fade into an anonymity as deep as that of his humblest subjects.

The attribution was now lost beyond trace. At least a dozen kings might have inscribed those haughty lines. Some had reigned for years, some only for weeks, and few indeed had died peacefully in their beds. No one would ever know if the king who felt it needless to give his name was Mahatissa II, or Bhatikabhaya, or Vijayakumara III, or Gajabahukagamani, or Candamukhasiva, or Moggallana I, or Kittisena, or Sirisamghabodhi . . . or some other monarch not even recorded in the long and tangled history of Taprobane.

The attendant operating the little elevator was astonished to see his distinguished visitor, and greeted Rajasinghe deferentially. As the cage slowly ascended the full fifteen meters, the visitor remembered how he would once have spurned it for the spiral stairway, up which Dravindra and Jaya were bounding even now in the thoughtless exuberance of youth.

The elevator clicked to a halt, and he stepped onto the small steel platform built out from the face of the cliff. Below and behind was a hundred meters of empty space, but the strong wire mesh gave ample security. Not even the most determined suicide could escape from the cage, large enough to hold a dozen people, that was clinging to the underside of the eternally breaking wave of stone.

Here in this accidental indentation, where the rock face formed a shallow cave, and so protected them from the elements, were the survivors of King Kalidasa's heavenly court. Rajasinghe greeted them silently as he sank gratefully into the chair that was offered by the official guide.

"I would like," he said quietly, "to be left alone for ten minutes. Jaya—Dravindra—see if you can head off the tourists."

His companions looked at him doubtfully; so did the guide, who was supposed never to leave the frescoes unguarded. But, as usual, Ambassador Rajasinghe had his way, without even raising his voice.

"*Ayu bowan,*" he greeted the silent figures when he was alone at last. "I'm sorry to have neglected you for so long."

He waited politely for an answer, but they paid no more attention to him than to all their other admirers for the last twenty centuries. Rajasinghe was not discouraged; he was used to their indifference. Indeed, it added to their charm.

"I have a problem, my dears," he continued. "You have watched all the invaders of Taprobane come and go, since Kalidasa's time. You have seen the jungle flow like a tide around Yakkagala, and then retreat before the ax and the plow. But nothing has really changed in all those years. Nature has been kind to little Taprobane, and so has History; it has left her alone. . . .

"Now the centuries of quiet may be drawing to a close. Our land may become the center of the world . . . of many worlds. The great mountain you have watched so long, there in the south, may be the key to the universe. If that is so, the Taprobane we knew and loved will cease to exist.

"Perhaps there is not much that I can do. But I have *some* power to help, or to hinder. I still have many friends. If I wish, I can delay this dream—or nightmare—at least beyond my lifetime. Should I do so? Or should I give aid to this man, whatever his real motives may be?"

He turned to his favorite, the only one who did not avert her eyes when he gazed upon her. All the other maidens stared into the distance, or examined the flowers in their hands; but the one he had loved since his youth seemed, from a certain angle, to catch his glance.

"Ah, Karuna! It's not fair to ask such questions. What could you possibly know of the *real* worlds beyond the sky, or of men's need to reach them? Even though you were once a goddess, Kalidasa's heaven was only an illusion.

"Well, whatever strange futures you may see, I shall not share them. We have known each other a long time—by my standards, if not by yours. While I can, I shall watch you from the villa; but I do not think that we will meet again. Farewell—and thank you, beautiful ones, for all the pleasure you have brought me down the years. Give my greetings to those who come after me."

Yet as he descended the spiral stairs—ignoring the elevator—Rajasinghe did not feel at all in a valedictory mood. On the contrary, it seemed to him that he had shed quite a few of his years (and, after all, seventy-two was not *really* old). He could tell that Dravindra and Jaya had noticed the spring in his step, by the way their faces lit up.

Perhaps his retirement had been getting a little dull. Perhaps both he and Taprobane needed a breath of fresh air to blow away the cobwebs—just as the

monsoon brought renewed life after the months of tor-
pid, heavy skies.

Whether Morgan succeeded or not, his was an enterprise to fire the imagination and stir the soul. Kalidasa would have envied—and approved.

II

___

THE
TEMPLE

"While the different religions wrangle with one another as to which of them is in possession of the truth, in our view the truth of religion may be altogether disregarded. . . . If one attempts to assign to religion its place in man's evolution, it seems not so much to be a lasting acquisition, as a parallel to the neurosis which the civilized individual must pass through on his way from childhood to maturity."

Sigmund Freud
New Introductory Lectures on Psycho-Analysis, 1932

"Of course man made God in his own image; but what was the alternative? Just as a real understanding of geology was impossible until we were able to study other worlds besides earth, so a valid theology must await contact with extraterrestrial intelligences. There can be no such subject as comparative religion as long as we study only the religions of man."

El Hadj Mohammed ben Selim
Professor of Comparative Religion
Inaugural Address, Brigham Young University, 1998

"We must await, not without anxiety, the answers to the following questions: (a) what, if any, are the religious concepts of entities with zero, one, two, or more than two 'parents'; (b) is religious belief found only among organisms that have close contact with their direct progenitors during their formative years?

"If we find that religion occurs exclusively among intelligent analogs of apes, dolphins, elephants, dogs, etc., but **not** among extraterrestrial computers, termites, fish, turtles, or social amoebae, we may have to draw some painful conclusions. . . . Perhaps both love and religion can arise only among mammals, and for much the same reasons. This is also suggested by a study of their pathologies. Anyone who doubts the connection between religious fanaticism and perversion should take a long, hard look at the **Malleus maleficarum** or Huxley's **The Devils of Loudun.**"

Ibid.

"Dr. Charles Willis's notorious remark (Hawaii, 1970) that 'religion is a by-product of malnutrition' is not, in itself, much more helpful than Gregory Bateson's somewhat indelicate one-syllable refutation. What Dr. Willis apparently meant was: (1) the hallucinations caused by voluntary or involuntary starvation are readily interpreted as religious visions; (2) hunger in **this** life encourages belief in a compensatory afterlife, as a, perhaps essential, psychological survival mechanism. . . .

"It is indeed one of the ironies of fate that research into the so-called consciousness-expanding drugs proved that they did exactly the opposite, by leading to the detection of the naturally occurring 'apothetic' chemicals in the brain. The discovery that the most devout adherent of any faith could be converted to any other by a judicious dose of 2-4-7 **ortho-para**-theosamine was, perhaps, the most devastating blow ever received by religion.

"Until, of course, the advent of Starglider. . . ."

R. Gabor
The Pharmacological Basis of Religion
Miskatonic University Press, 2069

12

STARGLIDER

Something of the sort had been expected for a hundred years, and there had been many false alarms. Yet when it finally happened, mankind was taken by surprise.

The radio signal from the direction of Alpha Centauri was so powerful that it was first detected as interference on normal commercial circuits. This was highly embarrassing to all the radio astronomers, who for so many decades had been seeking intelligent messages from space, especially because they had long ago dismissed the triple system of Alpha, Beta, and Proxima Centauri from serious consideration.

At once, every radio telescope that could scan the Southern Hemisphere was focused upon Centaurus. Within hours, a still more sensational discovery was made. The signal was not coming from the Centaurus system at all—but from a point half a degree away. *And it was moving*.

That was the first hint of the truth. When it was confirmed, all the normal business of mankind came to a halt.

The power of the signal was no longer surprising. Its source was already well inside the solar system, and moving sunward at six hundred kilometers a second. The long-awaited, long-feared visitors from space had arrived at last. . . .

Yet for thirty days the intruder did nothing, as it

fell past the outer planets, broadcasting an unvarying series of pulses that merely announced "Here I am!" It made no attempt to answer the signals beamed at it, nor did it make any adjustments to its natural, cometlike orbit. Unless it had slowed down from some much higher speed, its voyage from Centaurus must have lasted two thousand years. Some found this reassuring, since it suggested that the visitor was a robot space probe; others were disappointed, feeling that the absence of real, live extraterrestrials would be an anticlimax.

The whole spectrum of possibilities was argued, *ad nauseam,* in all the media of communications, all the parliaments of man. Every plot that had ever been used in science fiction, from the arrival of benevolent gods to an invasion of bloodsucking vampires, was disinterred and solemnly analyzed. Lloyds of London collected substantial premiums from people insuring against every possible future—including some in which there would have been little chance of collecting a penny.

Then, as the alien passed the orbit of Jupiter, man's instruments began to learn something about it. The first discovery created a short-lived panic. The object was five *hundred* kilometers in diameter—the size of a small moon. Perhaps, after all, it was a mobile world, carrying an invading army. . . .

This fear vanished when more precise observations showed that the solid body of the intruder was only a few meters across. The five-hundred-kilometer halo around it was something familiar—a flimsy, slowly revolving parabolic reflector, the exact equivalent of the astronomers' orbiting radio telescopes. Presumably this was the antenna through which the visitor kept in touch with its distant base. And through which, even now, it was doubtless beaming back its discoveries as it scanned the solar system and eavesdropped upon the radio, television, and data broadcasts of mankind.

Then came yet another surprise. That asteroid-sized antenna was *not* pointed in the direction of Alpha Centauri, but toward a totally different part of the sky. It began to look as if the Centaurus system was merely the vehicle's last port of call, not its origin.

The astronomers were still brooding over this when they had a remarkable stroke of luck. A solar weather probe on routine patrol beyond Mars became suddenly dumb, but recovered its radio voice a minute later. When the records were examined, it was found that the instruments had been momentarily paralyzed by intense radiation. The probe had cut right across the visitor's beam—and it was then a simple matter to calculate precisely where it was aimed.

There was nothing in that direction for fifty-two light-years, except a very faint—and presumably very old—red dwarf star, one of those abstemious little suns that would still be shining peacefully billions of years after the galaxy's splendid giants had burned themselves out. No radio telescope had ever examined it closely; now all those that could be spared from the approaching visitor were focused upon its suspected origin.

And there it was, beaming a sharply tuned signal in the one-centimeter band. The makers were still in contact with the vehicle they had launched, thousands of years ago; but the messages it must be receiving now were from only half a century in the past.

As it came within the orbit of Mars, the visitor showed its first awareness of mankind, in the most dramatic and unmistakable way that could be imagined. It started transmitting standard 3075-line television pictures, interleaved with video text in fluent though stilted English and Mandarin. The first cosmic conversation had begun—and not, as had always been imagined, with a delay of decades, but only minutes.

13

SHADOW AT DAWN

Morgan had left his hotel in Ranapura at 4:00 A.M. on a clear, moonless night. He was not too happy about the choice of time, but Professor Sarath, who had made all the arrangements, had promised him that it would be well worth while. "You won't understand anything about Sri Kanda," he had said, "unless you have watched the dawn from the summit. And Buddy —er, the Maha Thero—won't receive visitors at any other time. He says it's a splendid way of discouraging the merely curious." So Morgan had acquiesced with as much good grace as possible.

To make matters worse, the Taprobanean driver had persisted in carrying on a brisk, though rather one-sided, conversation, apparently designed to establish a complete profile of his passenger's personality. This was all done with such ingenuous good nature that it was impossible to take offense, but Morgan would have preferred silence.

He also wished, sometimes devoutly, that his driver would pay rather more attention to the countless hairpin bends around which they zipped in the near-darkness. Perhaps it was just as well that he could not see all the cliffs and chasms they were negotiating as the car climbed up through the foothills. This road was a triumph of nineteenth-century military engineering —the work of the last colonial power, built in the final campaign against the proud mountain folk of the interior. But it had never been converted to automatic operation, and there were times when Morgan wondered if he would survive the journey.

And then, suddenly, he forgot his fears and his annoyance at the loss of sleep.

"There it is!" said the driver proudly as the car rounded the flank of a hill.

Sri Kanda itself was completely invisible in a darkness that as yet bore no hint of the approaching dawn. Its presence was revealed by a thin ribbon of light, zigzagging back and forth under the stars, hanging as if by magic in the sky. Morgan knew that he was merely seeing the lamps set two hundred years ago to guide pilgrims as they ascended the longest stairway in the world, but in its defiance of logic and gravity it appeared almost a prevision of his own dream. Ages before he was born, inspired by philosophies he could barely imagine, men had begun the work he hoped to finish. They had, quite literally, built the first crude steps on a road to the stars.

No longer feeling drowsy, Morgan watched as the band of light drew closer and resolved itself into a necklace of innumerable twinkling beads. Now the mountain was becoming visible, as a black triangle eclipsing half the sky. There was something sinister about its silent, brooding presence. Morgan could almost imagine that it was indeed the abode of gods who knew of his mission, and were gathering their strength against him.

These ominous thoughts were entirely forgotten when they arrived at the cable-car terminus and Morgan discovered to his surprise—it was only 5:00 A.M.—that at least a hundred people were milling around in the little waiting room. He ordered welcome hot coffee for himself and his garrulous driver, who, rather to his relief, showed no interest in making the ascent. "I've done it at least twenty times," he said with perhaps exaggerated boredom. "*I'm* going to sleep in the car until you come down."

Morgan purchased his ticket, did a quick calculation, and estimated that he would be in the third or fourth load of passengers. He was glad that he had taken Sarath's advice and slipped a thermocoat in his pocket. At a mere two-kilometer altitude, it was quite cold. At the summit, three kilometers higher, it must be freezing.

As he slowly shuffled forward in the rather subdued and sleepy line of visitors, Morgan noted with amusement that he was the only one *not* carrying a camera. Where were the genuine pilgrims? he wondered. Then he remembered; they would not be here. There was no easy way to heaven, or nirvana, or whatever it was that the faithful sought. Merit was acquired solely by one's own efforts, not with the aid of machines. An interesting doctrine, and one containing much truth; but there were also times when only machines could do the job.

At last, he got a seat in the car, and with a considerable creaking of cables they were on their way. Once again, Morgan felt that eerie sense of anticipation. The elevator he was planning would hoist loads more than ten thousand times as high as this primitive system, which probably dated right back to the twentieth century. And yet, when all was said, its basic principles would be much the same.

Outside the swaying car was total darkness, except when a section of illuminated stairway came into view. It was completely deserted, as if the countless millions who had toiled up the mountain during the last three thousand years had left no successor. But then Morgan realized that those making the ascent on foot would already be far above on their appointment with the dawn; they would have left the lower slopes of the mountain hours ago.

At the four-kilometer level the passengers had to

change cars and walk a short distance to another cable
station, but the transfer involved little delay. Now
Morgan was glad of his coat, and wrapped its
metalized fabric closely around his body. There was
frost underfoot, and already he was breathing deeply
in the thin air. He was not at all surprised to see racks
of oxygen cylinders in the small terminus, with instructions for their use prominently displayed.

And now at last, as they began the final ascent,
there came the first intimation of the approaching day.
The eastern stars still shone with undiminished glory—
Venus most brilliantly of all—but a few thin, high
clouds began to glow faintly with the coming dawn.
Morgan looked anxiously at his watch, and wondered
if he would be in time. He was relieved to see that
daybreak was still thirty minutes away.

One of the passengers suddenly pointed to the immense stairway, sections of which were occasionally
visible beneath them as it zigzagged back and forth up
the mountain's now rapidly steepening slopes. It was
no longer deserted; moving with dreamlike slowness,
dozens of men and women were toiling painfully up
the endless steps. Every minute, more and more came
into view. For how many hours, Morgan wondered,
had they been climbing? Certainly all through the
night, and perhaps much longer—for many of the pilgrims were quite elderly, and could hardly have managed the ascent in a single day. He was surprised to see
that so many still believed.

A moment later, he saw the first monk—a tall,
saffron-robed figure moving with a gait of metronome-
like regularity, looking neither to the right nor to the
left, and completely ignoring the car floating above his
shaven head. He also appeared capable of ignoring the
elements, for his right arm and shoulder were bare to
the freezing wind.

The cable car was slowing down as it approached
the terminus. Presently it made a brief halt, disgorged

its numbed passengers, and set off again on its long descent. Morgan joined the crowd of two or three hundred people huddling in a small amphitheater cut in the western face of the mountain. They were all staring out into the darkness, though there was nothing to see but the ribbon of light winding down into the abyss. Some belated climbers on the last section of the stairway were making a final effort, as faith strove to overcome fatigue.

Morgan looked again at his watch; ten minutes to go. He had never before been among so many silent people. Camera-carrying tourists and devout pilgrims were united now in the same hope. The weather was perfect; soon they would know if they had made this journey in vain.

There came a delicate tinkling of bells from the temple, invisible in the darkness a hundred meters above their heads; and at the same instant, all the lights along that unbelievable stairway were extinguished.

Now they could see, as they stood with their backs toward the hidden sunrise, that the first faint gleam of day lay on the clouds far below; but the immense bulk of the mountain still delayed the approaching dawn.

Second by second, the light was growing on either side of Sri Kanda, as the sun outflanked the last strongholds of the night. Then there came a low murmur of awe from the patiently waiting crowd.

One moment there was nothing. Then it was *there,* stretching half the width of Taprobane—a perfectly symmetrical, sharp-edged triangle of deepest blue. The mountain had not forgotten its worshippers. There lay its famous shadow across the sea of clouds, a symbol for each pilgrim to interpret as he pleased.

It seemed almost solid in its rectilinear perfection, like some overturned pyramid rather than a mere phantom of light and shade. As the brightness grew around it, and the first direct rays of the sun struck past the flanks of the mountain, it appeared by contrast to grow even darker and denser. Yet through the thin veil of cloud responsible for its brief existence, Morgan could dimly discern the lakes and hills and forests of the awakening land.

The apex of that misty triangle must be racing toward him at enormous speed as the sun rose vertically behind the mountain, but Morgan was conscious of no movement. Time seemed to have been suspended; this was one of the rare moments of his life when he gave no thought to the passing minutes. The shadow of eternity lay upon his soul, as did that of the mountain upon the clouds.

Now it was fading swiftly, the darkness draining from the sky like a stain dispersing in water. The ghostly, glimmering landscape below was hardening into reality. Halfway to the horizon, there was an explosion of light as the sun's rays struck upon some building's eastern windows. And beyond that—unless his eyes had tricked him—Morgan could make out the faint, dark band of the encircling sea.

Another day had come to Taprobane.

Slowly, the visitors dispersed. Some returned to the cable-car terminus, while others, more energetic, headed for the stairway, in the mistaken belief that the descent was easier than the climb. Most of them would be thankful enough to catch the car again at the lower station; few indeed would make it all the way down.

Only Morgan continued upward, followed by many curious glances, along the short flight of steps that led to the monastery and to the very summit of the mountain. By the time he had reached the smoothly plastered outer wall—now beginning to glow softly in the first direct rays of the sun—he was short of breath, and was glad to lean for a moment against the massive wooden door.

Someone must have been watching. Before he could find a bell push or signal his presence in any way, the door swung silently open, and he was welcomed by a yellow-robed monk, who saluted him with clasped hands.

"*Ayu bowan,* Dr. Morgan. The Mahanayake Thero will be glad to see you."

14

THE EDUCATION OF STARGLIDER

Extract from *Starglider Summaries,* First Edition, 2071

"We now know that the interstellar spaceprobe generally referred to as Starglider is completely autonomous, operating according to general instructions programed into it sixty thousand years ago. While it is cruising between suns, it uses its five-hundred-kilometer antenna to send information back to its base at a relatively slow rate, and to receive occasional updates from Starholme, to adopt the lovely name coined by the poet Llewellyn ap Cymru.

"While it is passing through a solar system, however, it is able to tap the energy of a sun, and so its rate of information transfer increases enormously. It also 'recharges its batteries,' to use a doubtless crude analogy. And because, like our own early Pioneers and Voyagers, it employs the gravitational fields of the heavenly bodies to deflect it from star to star, it will operate indefinitely unless mechanical failure or cosmic accident terminates its career.

"Centaurus was its eleventh port of call. After it had rounded our sun like a comet, its new course was aimed precisely at Tau Ceti, twelve light-years away. If there is anyone there, it will be ready to start its next conversation soon after A.D. 8100. . . .

"Starglider combines the functions of both ambassador and explorer. When, at the end of one of its millennial journeys, it discovers a technological culture, it makes friends with the natives and starts to trade information, in the only form of interstellar commerce that may ever be possible. Before it departs again on its endless voyage, after its brief transit of their solar system, Starglider gives the location of its home world —already awaiting a direct call from the newest member of the galactic communications network.

"In our case, we can take some pride in the fact that, even before it had transmitted any star charts, we had identified its parent sun and even beamed our first transmissions to it. Now we have only to wait one hundred and four years for an answer. How incredibly lucky we are, to have neighbors so close at hand!"

It was obvious from its first messages that Starglider understood the meaning of several thousand basic English and Chinese words, which it had deduced from an analysis of television, radio, and, especially, broadcast video-text services. But what it had picked up during its approach was a very unrepresentative sample from the whole spectrum of human culture; it contained little advanced science, still less advanced mathematics, and only a random selection of literature, music, and the visual arts.

Like any self-taught genius, therefore, Starglider had huge gaps in its education. On the principle that it was better to give too much than too little, as soon as contact was established, Starglider was presented with the *Oxford English Dictionary*, the *Great Chinese Dictionary* (Mandarin edition), and the *Encyclopaedia Terrae*. Their digital transmission required little more than fifty minutes, and it was notable that immediately thereafter Starglider was silent for almost four hours— its longest period off the air. When it resumed contact, its vocabulary was immensely enlarged, and more than ninety-nine percent of the time it could pass the Turing test with ease—that is, there was no way of telling from the messages received that Starglider was a machine, and not a highly intelligent human.

There were occasional giveaways—for example, incorrect use of ambiguous words, and the absence of emotional content in the dialogue. This was only to be expected; unlike advanced terrestrial computers, which could replicate the emotions of their builders, when necessary, Starglider's feelings and desires were presumably those of a totally alien species, and therefore largely incomprehensible to man.

And, of course, vice versa. Starglider could understand precisely and completely what was meant by "the square on the hypotenuse equals the sum of the squares on the other two sides." But it could scarcely have the faintest glimmer of what lay in Keats's mind when he wrote:

> Charm'd magic casements, opening on the foam
> Of perilous seas, in faery lands forlorn. . . .

Still less

> Shall I compare thee to a summer's day?
> Thou art more lovely and more temperate. . . .

Nevertheless, in the hope of correcting this deficiency, Starglider was also presented with thousands of hours of music, drama, and scenes from terrestrial life, both human and otherwise. By general agreement, a certain amount of censorship was enforced here. Although mankind's propensity for violence and warfare could hardly be denied (it was too late to recall the *Encyclopaedia*), only a few carefully selected examples were broadcast. And, until Starglider was safely out of range, the normal fare of the video networks was uncharacteristically bland.

For centuries—perhaps, indeed, until it had reached its next target—philosophers would be debating Starglider's *real* understanding of human affairs and problems. But on one point there was no serious disagreement. The hundred days of its passage through the solar system altered irrevocably men's views of the universe, its origin, and their place in it.

Human civilization could never be the same after Starglider had gone.

15

BODHIDHARMA

As the massive door, carved with intricate lotus patterns, clicked softly shut behind him, Morgan felt that he had entered another world. This was by no means the first time he had been on ground once sacred to some great religion. He had seen Notre-Dame, Hagia Sophia, Stonehenge, the Parthenon, Karnak, Saint Paul's, and at least a dozen other major temples and mosques. But he had viewed them all as frozen relics of the past, splendid examples of art or engineering but with no relevance to the modern mind. The faiths that had created and sustained them had all passed into oblivion, though some had survived until well into the twenty-second century.

But here, it seemed, time had stood still. The hurricanes of history had blown past this lonely citadel of faith, leaving it unshaken. As they had done for three thousand years, the monks still prayed, and meditated, and watched the dawn.

During his walk across the worn flagstones of the courtyard, polished smooth by the feet of innumerable pilgrims, Morgan experienced a sudden and wholly uncharacteristic indecision. In the name of progress, he was attempting to destroy something ancient and noble; and something that he would never fully understand.

The sight of the great bronze bell, hanging in a campanile that grew out of the monastery wall, stopped

Morgan in his tracks. Instantly, his engineer's mind estimated its weight at not less than five tons, and it was obviously very old. How on earth . . . ?

The monk noticed his curiosity, and gave a smile of understanding.

"Two thousand years old," he said. "It was a gift from Kalidasa the Accursed, which we felt it expedient not to refuse. According to legend, it took ten years to carry it up the mountain—and the lives of a hundred men."

"When is it used?" asked Morgan, after he had digested this information.

"Because of its hateful origin, it is sounded only in time of disaster. I have never heard it, nor has any living man. It tolled once, without human aid, during the great earthquake of 2017. And the time before *that* was 1522, when the Iberian invaders burned the Temple of the Tooth and seized the Sacred Relic."

"So after all that effort—it's never been used?"

"Perhaps a dozen times in the last two thousand years. Kalidasa's doom still lies upon it."

That might be good religion, Morgan could not help thinking, but hardly sound economics. He wondered irreverently how many monks had succumbed to the temptation of tapping the bell, ever so gently, just to hear for themselves the unknown timbre of its forbidden voice. . . .

They were walking now past a huge boulder, up which a short flight of steps led to a gilded pavilion. This, Morgan realized, was the very summit of the mountain. He knew what the shrine was supposed to hold, but once again the monk enlightened him.

"The footprint," he said. "The Muslims believed it was Adam's; he stood here after he was expelled from Paradise. The Hindus attributed it to Siva or Saman. But to the Buddhists, of course, it was the imprint of the Enlightened One."

"I notice your use of the past tense," Morgan said in a carefully neutral voice. "What is the belief now?"

The monk's face showed no emotion as he replied: "The Buddha was a man, like you and me. The impression in the rock—and it is *very* hard rock—is two meters long."

That seemed to settle the matter, and Morgan had no further questions while he was led along a short cloister that ended at an open door. The monk knocked, but did not wait for any response as he waved the visitor to enter.

Morgan had half expected to find the Mahanayake Thero sitting cross-legged on a mat, probably surrounded by incense and chanting acolytes. There was, indeed, just a hint of incense in the chill air, but the chief incumbent of the Sri Kanda Maha Vihara sat behind a perfectly ordinary office desk equipped with standard display and memory units. The only unusual item in the room was the head of the Buddha, slightly larger than life, on a plinth in one corner. Morgan could not tell whether it was real or merely a projection.

Despite his conventional setting, there was little likelihood that the head of the monastery would be mistaken for any other type of executive. Quite apart from the inevitable yellow robe, the Mahanayake Thero had two features that, in this age, were extremely rare: he was completely bald, and he was wearing spectacles.

Both, Morgan assumed, were by deliberate choice. Since baldness could be so easily cured, that shining ivory dome must have been shaved or depilated. And he could not remember when he had last seen spectacles, except in historical recordings or dramas.

The combination was fascinating, and disconcerting. Morgan found it virtually impossible to guess the Mahanayake Thero's age. It could be anything from a mature forty to a well-preserved eighty. And those lenses, transparent though they were, somehow concealed the thoughts and emotions behind them.

"*Ayu bowan,* Dr. Morgan," said the High Priest, gesturing to the only empty chair. "This is my secretary, the Venerable Parakarma. I trust you won't mind if he makes notes."

"Of course not," said Morgan, inclining his head toward the remaining occupant of the small room. He noticed that the younger monk had flowing hair and an impressive beard. Presumably, shaven pates were optional.

"So, Dr. Morgan," the Mahanayake Thero continued, "you want our mountain."

"I'm afraid so, Your—er—Reverence. Part of it, at any rate."

"Out of *all* the world—these few hectares?"

"The choice is not ours, but Nature's. The earth terminus has to be on the equator, and at the greatest possible altitude, where the low air density minimizes wind forces."

"There are higher equatorial mountains in Africa and South America."

Here we go again, Morgan thought, groaning silently. Bitter experience had taught him that it was almost impossible to make laymen, however intelligent and interested, appreciate this problem, and he anticipated even less success with these monks. If only the earth were a nice, symmetrical body, with no dents and bumps in its gravitational field . . .

"Believe me," he said fervently, "we've looked at all the alternatives. Cotopaxi and Mount Kenya—and even Kilimanjaro, though that's three degrees south —would be fine except for one fatal flaw. When a satellite is established in the stationary orbit, it won't stay *exactly* over the same spot. Because of gravitational irregularities, which I won't go into, it will slowly drift along the equator. So all our synchronous satellites and space stations have to burn propellant to keep them on station. Luckily, the amount involved is quite small.

"But you can't keep nudging millions of tons—especially when they're in the form of slender rods tens of thousands of kilometers long—back into position. And there's no need to. Fortunately for us—"

"Not for *us*," interjected the Mahanayake Thero, almost throwing Morgan off his stride.

"—there are two stable points on the synchronous orbit. A satellite placed at them will *stay* there. It won't drift away. Just as if it's stuck at the bottom of an invisible valley . . .

"One of those points is out over the Pacific, so it's no use to us. The other is directly above our heads."

"Surely a few kilometers one way or the other would make no difference. There are other mountains in Taprobane."

"None more than half the height of Sri Kanda—which brings us down to the level of critical wind forces. True, there are not many hurricanes exactly on the equator. But there are enough to endanger the structure, at its very weakest point."

"We can control the winds."

It was the first contribution the young secretary had made to the discussion, and Morgan looked at him with heightened interest.

"To some extent, yes. Naturally, I have discussed this point with Monsoon Control. They say that absolute certainty is out of the question—especially with hurricanes. The best odds they will give me are fifty to one. That's not good enough for a trillion-dollar project."

The Venerable Parakarma seemed inclined to argue.

"There is an almost forgotten branch of mathematics, called catastrophe theory, which could make meteorology a really precise science. I am confident that—"

"I should explain," the Mahanayake Thero interjected blandly, "that my colleague was once rather celebrated for his astronomical work. I imagine you have heard of Dr. Choam Goldberg."

Morgan felt that a trap door had been opened beneath him. He should have been warned! Then he recalled that Professor Sarath had indeed told him, with a twinkle in his eye, that he should "watch out for Buddy's private secretary—he's a very smart character."

Morgan wondered if his cheeks were burning as the Venerable Parakarma, alias Dr. Choam Goldberg, looked back at him with a distinctly unfriendly expression. So he had been trying to explain orbital instabilities to these innocent monks; the Mahanayake Thero had probably received much better briefing on the subject than he had given.

He remembered that the world's scientists were neatly divided on the subject of Dr. Goldberg, into those who were *sure* that he was crazy, and those who had not yet made up their minds. He had been one of the most promising young men in the field of astrophysics when, five years ago, he had announced, "Now that Starglider has effectively destroyed all traditional religions, we can at last pay serious attention to the concept of God."

And with that, he had disappeared from public view.

16

CONVERSATIONS WITH STARGLIDER

Of all the thousands of questions put to Starglider during its transit of the solar system, those whose answers were most eagerly awaited concerned the living creatures and civilizations of other stars. Contrary to some expectations, the robot answered willingly, though it admitted that its last update on the subject had been received over a century ago.

Considering the immense range of cultures produced on earth by a single species, it was obvious that there would be even greater variety among the stars, where every conceivable type of biology might occur. Several thousand hours of fascinating—often incomprehensible, sometimes horrifying—scenes of life on other planets left no doubt that this was the case.

Nevertheless, the Starholmers had managed a rough classification of cultures according to their standards of technology—perhaps the only objective basis possible. Humanity was interested to discover that it came in Category Five on a scale that used these approximate stages: 1. Stone tools. 2. Metals, fire. 3. Writing, handicrafts, ships. 4. Steam power, basic science. 5. Atomic energy, space travel.

When Starglider had begun its mission, sixty thousand years ago, its builders were, like the human race, still in Category Five. They had now graduated to Six, characterized by the ability to convert matter completely into energy, and to transmute *all* elements on an industrial scale.

"And is there a Category Seven?" Starglider was immediately asked. The reply was a brief "Affirmative." When pressed for details, the probe explained: "I am not allowed to describe the technology of a higher-grade culture to a lower one." There the matter remained, right up to the moment of the final message, despite all the leading questions designed by the most ingenious legal brains of earth.

By that time, Starglider was more than a match for any terrestrial logician. This was partly the fault of the University of Chicago's Department of Philosophy. In a fit of monumental *hubris,* it had clandestinely transmitted the whole of the *Summa Theologica,* with disastrous results. . . .

"2069 June 02 GMT 1934. Message 1946. Sequence 2. Starglider to Earth.
"I have analyzed the arguments of your Saint Thomas Aquinas as requested in your message 145 sequence 3 of 2069 June 02 GMT 1842. Most of the content appears to be sense-free random noise, and so devoid of information, but the print-out that follows lists 192 fallacies expressed in the symbolic logic of your reference Mathematics 43 of 2069 May 29 GMT 0251.

"Fallacy 1 . . . [there followed a seventy-five-page printout]."

As the log timings show, it took Starglider less than an hour to demolish Saint Thomas. Although philosophers were to spend the next several decades arguing over the analysis, they found only two errors; and those could have been due to a misunderstanding of terminology.

It would have been most interesting to know what fraction of its processing circuits Starglider applied to this task. Unfortunately, no one thought of asking before the probe had switched to cruise mode and broken contact. By then, even more deflating messages had been received. . . .

"2069 June 04 GMT 0759. Message 9056. Sequence 2. Starglider to Earth.
"I am unable to distinguish clearly between your religious ceremonies and apparently identical behavior at the sporting and cultural functions you have transmitted to me. I refer you particularly to the Beatles, 1956; the World Soccer Final, 2047; and the farewell appearance of the Johann Sebastian Clones, 2056."

"2069 June 05 GMT 2038. Message 4675. Sequence 2. Starglider to Earth.
"My last update on this matter is 175 years old, but if I understand you correctly, the answer is as follows. Behavior of the type you call religious occurred among 3 of the 15 known Category One cultures, 6 of the 28 Category Two cultures, 5 of the 14 Category Three cultures, 2 of the 10 Category Four cultures, and 3 of the 174 Category Five cultures. You will appreciate that we have many more examples of Category Five, because only they can be detected over astronomical distances."

"2069 June 06 GMT 1209. Message 5897. Sequence 2. Starglider to Earth.
"You are correct in deducing that the 3 Category Five cultures that engaged in religious activities had two-parent reproduction, and the young remained in family groups for a large fraction of their lifetime. How did you arrive at this conclusion?"

"2069 June 08 GMT 1537. Message 6943. Sequence 2. Starglider to Earth.

"The hypothesis you refer to as God, though not disprovable by logic alone, is unnecessary for the following reason.

"If you assume that the universe can be quote explained unquote as the creation of an entity known as God, he must obviously be of a higher degree of organization than his product. Thus you have *more* than doubled the size of the original problem, and have taken the first step on a diverging infinite regress. William of Ockham pointed out as recently as your fourteenth century that entities should not be multiplied unnecessarily. I cannot therefore understand why this debate continues."

"2069 June 11 GMT 0684. Message 8964. Sequence 2. Starglider to Earth.
"Starholme informed me 456 years ago that the origin of the universe has been discovered but that I do not have the appropriate circuits to comprehend it. You must communicate directly for further information.

"I am now switching to cruise mode and must break contact. Good-by."

In the opinion of many, that final and most famous of all its thousands of messages proved that Starglider had a sense of humor. Why else would it have waited until the very end to explode such a philosophical bombshell? Or was the entire conversation all part of a careful plan, designed to put the human race in the right frame of reference for the time when the first direct messages from Starholme arrived, in, presumably, one hundred and four years?

There were some who suggested following Starglider, since it was carrying out of the solar system not only immeasurable stores of knowledge, but also the treasures of a technology centuries ahead of anything possessed by man. Although no spaceship existed that could overtake Starglider—*and* return again to earth after matching its enormous velocity—one could certainly be built.

However, wiser counsels prevailed. Even a robot space probe might have very effective defenses against boarders—including, as a last resort, the ability to self-destruct. But the most telling argument was that its builders were only fifty-two light-years away. During the millennia since they had launched Starglider, their spacefaring ability must have improved enormously. If the human race did anything to provoke them, they might arrive, slightly annoyed, in a few hundred years.

Meanwhile, among all its countless other effects upon human culture, Starglider had brought to its climax a process that was already well under way. It had put an end to the billions of words of pious gibberish with which apparently intelligent men had addled their minds for centuries.

17

PARAKARMA

As he quickly checked back on the conversation, Morgan decided that he had not made a fool of himself. Indeed, the Mahanayake Thero might have lost a tactical advantage by revealing the identity of the Venerable Parakarma. Yet it was no particular secret; perhaps he thought that Morgan already knew.

At this point, there was a rather welcome interruption, as two young acolytes filed into the office, one carrying a tray loaded with small dishes of rice, fruits, and what appeared to be thin pancakes, while the other followed with the inevitable pot of tea. There was nothing that looked like meat. After his long night, Morgan would have welcomed a couple of eggs, but he assumed that they, too, were forbidden. No—that was too strong a word. Sarath had told him that the Order prohibited nothing, believing in no absolutes. But it had a nicely calibrated scale of toleration, and the taking of life—even potential life—was very low on the list.

As he started to sample the various items, most of them quite unknown to him, Morgan looked inquiringly at the Mahanayake Thero, who shook his head.

"We do not eat before noon. The mind functions more clearly in the morning hours, and so should not be distracted by material things."

As he nibbled at some quite delicious papaya, Morgan considered the philosophical gulf represented by that simple statement. To him, an empty stomach could be most distracting, completely inhibiting the higher mental functions. Having always been blessed with good health, he had never tried to dissociate mind and body, and saw no reason why one should make the attempt.

While Morgan was eating his exotic breakfast, the Mahanayake Thero excused himself, and for a few minutes his fingers danced, with dazzling speed, over the keyboard of his console. Since the read-out was in full view, politeness compelled Morgan to look elsewhere. Inevitably, his eyes fell upon the head of the Buddha.

It was probably real, for the plinth cast a faint shadow on the wall behind. Yet even that was not conclusive. The plinth might be solid enough, and the head a projection carefully positioned on top of it. The trick was a common one.

Here was a work of art that, like the Mona Lisa, both mirrored the emotions of the observer and imposed its own authority upon them. La Gioconda's eyes were open, however, though what they were looking at no one would ever know. The eyes of the Buddha were completely blank—empty pools in which a man might lose his soul, or discover a universe.

Upon the lips there lingered a smile even more ambiguous than the Mona Lisa's. Yet was it really a smile, or merely a trick of the lighting? Already, it was gone, replaced by an expression of superhuman tranquillity. Morgan could not tear his eyes away from that hypnotic countenance, and only the familiar rustling whirr of a hard-copy read-out from the console brought him back to reality—if this *was* reality. . . .

"I thought you might like a souvenir of your visit," said the Mahanayake Thero.

As Morgan accepted the proffered sheet, he was surprised to see that it was archival-quality parchment, not the usual flimsy paper destined to be thrown away after a few hours of use. He could not read a single word. Except for an unobtrusive alphanumeric reference in the bottom left-hand corner, it was all in the flowery curlicues that he could now recognize as Taprobani script.

"Thank you," he said, with as much irony as he could muster. "What is it?" He had a good idea; legal documents had a close family resemblance, whatever their languages, or eras.

"A copy of the agreement between King Ravindra and the Mahanayake Sangha, dated Vesak, A.D. 854 of your calendar. It defines the ownership of the temple land—in perpetuity. The rights set out in this document were even recognized by the invaders."

"By the Caledonians and the Hollanders, I believe. But *not* by the Iberians."

If the Mahanayake Thero was surprised by the thoroughness of Morgan's briefing, not even the twitch of an eyebrow betrayed the fact.

"*They* were hardly respecters of law and order, particularly where other religions were concerned. I trust that their philosophy of might equals right does not appeal to you."

Morgan gave a somewhat forced smile.

"It certainly does not," he answered. But where did one draw the line? he asked himself silently. When the overwhelming interests of great organizations were at stake, conventional morality often took second place. The best legal minds on earth, human and electronic, would soon be focused upon this spot. If they could not find the right answers, a very unpleasant situation might develop—one that could make him a villain, not a hero.

"Since you have raised the subject of the 854 agreement, let me remind you that it refers only to the land *inside* the temple boundaries—which are clearly defined by the walls."

"Correct. But they enclose the entire summit."

"You have no control over the ground outside this area."

"We have the rights of any owner of property. If the neighbors create a nuisance, we would have legal redress. This is not the first time the point has been raised."

"I know. In connection with the cable-car system."

A faint smile played over the Mahanayake Thero's lips. "You have done your homework," he commended. "Yes, we opposed it vigorously, for a number of reasons—though I admit that now it is here, we have often been thankful for it." He paused thoughtfully, then added, "There have been some problems, but we have been able to coexist. Casual sightseers and tourists are content to stay on the lookout platform; *genuine* pilgrims, of course, we are always happy to welcome at the summit."

"Then perhaps some accommodation could be worked out in this case. A few hundred meters of altitude would make no difference to us. We could leave the summit untouched, and carve out another plateau, like the cable-car terminus."

Morgan felt distinctly uncomfortable under the prolonged scrutiny of the two monks. He had little doubt that they recognized the absurdity of the suggestion, but for the sake of the record he had to make it.

"You have a most peculiar sense of humor, Dr. Morgan," the Mahanayake Thero replied at last. "What would be left of the spirit of the mountain—of the solitude we have sought for three thousand years —if this monstrous device is erected here? Do you expect us to betray the faith of all the millions who have come to this sacred spot, often at the cost of their health—even their lives?"

"I sympathize with your feelings," Morgan answered. (But was he lying? he wondered.) "We would, of course, do our best to minimize any disturbance. All the support facilities will be buried inside the mountain. Only the elevator would emerge, and from any distance it would be quite invisible. The general aspect of the mountain would be totally unchanged. Even your famous shadow, which I have just admired, would be virtually unaffected."

The Mahanayake Thero turned to his colleague as if seeking confirmation. The Venerable Parakarma looked straight at Morgan and said: "What about noise?"

Damn, Morgan thought; my weakest point. The payloads would emerge from the mountain at several hundred kilometers an hour. The more velocity they could be given by the ground-based system, the less the strain on the suspended tower. Of course, passengers couldn't take more than half a gee or so, but the capsules would still pop out at a substantial fraction of the speed of sound.

"There will be some aerodynamic noise," Morgan admitted. "But nothing like that near a large airport."

"Very reassuring," said the Mahanayake Thero. Morgan was certain that he was being sarcastic, though he could detect no trace of irony in his voice. He was either displaying an Olympian calm or testing his visitor's reactions. The younger monk, on the other hand, made no attempt to conceal his anger.

"For years," he said with indignation, "we have been protesting about the disturbance caused by re-entering spacecraft. Now you want to generate shock waves in . . . in our back garden."

"Our operations will *not* be transsonic, at this altitude," Morgan replied firmly. "And the tower structure will absorb most of the sound energy. In fact," he added, trying to press what he had suddenly seen as an advantage, "in the long run, we'll help to eliminate re-entry booms. The mountain will actually be a quieter place."

"I understand. Instead of occasional concussions, we will have a steady roar."

I'm not getting anywhere with *this* character, thought Morgan; and I'd expected the Mahanayake Thero to be the biggest obstacle. . . .

Sometimes, it was best to change the subject entirely. He decided to dip one cautious toe into the quaking quagmire of theology.

"Isn't there something appropriate," he said earnestly, "in what we are trying to do? Our purposes may be different, but the net results have much in common. What we hope to build is only an extension of your stairway. If I may say so, we're continuing it —all the way to heaven."

For a moment, the Venerable Parakarma seemed taken aback at such effrontery. Before he could recover, his superior answered smoothly:

"An interesting concept. But our philosophy does not believe in heaven. Such salvation as may exist can be found only in *this* world, and I sometimes wonder at your anxiety to leave it. Do you know the story of the Tower of Babel?"

"Vaguely."

"I suggest you look it up in the old Christian Bible —Genesis 11. That, too, was an engineering project to scale the heavens. It failed, owing to difficulties in communication."

"Though we will have our problems, I don't think *that* will be one of them."

But looking at the Venerable Parakarma, Morgan was not so sure. Here was a communications gap that seemed in some ways greater than that between Homo sapiens and Starglider. They spoke the same language, but there were gulfs of incomprehension that might never be spanned.

"May I ask," continued the Mahanayake Thero with imperturbable politeness, "how successful you were with the Department of Parks and Forests?"

"They were extremely co-operative."

"I am not surprised. They are chronically under-budgeted, and any new source of revenue would be welcome. The cable system was a financial windfall, and doubtless they hope your project will be an even bigger one."

"They will be right. And they have accepted the fact that it won't create any environmental hazards."

"Suppose it falls down?"

Morgan looked the monk straight in the eye.

"It won't," he said, with all the authority of the man whose inverted rainbow now linked two continents.

But he knew, and the implacable Parakarma must also know, that absolute certainty was impossible in such matters. Two hundred and two years ago, on 7 November 1940, that lesson had been driven home in a way that no engineer could ever forget.

Morgan had few nightmares, but that was one of them. Even at this moment the computers at Terran Construction were trying to exorcise it.

But all the computing power in the universe could provide no protection against the problems he had *not* foreseen—the nightmares that were still unborn.

18

THE GOLDEN BUTTERFLIES

Despite the brilliant sunlight and the magnificent views that assailed him from every side, Morgan was fast asleep before the car had descended into the lowlands. Even the innumerable hairpin bends failed to keep him awake—but he was snapped back into consciousness when the brakes were slammed on and he was pitched forward against his seat belt.

For a moment of utter confusion, he thought that he must still be dreaming. The breeze blowing gently through the half-open windows was so warm and humid that it might have escaped from a Turkish bath; yet the car had apparently come to a halt in the midst of a blinding snowstorm.

Morgan blinked, screwed up his eyes, and opened them to reality. This was the first time he had ever seen *golden* snow.

A dense swarm of butterflies was crossing the road, headed due east in a steady, purposeful migration. Some had been sucked into the car, and fluttered around frantically until Morgan waved them out; many more had plastered themselves on the windshield. With what were doubtless a few choice Taprobani expletives, the driver emerged and wiped the glass clear. By the time he had finished, the swarm had thinned out to a handful of isolated stragglers.

"Did they tell you about the legend?" he asked, glancing back at his passenger.

"No," said Morgan curtly. He was not at all interested, being anxious to resume his interrupted nap.

"The Golden Butterflies—they're the souls of Kalidasa's warriors, the army he lost at Yakkagala."

Morgan gave an unenthusiastic grunt, hoping that the driver would get the message; but he continued remorselessly.

"Every year, around this time, they head for the mountain, and they all die on its lower slopes. Sometimes you'll meet them halfway up the cable ride, but that's the highest they get. Which is lucky for the vihara."

"The vihara?" asked Morgan sleepily.

"The temple. If they ever reach it, Kalidasa will have conquered, and the bhikkus—the monks—will have to leave. That's the prophecy—it's carved on a stone slab in the Ranapura Museum. I can show it to you."

"Some other time," said Morgan hastily as he settled back into the padded seat. But it was many kilometers before he could doze off again, because there was something haunting about the image that the driver had conjured up.

He would remember it often in the months ahead—when waking, and in moments of stress or crisis. Once again he would be immersed in that golden snowstorm, as the doomed millions spent their energies in a vain assault upon the mountain and all that it symbolized.

Even now, at the very beginning of his campaign, the image was too close for comfort.

19

BY THE SHORES OF LAKE SALADIN

"Almost all the Alternative History computer simulations suggested that the Battle of Tours (A.D. 732) was one of the crucial disasters of mankind. Had Charles Martel been defeated, Islam might have resolved the internal differences that were tearing it apart and gone on to conquer Europe. Thus centuries of Christian barbarism would have been avoided, the Industrial Revolution would have started almost a thousand years earlier, and by now we would have reached the nearer stars instead of merely the farther planets. . . .

"But fate ruled otherwise, and the armies of the Prophet turned back into Africa. Islam lingered on, a fascinating fossil, until the end of the twentieth century. Then, abruptly, it was dissolved in oil . . ."

Chairman's Address
Toynbee Bicentennial Symposium
London, 2089

"Did you know," said Sheik Farouk Abdullah, "that I have now appointed myself Grand Admiral of the Sahara Fleet?"

"It wouldn't surprise me, Mr. President," Morgan answered as he gazed out across the sparkling blue expanse of Lake Saladin. "If it's not a naval secret, how many ships do you have?"

"Ten at the moment. The largest is a thirty-meter hydro-skimmer run by the Red Crescent. It spends every weekend rescuing incompetent sailors. My people still aren't much good on the water—look at that idiot trying to tack! After all, two hundred years really isn't long enough to switch from camels to boats."

"You had Cadillacs and Rolls-Royces in between. Surely that should have eased the transition."

"And we still have them. My great-great-*great*-grandfather's Silver Ghost is just as good as new. But I must be fair—it's the visitors who get into trouble, trying to cope with our local winds. *We* stick to powerboats. And next year I'm getting a submarine guaranteed to reach the lake's maximum depth of seventy-eight meters."

"Whatever for?"

"*Now* they tell us that the Erg was full of archaeological treasures. Of course, no one bothered about them before it was flooded."

It was no use trying to hurry the President of ANAR—the Autonomous North African Republic—and Morgan knew better than to attempt it. Whatever the constitution might say, Sheik Abdullah controlled more power and wealth than almost any single individual on earth. More to the point, he understood the uses of both.

He came of a family that was not afraid to take risks, and seldom had cause to regret them. Its first and most famous gamble—which had incurred the hatred of the whole Arab world for almost half a century—was the investment of its abundant petro-dollars in the science and technology of Israel. That farsighted act had led directly to the mining of the Red Sea, the defeat of the deserts, and, very much later, to the Gibraltar Bridge. . . .

"I don't have to tell you, Van," said the Sheik at last, "how much your new project fascinates me. And after all that we went through together while the

Bridge was being built, I know that you could do it—
given the resources."

"Thank you."

"But I have a few questions. I'm not clear why
there's Midway Station—and why it's at a height of
twenty-five thousand kilometers."

"Several reasons. We need a major power plant at
about that level, which would involve fairly massive
construction there in any case. Then it occurred to us
that seven hours was too long to stay cooped up in a
rather cramped cabin, and splitting the journey would
give a number of advantages. We wouldn't have to
feed the passengers in transit; they could eat and
stretch their legs at the station. We could also optimize
the vehicle design. Only the capsules on the lower
section would have to be streamlined. Those on the
upper run could be much simpler and lighter. Midway
Station would serve not only as a transfer point, but
also as an operations and control center—and ultimately, we believe, as a major tourist attraction and
resort in its own right."

"But it's *not* midway! It's almost—ah—two thirds of
the distance up to stationary orbit."

"True. The mid-point would be at eighteen thousand, not twenty-five. But there's another factor:
safety. If the section above is severed, Midway Station
won't crash back to earth."

"Why not?"

"It will have enough momentum to maintain a stable
orbit. Of course, it will fall earthward, but it will
always remain clear of the atmosphere. So it will be
perfectly safe. It will simply become a space station,
moving in a ten-hour elliptical orbit. Twice a day, it
will be right back where it started from, and eventually
it could be reconnected. In theory, at least . . ."

"And in practice?"

"Oh, I'm sure it could be done. Certainly the people
and equipment on the station could be saved. But we

wouldn't have even that option if we established it at a lower altitude. *Anything* falling from below the twenty-five-thousand-kilometer limit hits the atmosphere and burns up in five hours, or less."

"Do you propose advertising this fact to passengers on the Earth-Midway run?"

"We hope they will be too busy admiring the view to worry about it."

"You make it sound like a scenic elevator."

"Why not? Except that the tallest scenic ride on earth goes up a mere three kilometers! We're talking about something ten thousand times higher."

There was a considerable pause while Sheik Abdullah thought this over.

"We missed an opportunity," he said at last. "We could have had *five*-kilometer scenic rides up the piers of the Bridge."

"They were in the original design, but we dropped them for the usual reason—economy."

"Perhaps we made a mistake. They could have paid for themselves. And I've just realized something else. If this . . . hyperfilament . . . had been available at the time, I suppose the Bridge could have been built for half the cost."

"I wouldn't lie to you, Mr. President. Less than a fifth. But construction would have been delayed more than twenty years, so you haven't lost by it."

"I must talk that over with my accountants. Some of them still aren't convinced it was a good idea, even though the traffic growth rate is ahead of projection. But I keep telling them that money isn't everything— the republic *needed* the Bridge psychologically and culturally, as well as economically. Did you know that eighteen percent of the people who drive across it do so just because it's there, not for any other reason? And then they go straight back again, despite having to pay the toll both ways."

"I seem to recall," said Morgan dryly, "giving you

similar arguments a long time ago. You weren't easy to convince."

"True. I remember that the Sydney Opera House was your favorite example. You liked to point out how many times *that* had paid for itself—even in hard cash, let alone prestige."

"And don't forget the Pyramids."

The Sheik laughed.

"What did you call them? The best investment in the history of mankind?"

"Precisely. Still paying tourist dividends after four thousand years."

"Hardly a fair comparison, though. Their running costs don't compare with those of the Bridge . . . much less your proposed Tower's."

"The Tower may last longer than the Pyramids. It's in a far more benign environment."

"That's a very impressive thought. You *really* believe that it will operate for several thousand years?"

"Not in its original form, of course. But in principle, yes. Whatever technical developments the future brings, I don't believe there will ever be a more efficient, more economical way of reaching space. Think of it as another bridge. But this time, a bridge to the stars—or at least to the planets."

"And once again, you'd like us to help finance it. We'll still be paying for the *last* bridge for another twenty years. It's not as if your Space Elevator was on our territory, or was of direct importance to us."

"But I believe it is, Mr. President. Your republic is a part of the terran economy, and the cost of space transportation is now one of the factors limiting its growth. If you've looked at those estimates for the 50's and 60's . . ."

"I have—I have. Very interesting. But though we're not exactly poor, we couldn't raise a fraction of the funds needed. Why, it would absorb the entire gross world product for a couple of years!"

"And pay it back every fifteen, forever afterward."

"If your projections are correct."

"They were for the Bridge. But you're right, of course, and I don't expect ANAR to do more than start the ball rolling. Once you've shown your interest, it will be that much easier to get other support."

"Such as?"

"The World Bank. The planetary banks. The federal government."

"And your own employers, the Terrann Construction Corporation? What are you *really* up to, Van?"

Here it comes, thought Morgan, almost with a sigh of relief. Now at last he could talk frankly with someone he could trust, someone who was too big to be involved in petty bureaucratic intrigues, but who could thoroughly appreciate their finer points.

"I've been doing most of this work in my own time —I'm on vacation right now. And incidentally, that's just how the Bridge started! I don't know if I ever told you that I was once officially ordered to forget it. . . . I've learned a few lessons in the past fifteen years."

"This report must have taken a good deal of computer time. Who paid for that?"

"Oh, I have considerable discretionary funds. And my staff is always doing studies that nobody else can understand. To tell the truth, I've had quite a little team playing with the idea for several months. They're so enthusiastic that they spend most of their free time on it as well. But now we have to commit ourselves—or abandon the project."

"Does your esteemed chairman know about this?"

Morgan smiled, without much humor.

"Of course not, and I don't want to tell him until I've worked out all the details."

"I can appreciate some of the complications," said the President shrewdly. "One of them, I imagine, is insuring that Senator Collins doesn't invent it first."

"He can't do *that*—the idea is about two hundred

years old. But he, and a lot of other people, could slow it down. I want to see it happen in my lifetime."

"And of course you intend to be in charge. . . . Well, what exactly would you like us to do?"

"This is merely one suggestion, Mr. President—you may have a better idea. Form a consortium—perhaps including the Gibraltar Bridge Authority, the Suez and Panama corporations, the English Channel Company, the Bering Dam Corporation. . . . Then, when it's all wrapped up, approach TCC with a request for a feasibility study. At this stage, the investment will be negligible."

"Meaning?"

"Less than a million. Especially since I've already done ninety percent of the work."

"And then?"

"Thereafter, with *your* backing, Mr. President, I can play it by ear. I might stay with TCC. Or I might resign and join the consortium—call it Astroengineering. It would all depend on circumstances. I would do whatever seemed best for the project."

"That seems a reasonable approach. I think we can work something out."

"Thank you, Mr. President," Morgan answered with heartfelt sincerity. "But there's one annoying roadblock we have to tackle at once—perhaps even before we set up the consortium. We have to go to the World Court and establish jurisdiction over the most valuable piece of real estate on earth."

20

THE BRIDGE THAT DANCED

Even in this age of instantaneous communication and swift global transport, it was convenient to have a place that one could call one's office. Not everything could be stored in patterns of electronic charges; there were still such items as good old-fashioned books, professional certificates, awards and honors, engineering models, samples of material, artists' renderings of projects (not as accurate as a computer's, but very ornamental), and, of course, the wall-to-wall carpet that every senior bureaucrat needed to soften the impact of external reality.

Morgan's office, which he saw, on the average, ten days per month, was on the sixth or LAND floor of the sprawling Terran Construction Corporation headquarters in Nairobi. The floor below was SEA; that above it, ADMINISTRATION—meaning Chairman Collins and his empire. The architect, in a fit of naive symbolism, had devoted the top floor to SPACE. There was even a small observatory on the roof, with a thirty-centimeter telescope, which was always out of order because it was used only during office parties, and frequently for very nonastronomical purposes. The upper rooms of the Triplanetary Hotel, only a kilometer away, were a favorite target, since they often held some extremely strange forms of life—or, at any rate, of behavior.

Since Morgan was in continuous touch with his two

secretaries—one human, the other electronic—he expected no surprises when he walked into his office after the brief flight from ANAR. By the standards of an earlier age, his was an extraordinarily small organization. He had fewer than three hundred men and women under his direct control; but the computing and information-processing power at their command could not be matched by the merely human population of the entire planet.

"Well, how did you get on with the Sheik?" asked Warren Kingsley, his deputy and long-time friend, as soon as they were alone together.

"Very well. I think we have a deal. But I still can't believe that we're held up by such a stupid problem. What does the Legal Department say?"

"We'll definitely have to get a World Court ruling. If the Court agrees that it's a matter of overwhelming public interest, our reverend friends will have to move . . . . Though if they decide to be stubborn, there would be a nasty situation. Perhaps you should send a small earthquake to help them make up their minds."

The fact that Morgan was on the board of General Tectonics was an old joke between him and Kingsley; but GT—perhaps fortunately—had never found a way of controlling and directing earthquakes, nor did it ever expect to do so. The best that it could hope for was to predict them, and to bleed off their energies harmlessly before they could do major damage. Even here, its record of success was not much better than seventy-five percent.

"A nice idea," said Morgan. "I'll think it over. Now, what about our other problem?"

"All set to go. Do you want it now?"

"Okay—let's see the worst."

The office windows darkened, and a grid of glowing lines appeared in the center of the room.

"Watch this, Van," said Kingsley. "Here's the regime that gives trouble."

Rows of letters and numbers materialized in the empty air—velocities, payloads, accelerations, transit times. Morgan absorbed them at a glance. The globe of the earth, with its circles of longitude and latitude, hovered just above the carpet; and rising from it, to little more than the height of a man, was the luminous thread that marked the position of the Orbital Tower.

"Five hundred times normal speed; lateral scale exaggeration fifty. Here we go."

Some invisible force had started to pluck at the line of light, drawing it away from the vertical. The disturbance was moving upward as it mimicked, via the computer's millions of calculations a second, the ascent of a payload through the earth's gravitational field.

"What's the displacement?" asked Morgan as his eyes strained to follow the details of the simulation.

"Now about two hundred meters. It gets to three before—"

The thread snapped. In the leisurely slow-motion that represented real speeds of thousands of kilometers an hour, the two segments of the severed tower began to curl away from each other—one bending back to earth, the other whipping upward to space. But Morgan was no longer fully conscious of this imaginary disaster, existing only in the mind of the computer. Superimposed upon it now was the reality that had haunted him for years.

He had seen that two-century-old film at least fifty times, and there were sections that he had examined frame by frame, until he knew every detail by heart. It was, after all, the most expensive movie footage ever shot, at least in peacetime. It had cost the State of Washington several million dollars a minute. . . .

There stood the slim (too slim!) and graceful bridge, spanning the canyon. It bore no traffic, but a single car had been abandoned midway by its driver.

And no wonder, for the bridge was behaving as none before in the whole history of engineering.

It seemed impossible that thousands of tons of metal could perform such an aerial ballet. One could more easily believe that the bridge was made of rubber than of steel. Vast, slow undulations, meters in amplitude, were sweeping along the entire width of the span, so that the roadway suspended between the piers twisted back and forth like an angry snake. The wind blowing down the canyon was sounding a note far too low for any human ears to detect, as it hit the natural frequency of the beautiful, doomed structure. For hours, the torsional vibrations had been building up, but no one knew when the end would come. Already, the protracted death throes were a testimonial that the unlucky designers could well have forgone.

Suddenly, the supporting cables snapped, flailing upward like murderous steel whips. Twisting and turning, the roadway pitched into the river, fragments of the structure flying in all directions. Even when projected at normal speed, the final cataclysm looked as if shot in slow motion; the scale of the disaster was so large that the human mind had no basis of comparison. In reality, it lasted perhaps five seconds. At the end of that time, the Tacoma Narrows Bridge had earned an inexpungable place in the history of engineering. Two hundred years later, there was a photograph of its last moments on the wall of Morgan's office, bearing the caption "One of our less successful products."

To Morgan, that was no joke, but a permanent reminder that the unexpected could always strike from ambush. When the Gibraltar Bridge was being designed, he had gone carefully through Theodore von Kármán's classic analysis of the Tacoma Narrows disaster, learning all he could from one of the most expensive mistakes of the past. There had been no serious vibrational problems even in the worst gales that had come roaring in from the Atlantic, though the roadway had moved a hundred meters from the centerline—precisely as calculated.

But the Space Elevator was such a leap forward into the unknown that some unpleasant surprises were a virtual certainty. Wind forces in the atmospheric section were easy to estimate, but it was also necessary to take into account the vibrations induced by the stopping and starting of the payloads—and even, on so enormous a structure, by the tidal effects of the sun and the moon. And not only individually, but acting all together; with, perhaps, an occasional earthquake to complicate the picture, in the so-called worst-case analysis.

"All the simulations, in this tons-of-payload-per-hour regime, give the same result. The vibrations build up until there's a fracture at around five hundred kilometers. We'll have to increase the damping—drastically."

"I was afraid of that. How much do we need?"

"Another ten megatons."

Morgan could take some gloomy satisfaction from the figure. That was close to the guess he had made, using his engineer's intuition and the mysterious resources of his subconscious. Now the computer had confirmed it. They would have to increase the "anchor" mass in orbit by ten million tons.

Even by terrestrial earth-moving standards, such a mass was hardly trivial. It was equivalent to a sphere of rock about two hundred meters across. Morgan had a sudden image of Yakkagala, as he had last seen it, looming against the Taprobanean sky. Imagine lifting *that* forty thousand kilometers into space! Fortunately, it might not be necessary; there were alternatives.

Morgan always let his subordinates do their thinking for themselves. It was the only way to establish responsibility, it took much of the load off him, and on many occasions his staff arrived at solutions he had overlooked.

"What do you suggest, Warren?" he asked quietly.

"We *could* use one of the lunar freight launchers, and shoot up ten megatons of moon rock. It would be a long and expensive job, and we'd need a large space-based operation to catch the material and steer it into final orbit. There would also be a psychological problem—"

"Yes, I can appreciate that. We don't want another San Luiz Domingo."

San Luiz had been the—fortunately small—South American village that had received a stray cargo of processed lunar metal intended for a low-orbit space station. The terminal guidance had failed, resulting in the first man-made meteor crater—and two hundred and fifty deaths. Ever since that, the population of planet earth had been very sensitive on the subject of celestial target practice.

"A much better answer is to catch an asteroid. We're running a search for those with suitable orbits, and have found three promising candidates. What we really want is a carbonaceous one. Then we can use it for raw material when we set up the processing plant. Killing two birds with one stone."

"A rather large stone, but that's probably the best idea. Forget the lunar launcher—a million ten-ton shots would tie it up for years, and some of them would be bound to go astray. If you can't find a large enough asteroid, we can send the extra mass up by the elevator itself—though I hate wasting all that energy if it can be avoided."

"It may be the cheapest way. With the efficiency of the latest fusion plants, it will take only twenty dollars' worth of electricity to lift a ton up to orbit."

"Are you sure of that figure?"

"It's a firm quotation from Central Power."

Morgan was silent for a few minutes. Then he

said: "The aerospace engineers really are going to
hate me." Almost as much, he added to himself, as the
Venerable Parakarma.

No—that was not fair. Hate was an emotion no
longer possible to a true follower of the doctrine.
What he had seen in the eyes of former Dr. Choam
Goldberg was merely implacable opposition. But that
could be equally dangerous.

21

JUDGMENT

One of Paul Sarath's more annoying specialties was the sudden call, gleeful or gloomy, as the case might be, which invariably consisted of the words: "Have you heard the news?" Though Rajasinghe had often been tempted to give the general-purpose answer "Yes—I'm not at all surprised," he had never had the heart to rob Sarath of his simple pleasure.

"What is it *this* time?" he answered, without much enthusiasm.

"Maxine's on Global Two, talking to Senator Collins. I think our friend Morgan is in trouble. Call you back."

Sarath's excited image faded from the screen, to be replaced a few seconds later by Maxine Duval's, as Rajasinghe switched to the news-analysis channel. She was sitting in her familiar studio, talking to the Chairman of the Terran Construction Corporation, who seemed to be in a mood of barely suppressed indignation, probably synthetic.

"Senator Collins, now that the World Court ruling has been given—"

Rajasinghe shunted the entire program to RECORD, with a muttered "I thought that wasn't until Friday." As he turned off the sound and activated his private link with ARISTOTLE, he exclaimed, "My God, it *is* Friday!"

As always, Ari was on line at once.

"Good morning, Raja. What can I do for you?"

That beautiful, dispassionate voice, untouched by human glottis, had never changed in the forty years that he had known it. Decades, perhaps centuries, after he was dead, it would be talking to other men just as it had spoken to him. (For that matter, how many conversations was it having at this very moment?) Once, this knowledge had depressed Rajasinghe; now, it no longer mattered. He did not envy ARISTOTLE'S immortality.

"Good morning, Ari. I'd like today's World Court ruling on the Astroengineering Corporation *versus* the Sri Kanda Vihara case. The summary will do. Let me have the full print-out later."

"Decision 1. Lease of temple site confirmed in perpetuity under Taprobanean and World law, as codified 2085. Unanimous ruling.

"Decision 2. The construction of the proposed Orbital Tower, with its attendant noise, vibration, and its impact upon a site of great historic and cultural importance would constitute a private nuisance, meriting an injunction under the law of torts. At this stage, public interest not of sufficient merit to affect the issue. Ruling 4 to 2, one abstention."

"Thank you, Ari. Cancel print-out. I won't need it. Good-by."

Well, that was that, just as he had expected. Yet he did not know whether to be relieved or disappointed.

Rooted as he was in the past, he was glad that old traditions were cherished and protected. If one thing had been learned from the bloody history of mankind, it was that only individual human beings mattered: however eccentric their beliefs might be, they must be safeguarded, so long as they did not conflict with wider but equally legitimate interests. What was it that the old poet had said? "There is no such thing as the State." Perhaps that was going a little too far; but it was better than the other extreme.

At the same time, Rajasinghe felt a mild sense of regret. He had half convinced himself (was this merely co-operating with the inevitable?) that Morgan's fantastic enterprise might be just what was needed to prevent Taprobane (and perhaps the whole world, though *that* was no longer his responsibility) from sinking into a comfortable, self-satisfied decline. Now the Court had closed that particular avenue, at least for many years.

He wondered what Duval would have to say on the subject, and switched over to delayed playback. On Global Two (sometimes referred to as the Land of Talking Heads), Senator Collins was still gathering momentum.

"—undoubtedly exceeding his authority and using the resources of his division on projects that did not concern it."

"But surely, Senator, aren't you being somewhat legalistic? As I understand it, hyperfilament was developed for *construction* purposes, especially bridges. And isn't this a kind of bridge? I've heard Dr. Morgan use that analogy, though he also calls it a tower."

"*You're* being legalistic now, Maxine. I prefer the name 'Space Elevator.' And you're quite wrong about hyperfilament. It's the result of two hundred years of aerospace research. The fact that the final breakthrough came in the *Land* Division of my—ah—organization is irrelevant, though naturally I'm proud that my scientists were involved."

"You consider that the whole project should be handed over to the Space Division?"

"What project? This is merely a design study—one of hundreds that are always going on at TCC. I never hear about a fraction of them, and I don't want to—until they reach the stage when some major decision has to be made."

"Which is not the case here?"

"Definitely not. My space-transportation experts say that they can handle all projected traffic increases —at least for the foreseeable future."

"Meaning precisely?"

"Another twenty years."

"And what happens then? The Tower will take that long to build, according to Dr. Morgan. Suppose it isn't ready in time?"

"Then we'll have something else. My staff is looking into *all* the possibilities, and it's by no means certain that the Space Elevator is the right answer."

"The idea, though, is fundamentally sound?"

"It appears to be, though further studies are required."

"Then surely you should be grateful to Dr. Morgan for his initial work."

"I have the utmost respect for Dr. Morgan. He is one of the most brilliant engineers in my organization—if not in the world."

"I don't think, Senator, that quite answers my question."

"Very well; I *am* grateful to Dr. Morgan for bringing this matter to our notice. But I do not approve of the way in which he did it. If I may be blunt, he tried to force my hand."

"How?"

"By going outside my organization—*his* organization—and thus showing a lack of loyalty. As a result of his maneuverings, there has been an adverse World Court decision, which inevitably has provoked much unfavorable comment. In the circumstances, I have had no choice but to request—with the utmost regret —that he tender his resignation."

"Thank you, Senator Collins. As always, it's been a pleasure talking to you."

"You sweet liar," said Rajasinghe as he switched

off and took the call that had been flashing for the last minute.

"Did you get it all?" asked Sarath. "So *that's* the end of Dr. Vannevar Morgan."

Rajasinghe looked thoughtfully at his old friend for a few seconds.

"You were always fond of jumping to conclusions, Paul. How much would you care to bet?"

III

THE
BELL

22

APOSTATE

"Driven to despair by his fruitless attempts to understand the universe, the sage Devadasa finally announced in exasperation:

" 'All statements that contain the word God are false.'

"Instantly, his least-favorite discipline, Somasiri, replied:

" 'The sentence I am now speaking contains the word God. I fail to see, oh Noble Master, how **that** simple statement can be false.'

"Devadasa considered the matter for several Poyas. Then he answered, this time with apparent satisfaction:

" 'Only statements that do **not** contain the word God can be true.'

"After a pause barely sufficient for a starving mongoose to swallow a millet seed, Somasiri replied:

" 'If this statement applies to itself, oh Venerable One, it cannot be true, because it contains the word God. But if it is **not** true—'

"At this point, Devadasa broke his begging bowl upon Somasiri's head, and should therefore be honored as the true founder of Zen."

From a fragment of the **Culavamsa,**
as yet undiscovered

In the late afternoon, when the stairway was no longer blasted by the full fury of the sun, the Venerable Parakarma began his descent. By nightfall, he would reach the highest of the pilgrim resthouses; and by the following day, he would have returned to the world of men.

The Mahanayake Thero had given neither advice nor discouragement, and if he was grieved by his colleague's departure, he had shown no sign. He had merely intoned, "All things are impermanent," clasped his hands, and given his blessing.

The Venerable Parakarma, who had once been Dr. Choam Goldberg, and might be so again, would have had great difficulty in explaining all his motives. "Right action" was easy to say; it was not so easy to discover.

At the Sri Kanda Maha Vihara he had found peace of mind—but that was not enough. With his scientific training, he was no longer content to accept the Order's ambiguous attitude toward God. Such indifference had come at last to seem worse than outright denial.

If such a thing as a rabbinical gene could exist, Dr. Goldberg possessed it. Like many before him, Goldberg-Parakarma had sought God through mathematics, undiscouraged even by the bombshell that Kurt Gödel, with the discovery of undecidable propositions, had exploded early in the twentieth century. He could not understand how anyone could contemplate the dynamic asymmetry of Euler's profound yet beautifully simple $e^{\pi i} + 1 = 0$ without wondering if the universe was the creation of some vast intelligence.

Having first made his name with a new cosmological theory that had survived almost ten years before being refuted, Goldberg had been widely acclaimed as another Einstein or N'goya. In an age of ultraspecialization, he had also managed to make notable ad-

vances in aero- and hydrodynamics—long regarded as
dead subjects, incapable of further surprises.

Then, at the height of his powers, he had experienced a religious conversion not unlike Pascal's, though
without so many morbid undertones. For the next
decade, he had been content to lose himself in saffron
anonymity, focusing his brilliant mind upon questions
of doctrine and philosophy. He did not regret the
interlude, and he was not even sure that he had
abandoned the Order; one day, perhaps, this great
stairway would see him again. But his God-given
talents were reasserting themselves. There was massive
work to be done, and he needed tools that could not be
found on Sri Kanda—or even, for that matter, on earth
itself.

He felt little hostility, now, toward Vannevar
Morgan. However inadvertently, the engineer had ignited the spark; in his blundering way, he, too, was an
agent of God. Yet, at all costs, the temple must be
protected. Whether or not the wheel of fate ever returned him to its tranquillity, Parakarma was implacably resolved upon that.

And so, like a new Moses bringing down from the
mountain laws that would change the destinies of men,
the Venerable Parakarma descended to the world he
had once renounced. He was blind to the beauties of
land and sky that were all around him. They were
utterly trivial compared to those that he alone could see
in the armies of equations that were marching through
his mind.

23

MOONDOZER

"Your trouble, Dr. Morgan," said the man in the wheelchair, "is that you're on the wrong planet."

"I can't help thinking," retorted Morgan, looking pointedly at his visitor's life-support system, "that much the same may be said of you."

The Vice President (Investments) of Narodny Mars gave an appreciative chuckle.

"At least I'm here only for a week. Then it's back to the moon, and a civilized gravity. Oh, I can walk if I really have to; but I prefer otherwise."

"If I may ask, why do you come to earth at all?"

"I do so as little as possible, but sometimes one has to be on the spot. Contrary to general belief, you can't do *everything* by remotes. I'm sure you are aware of that."

Morgan nodded; it was true enough. He thought of all the times when the texture of some material, the feel of rock or soil underfoot, the smell of a jungle, the sting of spray upon his face, had played a vital role in one of his projects. Someday, perhaps even these sensations could be transferred by electronics. Indeed, it had already been done so, crudely, on an experimental basis, and at enormous cost. But there was no substitute for reality; one should beware of imitations.

"If you've visited earth especially to meet me," Morgan replied, "I appreciate the honor. But if you're offering me a job on Mars, you're wasting your time.

I'm enjoying my retirement, meeting friends and relatives I haven't seen for years, and I've no intention of starting a new career."

"I find that surprising. After all, you're only fifty-two. How do you propose to occupy your time?"

"Easily. I could spend the rest of my life on any one of a dozen projects. The ancient engineers—the Romans, the Greeks, the Incas—they've always fascinated me, and I've never had time to study them. I've been asked to write and deliver a Global University course on design science. There's a textbook I'm commissioned to write on advanced structures. I want to develop some ideas about the use of active elements to correct dynamic loads—winds, earthquakes, and so forth. I'm still consultant for General Tectonics. And I'm preparing a report on the administration of TCC."

"At whose request? Not, I take it, Senator Collins."

"No," said Morgan, with a grim smile. "I thought it would be—useful. And it helps to relieve my feelings."

"I'm sure of it. But all these activities aren't really *creative*. Sooner or later, they'll pall—like this beautiful Norwegian scenery. You'll grow tired of looking at lakes and fir trees, just as you'll grow tired of writing and talking. You are the sort of man who will never be really happy, Dr. Morgan, unless you are shaping your universe."

Morgan did not reply. The prognosis was much too accurate for comfort.

"I suspect that you agree with me. What would you say if I told you that my bank is seriously interested in the Space Elevator project?"

"I'd be skeptical. When I approached its officers, they said it was a fine idea but they couldn't put any money into it at this stage. All available funds were needed for the development of Mars. It's the old story: we'll be glad to help you when you don't need any help."

"*That* was a year ago. Now there have been some

second thoughts. We'd like you to build the Space Elevator. But not on earth. *On Mars.* Are you interested?"

"I might be. Go on."

"Look at the advantages. Only a third of the gravity, so the forces involved are correspondingly smaller. The synchronous orbit is also closer—less than half the altitude here. So at the very start, the engineering problems are enormously reduced. Our people estimate that the Mars system would cost less than a tenth of the Terran one."

"That's quite possible, though I'd have to check it."

"And *that's* just the beginning. We have some fierce gales on Mars, despite our thin atmosphere—but mountains that get completely above them. Your Sri Kanda is only five kilometers high. We have Mons Pavonis—twenty-one kilometers, and exactly on the equator! Better still, there are no Martian monks with long-term leases sitting on the summit. . . .

"And there's one other reason why Mars might have been designed for a space elevator. Deimos is only three thousand kilometers above the stationary orbit. So we already have a couple of million megatons sitting in exactly the right place for the anchor."

"That will present some interesting problems in synchronization, but I see what you mean. I'd like to meet the people who worked all this out."

"You can't, in real time. They're all on Mars. You'll have to go there."

"I'm tempted, but I have a few other questions."

"Go ahead."

"Earth *must* have the elevator, for all the reasons you doubtless know. But it seems to me that Mars could manage without it. You have only a fraction of our space traffic, and a much smaller projected growth rate. Frankly, it doesn't make a great deal of sense to me."

"I was wondering when you'd ask."

"Well, I'm asking."

"Have you heard of Project Eos?"

"I don't think so."

"Eos—Greek for dawn—the plan to rejuvenate Mars."

"Oh, of course I know about that. It involves melting the polar caps, doesn't it?"

"Exactly. If we could thaw out all that water and CO_2 ice, several things would happen. The atmospheric density would increase, until men could work in the open without spacesuits. At a later stage, the air might even be made breatheable. There would be running water, small seas, and, above all, *vegetation*—the beginnings of a carefully planned biota. In a couple of centuries, Mars could be another Garden of Eden. It's the only planet in the solar system we can transform with known technology. Venus may always be too hot."

"And where does the elevator come into this?"

"We have to lift several million tons of equipment into orbit. The only practical way to heat up Mars is by solar mirrors, hundreds of kilometers across. And we'll need them *permanently*—first to melt the icecaps, and later to maintain a comfortable temperature."

"Couldn't you get all this material from your asteroid mines?"

"Some of it, of course. But the best mirrors for the job are made of sodium, and that's rare in space. We'll have to get it from the Tharsis salt beds—right by the foothills of Pavonis, luckily enough."

"And how long will all this take?"

"If there are no problems, the first stage could be complete in fifty years. Maybe by your hundredth birthday, which the actuaries say you have a thirty-nine-percent chance of seeing."

Morgan laughed.

"I admire people who do a thorough job of research."

"We wouldn't survive on Mars unless we paid attention to detail."

"Well, I'm favorably impressed, though I have a great many reservations. The financing, for example."

"That's my job, Dr. Morgan. I'm the banker. *You're* the engineer."

"Correct, but you seem to know a good deal about engineering, and I've had to learn a lot of economics —often the hard way. Before I'd even consider getting involved in such a project, I would want a detailed budget breakdown—"

"Which can be provided."

"—and *that* would just be the start. You may not realize that there's still a vast amount of research involved in half a dozen fields—mass production of the hyperfilament material, stability and control problems . . . . I could go on all night."

"That won't be necessary. Our engineers have read all your reports. What they are proposing is a small-scale experiment that will settle many of the technical problems, and prove that the principle is sound."

"There's no doubt about *that*."

"I agree, but it's amazing what difference a little practical demonstration can make. So this is what we would like you to do. Design the minimum possible system—just a wire with a payload of a few kilograms. Lower it from synchronous orbit to earth—yes, *earth*. If it works here, it will be easy on Mars. Then run something up it just to show that rockets are obsolete. The experiment will be relatively cheap, it will provide essential information and basic training, and, from our point of view, it will save years of argument. We can go to the government of earth, the Solar Fund, the other interplanetary banks—and just point to the demonstration."

"You really *have* worked all this out. When would you like my answer?"

"To be honest, in about five seconds. But obviously, there's nothing urgent about the matter. Take as long as seems reasonable."

"Very well. Give me your design studies, cost analyses, and all the other material you have. Once I've been through them, I'll let you have my decision in— oh, a week at the most."

"Thank you. Here's my number. You can get me at any time."

Morgan slipped the banker's ident card into the memory slot of his communicator and checked the ENTRY CONFIRMED on the visual display. Before he had returned the card, he had made up his mind.

Unless there was a fundamental flaw in the Martian analysis—and he would bet a large sum that it was sound—his retirement was over. He had often noted, with some amusement, that whereas he frequently thought long and hard over relatively trivial decisions, he had never hesitated for a moment at the major turning points of his career. He had always known what to do, and had seldom been wrong.

At this stage in the game, however, it was better not to invest too much intellectual or emotional capital in a project that might come to nothing. After the banker had rolled out on the first stage of his journey back to Port Tranquillity, via Oslo and Gagarin, Morgan found it impossible to settle down to any of the activities he had planned for the long northern evening. His mind was in a turmoil, scanning the whole spectrum of suddenly changed futures.

After a few minutes of restless pacing, he sat down at his desk and began to list priorities in a kind of reverse order, starting with the commitments he could most easily shed. Before long, he found it impossible to concentrate on such routine matters. Far down in the depths of his mind, something was nagging him, trying to attract his attention. When he tried to focus upon it, it promptly eluded him, like a familiar but momentarily forgotten word.

With a sigh of frustration, Morgan pushed himself away from the desk and walked out onto the veranda running along the western face of the hotel. Though it was very cold, the air was quite still and the sub-zero temperature was more of a stimulus than a discomfort. The sky was a blaze of stars, and a yellow crescent moon was sinking down toward its reflection in the fjord, whose surface was so dark and motionless that it might have been a sheet of polished ebony.

Thirty years ago, he had stood at almost this same spot, with a girl whose appearance he could no longer clearly recall. They had both been celebrating their first degrees, and that had been really all they had in common. It had not been a serious affair; they were young and enjoyed each other's company—and that had been enough.

Yet somehow that fading memory had brought him back to Trollshavn Fjord at this crucial moment of his life. What would the young student of twenty-two have thought, could he have known that his footsteps would lead him back to this place of remembered pleasures three decades in his future?

There was scarcely a trace of nostalgia or self-pity in Morgan's reverie—only a kind of wistful amusement. He had never for an instant regretted the fact that he and Ingrid had separated amicably, without even considering the usual one-year trial contract. She had gone on to make three men moderately miserable before finding herself a job with the Lunar Commission, and Morgan had lost track of her. Perhaps, even now, she was up there on that shining crescent, whose color almost matched her golden hair. . . .

So much for the past. Morgan turned his thoughts to the future. Where was Mars? He was ashamed to admit that he did not even know if it was visible tonight. As he ran his eye along the path of the ecliptic, from the moon to the dazzling beacon of Venus and beyond, he saw nothing in all that jeweled profusion that he could certainly identify as the red planet. It was exciting to think that in the not-too-distant future he—who had never even traveled beyond lunar orbit!—might be looking with his own eyes at those magnificent crimson landscapes, and watching the tiny moons pass swiftly through their phases. . . .

In that instant, the dream collapsed. Morgan stood for a moment paralyzed, before dashing back into the hotel, forgetting the splendor of the night.

There was no general-purpose console in his room, so he had to go down to the lobby to get the information he required. As luck would have it, the cubicle was occupied by an old lady, who took so long to find what she wanted that Morgan almost pounded on the door. But at last the sluggard left, with a mumbled apology, and Morgan was face to face with the accumulated art and knowledge of all mankind.

In his student days, he had won several retrieval championships, racing against the clock while digging out obscure items of information on lists prepared by ingeniously sadistic judges. ("What was the rainfall in the capital of the world's smallest national state on the day when the second-largest number of home runs was scored in college baseball?" was one that he recalled with particular affection.) His skill had improved with the years, and this was a perfectly straightforward question. The display came up in thirty seconds, in far more detail than he really needed.

Morgan studied the screen for a minute, then shook his head in baffled amazement.

"They couldn't *possibly* have overlooked that!" he muttered. "But what can they do about it?"

He pressed the HARD COPY button, and carried the thin sheet of paper back to his room for more detailed study. The problem was so stunningly, appallingly obvious that he wondered if he had overlooked some equally obvious solution and would be making a fool of himself if he raised the matter. Yet there was no possible escape. . . .

He looked at his watch: already after midnight. But this was something he had to settle at once.

To Morgan's relief, the banker had not pressed his DO NOT DISTURB button. He replied immediately, sounding a little surprised.

"I hope I didn't wake you up," said Morgan, not very sincerely.

"No—we're just about to land at Gagarin. What's the problem?"

"About ten teratons, moving at two kilometers a second. The inner moon, Phobos. It's a cosmic bulldozer, going past the elevator every eleven hours. I've not worked out the exact probabilities, but a collision is inevitable every few days."

There was silence for a long time from the other end of the circuit. Then the banker said: "I could have thought of that. So obviously someone has the answer. Perhaps we'll have to move Phobos."

"Impossible: the mass is far too great."

"I'll have to call Mars. The time delay's twelve minutes right now. I should have some sort of answer within the hour."

I hope so, Morgan said to himself. And it had better be good. . . . That is, if I *really* want this job.

24

THE FINGER OF GOD

Dendrobium macarthiae usually flowered with the coming of the southwest monsoon, but this year it was early. As Johan Rajasinghe stood in his orchid house admiring the intricate violet-pink blossoms, he remembered that last season he had been trapped by a torrential downpour for half an hour while examining the first blooms.

He looked anxiously at the sky. No, there was little danger of rain. It was a beautiful day, with thin, high bands of cloud moderating the fierce sunlight. But *that* was odd. . . .

Rajasinghe had never seen anything quite like it before. Almost vertically overhead, the parallel lanes of cloud were broken by a curious circular disturbance. It appeared to be a tiny cyclonic storm, only a few kilometers across, but it reminded Rajasinghe of something completely different—a knothole breaking through the grain of a smoothly planed board.

He abandoned his beloved orchids and stepped outside to get a better view of the phenomenon. Now he could see that the small whirlwind was moving slowly across the sky, the track of its passage clearly marked by the distortion of the cloud lanes.

One could easily imagine that the finger of God was reaching down from heaven, tracing a furrow through the clouds. Even Rajasinghe, who understood the basics of weather control, had no idea that such precision was now possible; but he could take modest pride in the fact that, almost forty years ago, he had played his part in its achievement.

It had not been easy to persuade the surviving superpowers to relinquish their orbital fortresses and to hand them over to the Global Weather Authority, in what was—if the metaphor could be stretched that far —the last and most dramatic example of beating swords into plowshares. Now the lasers that had once threatened mankind directed their beams into carefully selected portions of the atmosphere, or onto heat-absorbing target areas in remote regions of the earth. The energy they contained was trifling compared with that of the smallest storm; but so is the energy of the falling stone that triggers an avalanche, or the single neutron that starts a chain reaction.

Beyond that, Rajasinghe knew nothing of the technical details, except that they involved networks of monitoring satellites, and computers that held within their electronic brains a complete model of the earth's atmosphere, land surfaces, and seas. He felt rather like an awe-struck savage, gaping at the wonders of some advanced technology, as he watched the little cyclone move purposefully into the west, until it disappeared below the graceful line of palms just inside the ramparts of the pleasure gardens.

He glanced up at the invisible engineers and scientists racing around the world in their man-made heavens.

"Very impressive," he said. "But I hope you know *exactly* what you're doing."

25

ORBITAL ROULETTE

"I should have guessed," said the banker ruefully, "that it would be in one of those technical appendices that I never looked at. And now that you've seen the whole report, I'd like to know the answer. You've had *me* worrying ever since you raised the problem."

"It's brilliantly obvious," Morgan answered, "and I should have thought of it myself."

And I would have—eventually—he told himself with a fair degree of confidence. In his mind's eye he saw again those computer simulations of the whole immense structure, twanging like a cosmic violin string, as the hours-long vibrations raced from earth to orbit and were reflected back again. Superimposed on that he replayed from memory, for the hundredth time, the scratched movie of the dancing bridge. *There* were all the clues he needed.

"Phobos sweeps past the tower every eleven hours and ten minutes, but luckily it isn't moving in exactly the same plane—or we'd have a collision *every* time it went around. It misses on most revolutions, and the danger times are exactly predictable—to a thousandth of a second, if desired.

"Now the elevator, like any piece of engineering, isn't a completely rigid structure. It has natural vibration periods, which can be calculated almost as accurately as planetary orbits. So what your engineers propose to do is to *tune* the elevator, so that its normal oscillations—which can't be avoided anyway—always keep it clear of Phobos. Every time the satellite passes by the structure, it won't be there; it will have sidestepped the danger zone by a few kilometers."

There was a long pause on the other end of the circuit.

"I shouldn't say this," said the banker at last, "but my hair is standing on end."

Morgan laughed.

"Put as bluntly as this, it does sound like—what was it called?—Russian roulette. But remember, we're dealing with exactly predictable movements. We always know where Phobos will be, and we can control the displacement of the tower simply by the way we schedule traffic along it."

"Simply," thought Morgan, was hardly the right word, but anyone could see that it was possible. And then an analogy flashed into his mind that was so perfect, yet so incongruous, that he almost burst into laughter. No—it would *not* be a good idea to use it on the banker.

Once again, he was back at the Tacoma Narrows Bridge, but this time in a world of fantasy. There was a ship that had to sail beneath it, on a perfectly regular schedule. Unfortunately, the mast was a meter too tall. . . .

No problem. Just before it was due to arrive, a few heavy trucks would be sent racing across the bridge at intervals carefully calculated to match its resonant frequency. A gentle wave would sweep along the roadway from pier to pier, the crest timed to coincide with the arrival of the ship. And so the masthead would glide beneath, with whole centimeters to spare. . . . On a scale thousands of times larger, this was how Phobos would miss the structure towering out into space from Mons Pavonis.

"I'm glad to have your assurance," said the banker,

"but I think I'd do a private check on the position of Phobos before I took a trip."

"Then you'll be surprised to know that some of your bright young people—they're certainly bright, and I'm assuming they're young because of their sheer technical effrontery—want to use the critical periods as a tourist attraction. They think they could charge premium rates for views of Phobos sailing past at arm's length at a couple of thousand kilometers an hour. Quite a spectacle, wouldn't you agree?"

"I prefer to imagine it. But they may be right. . . . Anyway, I'm relieved to hear that there *is* a solution. I'm also happy to note that you approve of our engineering talent. Does this mean we can expect a decision soon?"

"You can have it now," said Morgan. "When can we start work?"

26

THE NIGHT BEFORE VESAK

It was still, after twenty-seven centuries, the most revered day of the Taprobanean calendar. At the May full moon, according to legend, the Buddha had been born, had achieved enlightenment, and had died. Though to most people Vesak now meant no more than did that other great annual holiday, Christmas, it continued to be a time for meditation and tranquillity.

For many years, Monsoon Control had guaranteed that there would be no rain on the nights of Vesak plus and minus one. And for almost as long, Rajasinghe had gone to the City of Gold two days before that full moon, on a pilgrimage that annually refreshed his spirit. He avoided Vesak itself; on that day, Ranapura was too crowded with visitors, some of whom would be guaranteed to recognize him, and disturb his solitude.

Only the sharpest eye could have noticed that the huge yellow moon lifting above the bell-shaped domes of the ancient dagobas was not yet a perfect circle. The light it gave was so intense that only a few of the most brilliant satellites and stars were visible in the cloudless sky. And there was not a breath of wind.

Twice, it was said, Kalidasa had stopped on this road when he had left Ranapura forever. The first halt was at the tomb of Hanuman, the loved companion of his boyhood; and the second was at the Shrine of the Dying Buddha.

Rajasinghe had often wondered what solace the haunted King had gathered—perhaps at this very spot, for it was the best point from which to view the immense figure carved from the solid rock. The reclining shape was so perfectly proportioned that one had to walk right up to it before its real size could be appreciated. From a distance, it was impossible to realize that the pillow upon which the Buddha rested his head was itself higher than a man.

Though Rajasinghe had seen much of the world, he knew no other spot so full of peace. Sometimes he felt that he could sit here forever, beneath the blazing moon, wholly unconcerned with the cares and turmoil of life. He had never tried to probe too deeply into the magic of the shrine, for fear that he would destroy it, but some of its elements were obvious enough. The very posture of the Enlightened One, resting at last with closed eyes after a long and noble life, radiated serenity. The sweeping lines of the robe were extraordinarily soothing and restful to contemplate; they appeared to flow from the rock, to form waves of frozen stone. And, like the waves of the sea, the natural rhythm of their curves appealed to instincts of which the rational mind knew nothing.

In timeless moments such as this, alone with the Buddha and the almost full moon, Rajasinghe felt that he could understand at last the meaning of nirvana—that state which can be defined only by negatives. Such emotions as anger, desire, greed no longer possessed any power; indeed, they were barely conceivable. Even the sense of personal identity seemed about to fade away, like a mist before the morning sun.

It could not last, of course. Presently he became aware of the buzzing of insects, the distant barking of dogs, the cold hardness of the stone upon which he was sitting. Tranquillity was not a state of mind that could be sustained for long. With a sigh, Rajasinghe got to his feet and began the walk back to his car, parked a hundred meters outside the temple grounds.

He was just entering the vehicle when he noticed the small white patch, so clearly defined that it might have been painted on the sky, rising over the trees to the west. It was the most peculiar cloud that Rajasinghe had ever seen—a perfectly symmetrical ellipsoid, so sharp-edged that it appeared almost solid. He wondered if someone was flying an airship through the skies of Taprobane; but he could see no fins, and there was no sound of engines.

Then, for a fleeting moment, he had a far wilder fancy. *The Starholmers had arrived at last. . . .*

But that, of course, was absurd. Even if they had managed to outrun their own radio signals, they could hardly have traversed the whole solar system—*and* descended into the skies of earth!—without triggering all the traffic radars in existence. The news would have broken hours ago.

Rather to his surprise, Rajasinghe felt a mild sense of disappointment. And now, as the apparition came closer, he could see that it undoubtedly was a cloud, because it was getting slightly frayed around the edges. Its speed was impressive; it seemed to be driven by a private gale, of which there was no trace here at ground level.

So the scientists of Monsoon Control were at it again, testing their mastery of the winds. What, Rajasinghe wondered, would they think of next?

27

ASHOKA STATION

How tiny the island looked from this altitude! Thirty-six thousand kilometers below, straddling the equator, Taprobane appeared not much bigger than the moon. The entire country seemed too small a target to hit; yet he was aiming for an area as its center about the size of a tennis court.

Even now, Morgan was not completely certain of his motives. For the purpose of this demonstration, he could just as easily have operated from Kinte Station and targeted Kilimanjaro or Mount Kenya. The fact that Kinte was at one of the most unstable points along the entire stationary orbit, and was always jockeying to remain over Central Africa, would not have mattered for the few days the experiment would last.

For a while, he had been tempted to aim at Chimborazo; the Americans had even offered to move Columbus Station, at considerable expense, to its precise longitude. But in the end, despite this encouragement, he had returned to his original objective—Sri Kanda.

It was fortunate for Morgan that, in this age of computer-assisted decisions, even a World Court ruling could be obtained in a matter of weeks. Naturally, the vihara had protested. Morgan had argued that a brief scientific experiment, conducted on grounds outside the temple premises, and resulting in no noise, pollution, or other form of interference, could not possibly constitute a tort. If he was prevented from carrying it out, all his earlier work would be jeopardized, he would have no way of checking his calculations, and a project vital to the Republic of Mars would receive a severe setback.

It was a plausible argument, and Morgan had believed most of it himself. So had the judges, by five to two. Though they were not supposed to be influenced by such matters, mentioning the litigious Martians was a clever move. The R.o.M. already had three complicated cases in progress, and the Court was somewhat tired of establishing precedents in interplanetary law.

But Morgan knew, in the coldly analytical part of his mind, that his action was not dictated by logic alone. He was not a man who accepted defeat gracefully; the gesture of defiance gave him a certain satisfaction. Yet at a deeper level he rejected this petty motivation; such a schoolboy gesture was unworthy of him. What he was *really* doing was building up his self-assurance, and reaffirming his belief in ultimate success. Though he did not know how or when, he was proclaiming to the world, and to the stubborn monks within their ancient walls: "I shall return."

Ashoka Station controlled virtually all communications, meteorology, environmental monitoring, and space traffic in the Hindu-Cathay region. If it ever ceased to function, a billion lives would be threatened with disaster and, if its services were not quickly restored, death. No wonder that Ashoka had two completely independent subsatellites, Bhaba and Sarabhai, a hundred kilometers away. If some unthinkable catastrophe destroyed all three stations, Kinte and Imhotep to the west or Confucius to the east could take over on an emergency basis. The human race had learned, from harsh experience, not to put all its eggs in one basket.

There were no tourists, vacationers, or transit passengers here, so far from earth. They did their business and sightseeing only a few thousand kilometers out, and left the high geosynchronous orbit to the scientists and engineers—not one of whom had ever before visited Ashoka on so unusual a mission, or with such unique equipment.

The key to Project Gossamer now floated in one of the station's medium-sized docking chambers, awaiting the final checkout before launch. There was nothing spectacular about it, and its appearance gave no hint of the man-years and the millions in money that had gone into its development.

The dull-gray cone, four meters long and two meters across the base, appeared to be made of solid metal. It required a close examination to reveal the tightly wound fiber covering the entire surface. Indeed, apart from an internal core, and the strips of plastic interleaving that separated the hundreds of layers, the cone was made of nothing but a tapering hyperfilament thread—forty thousand kilometers of it.

Two obsolete and totally different technologies had been revived for the construction of that unimpressive gray cone. Some three hundred years ago, submarine telegraphs had started to operate across the ocean beds. Men had lost fortunes before they had mastered the art of coiling thousands of kilometers of cable and playing it out at a steady rate from continent to continent, despite storms and all the other hazards of the sea.

Then, just a century later, some of the first primitive guided weapons had been controlled by fine wires spun out as they flew to their targets, at a few hundred kilometers an hour. Morgan was attempting a thousand times the range of those War Museum relics, and fifty times their velocity. However, he had some advantages. His missile would be operating in a perfect vacuum for all but the last hundred kilometers; and its target was not likely to take evasive action.

The Operations Manager, Project Gossamer, attracted Morgan's attention with a slightly embarrassed cough.

"We still have one minor problem, Dr. Morgan," she said. "We're quite confident about the lowering All the tests and computer simulations are satisfactory, as you've seen. It's reeling the filament *in* again that has Station Safety worried."

Morgan blinked rapidly. He had given little thought to the matter. It seemed obvious that winding the filament back again was a trivial problem compared to sending it out. All that was needed, surely, was a simple power-operated winch, with the special modifications needed to handle such a fine, variable-thickness material. But he knew that in space one should never take anything for granted, and that intuition—*especially* the intuition of an earth-based engineer—could be a treacherous guide.

Let's see—when the tests are concluded, he thought, we cut the earth end and Ashoka starts to wind the filament in. Of course, when you tug, however hard, at one end of a line forty thousand kilometers long, nothing happens for hours. It would take half a day for the impulse to reach the far end, and for the system to start moving as a whole. So we keep up the tension. . . . Oh!

"Somebody did a few calculations," continued the Operations Manager, "and realized that when we finally got up to speed, we'd have several tons heading toward the station at a thousand kilometers an hour. They didn't like *that* at all."

"Understandably. What do they want us to do?"

"Program a slower reeling-in, with a controlled-momentum budget. If the worst comes to the worst, they may make us move off station to do the windup."

"Will that delay the operation?"

"No. We've worked out a contingency plan for heaving the whole thing out of the airlock in five minutes, if we have to."

"And you'll be able to retrieve it easily?"

"Of course."

"I hope you're right. That little fishing line cost a lot of money—and I want to use it again."

But *where?* Morgan asked himself as he stared at the slowly waxing crescent earth. Perhaps it would be better to complete the Mars project first, even if it meant several years of exile. Once Pavonis was fully operational, earth would *have* to follow, and he did not doubt that, somehow, the last obstacles would be overcome.

Then the chasm across which he was now looking would be spanned, and the fame that Gustave Eiffel had earned three centuries ago would be utterly eclipsed.

28

THE FIRST LOWERING

There would be nothing to see for at least another twenty minutes. Nevertheless, everyone not needed in the control hut was already outside, staring up at the sky. Even Morgan found it hard to resist the impulse, and kept edging toward the open door.

Seldom more than a few meters from him was Maxine Duval's latest remote, a husky youth in his late twenties. Mounted on his shoulders were the usual tools of his trade—twin cameras in the traditional right forward, left backward arrangement, and above those a small sphere not much larger than a grapefruit. The antenna inside that sphere was doing very clever things, several thousand times a second, so that it was always locked on the nearest comsat despite all the antics of its bearer. At the other end of that circuit, sitting comfortably in her studio-office, Duval was seeing through the eyes of her distant alter ego and hearing with his ears—but not straining *her* lungs in the freezing air. This time, she had the better part of the bargain. It was not always the case.

Morgan had agreed to the arrangement with some reluctance. He knew that this was a historic occasion, and had accepted Duval's assurance that "my man won't get in the way." But he was keenly aware of all the things that could go wrong in such a novel experiment—especially during the last hundred kilometers of atmospheric entry. On the other hand, he also knew that Duval could be trusted to treat either failure or triumph without sensationalism.

Like all great reporters, Maxine Duval was not emotionally detached from the events that she observed. She could give all points of view, neither distorting nor omitting any facts she considered essential. Yet she made no attempt to conceal her own feelings, though she did not let them intrude.

She admired Morgan enormously, with the envious awe of someone who lacked all real creative ability. Ever since the building of the Gibraltar Bridge, she had waited to see what the engineer would do next; and she had not been disappointed.

But though she wished Morgan luck, she did not really like him. In her opinion, the sheer drive and ruthlessness of his ambition made him both larger than life and less than human. She could not help contrasting him with his deputy, Warren Kingsley. Now *there* was a thoroughly nice, gentle person ("and a better engineer than I am," Morgan had once told her, more than half seriously). But no one would ever hear of Kingsley; he would always be a dim and faithful satellite of his dazzling primary. As he was perfectly content to be.

It was Kingsley who had patiently explained to Duval the surprisingly complex mechanics of the descent. At first sight, it appeared simple enough to drop something straight down to the equator from a satellite hovering motionless above it. But astrodynamics was full of paradoxes. If you tried to slow down, you moved faster. If you took the shortest route, you burned up the most fuel. If you aimed in one direction, you traveled in another. . . . And *that* was merely allowing for gravitational fields. This time, the situation was much more complicated. No one had ever before tried to steer a space probe trailing forty thousand kilometers of wire. But the Ashoka program had worked perfectly, all the way down to the edge of the atmosphere. In a few minutes, the ground controller on Sri Kanda would take over for the final descent. No wonder Morgan looked tense.

"Van," said Duval softly but firmly over the private circuit. "Stop sucking your thumb. It makes you look like a baby."

Morgan registered indignation, then surprise—and finally relaxed with a slightly embarrassed laugh.

"Thanks for the warning," he said. "I'd hate to spoil my public image."

He looked with rueful amusement at the missing joint, wondering when self-appointed wits would stop chortling "Ha! The engineer hoist by his own petard!" After all the times he had cautioned others, he had grown careless and had managed to slash himself while demonstrating the properties of hyperfilament. There had been practically no pain, and surprisingly little inconvenience. One day he would do something about it; but he simply could not afford to spend a whole week hitched up to an organ regenerator, just for two centimeters of thumb.

"Altitude two five zero," said a calm, impersonal voice from the control hut. "Probe velocity one one six zero meters per second. Wire tension nine zero percent nominal. Parachute deploys in two minutes."

After his momentary relaxation, Morgan was once again tense and alert—like a boxer, Duval could not help thinking, watching an unknown but dangerous opponent.

"What's the wind situation?" he snapped.

Another voice answered, this time far from impersonal.

"I can't believe this," it said in worried tones. "But Monsoon Control has just issued a gale warning."

"This is no time for jokes."

"They're not joking. I've just checked back."

"But they guaranteed no gusts above thirty kilometers an hour!"

"They've just raised that to sixty—correction, eighty. Something's gone badly wrong. . . ."

"I'll say," Duval murmured to herself. She instructed her distant eyes and ears: "Fade into the woodwork. They won't want you around—but don't miss any· thing." Leaving her rem to cope with these somewhat contradictory orders, she switched to her excellent information service.

It took her less than thirty seconds to discover which meteorological station was responsible for the weather in the Taprobane area. And it was frustrating, but not surprising, to find that it was not accepting incoming calls from the general public.

Leaving her competent staff to break through that obstacle, she switched back to the mountain. And she was astonished to find how much, even in this short interval, conditions had worsened.

The sky had become darker; the microphones were picking up the faint, distant roar of the approaching gale. Duval had known such sudden changes of weather at sea, and more than once had taken advantage of them in her ocean racing. But this was unbelievably bad luck. She sympathized with Morgan, whose dreams and hopes might all be swept away by this unscheduled—this *impossible*—blast of air.

"Altitude two zero zero. Probe velocity one one five zero meters per second. Wire tension nine five percent nominal . . ."

So the tension was increasing—in more ways than one. The experiment could not be called off at this late stage; Morgan would simply have to go ahead, and hope for the best. Duval wished that she could speak to him, but knew better than to interrupt him during this crisis.

"Altitude one nine zero. Probe velocity one one zero zero. Wire tension one zero zero percent. First parachute deployment—NOW!"

So—the probe was committed; it was a captive of

the earth's atmosphere. Now the little fuel that remained must be used to steer it into the catching net spread out on the mountainside. The cables supporting that net were already thrumming as the wind tore through them.

Abruptly, Morgan emerged from the control hut and stared up at the sky. Then he turned and looked directly at the camera.

"Whatever happens, Maxine," he said slowly and carefully, "the test is already ninety-five percent successful. No—ninety-nine percent. We've made it for thirty-six thousand kilometers, and have fewer than two hundred to go."

Duval made no reply. She knew that the words were not intended for her, but for the figure in the complicated wheelchair just outside the hut. The vehicle proclaimed the occupant; only a visitor to earth would have need of such a device. The doctors could now cure virtually all muscular defects, but the physicists could not cure gravity.

How many powers and interests were now concentrated upon this mountaintop! The very forces of Nature, the Bank of Narodny Mars, the Autonomous North African Republic, Vannevar Morgan (no mean natural force himself)—and those gently implacable monks in their wind-swept aerie.

Duval whispered instructions to her patient rem, and the camera tilted smoothly upward. There was the summit, crowned by the dazzling white walls of the temple. Here and there along its parapets she could catch glimpses of orange robes fluttering in the gale. As she had expected, the monks were watching.

She zoomed toward them, close enough to see individual faces. Though she had never met the Mahanayake Thero (a request for an interview had been politely refused), she was confident that she would be able to identify him. But there was no sign of the prelate. Perhaps he was in the sanctum sanctorum, focusing his formidable will upon some spiritual exercise.

Duval was not sure if Morgan's chief antagonist indulged in anything so naïve as prayer. But if he had prayed for this miraculous storm, his request was about to be answered.

The Gods of the Mountain were awakening from their slumbers.

29

FINAL APPROACH

"With increasing technology goes increasing vulnerability. The more man conquers [sic] Nature the more liable he becomes to artificial catastrophes. . . . Recent history provides sufficient proof of this: for example, the sinking of Marina City (2127), the collapse of the Tycho B dome (2098), the escape of the Arabian iceberg from its towlines (2062), and the melting of the Thor reactor (2009). We can be sure that the list will have even more impressive additions in the future.

"Perhaps the most terrifying prospects are those that involve **psychological**, not just technological, factors. In the past, a mad bomber or sniper could kill only a handful of people; today, it would not be difficult for a deranged engineer to assassinate a city.

"The narrow escape of O'Neill Space Colony II from such a disaster in 2047 has been well documented. Such incidents, in theory at least, could be avoided by careful screening and fail-safe procedures, though all too often these live up only to the first half of the name.

"There is also a most interesting, but fortunately rare, event in which the individual concerned is in a position of such eminence, or has such unique powers, that no one realizes what he is doing until it is too late. The devastation created by such mad geniuses (there seems no other good term for them) can be world-wide, as in the case of A. Hitler (1889-1945). In a surprising number of instances, nothing is heard of their activities, thanks to a conspiracy of silence among their embarrassed peers.

"A classic example has recently come to light with the publication of Dame Maxine Duval's eagerly awaited and much postponed memoirs. Even now, some aspects of the matter are not entirely clear. . . ."

J. K. Golitsyn
Civilization and Its Malcontents
Prague, 2175

"Altitude one five zero. Probe velocity nine five. Repeat, nine five. Heat shield jettisoned."

So the probe had safely entered the atmosphere, and got rid of its excess speed. But it was far too soon to start cheering. Not only were there a hundred and fifty vertical kilometers to go, but three hundred horizontal ones—with a howling gale to complicate matters. Though the probe still carried a small amount of propellent, its freedom to maneuver was very limited. If the operator missed the mountain on the first approach, he could not go around and try again.

"Altitude one two zero. No atmospheric effects yet."

The little probe was spinning itself down from the sky like a spider decending its silken ladder. I hope, Duval thought, that they have enough wire. How infuriating if they run out only a few kilometers from the target! Just such tragedies had occurred with some of the first submarine cables.

"Altitude eight zero. Approach nominal. Tension one zero five percent. Some air drag."

So, the upper atmosphere was beginning to make itself felt, though as yet only to the sensitive instruments aboard the tiny vehicle.

A small, remotely controlled telescope had been set up beside the control truck and was now automatically tracking the still-invisible probe. Morgan walked toward it, and Duval's Rem followed him like a shadow.

"Anything in sight?" Duval whispered quietly, after a few seconds. Morgan shook his head impatiently, and kept on peering through the eyepiece.

"Altitude six zero. Moving off to the left. Tension one zero five percent—correction, one one zero percent."

Well within limits, thought Duval. But things were starting to happen up there on the other side of the stratosphere. Surely, Morgan had the probe in sight now.

"Altitude five five. Giving two-second impulse correction."

"Got it!" exclaimed Morgan. "I can see the jet."

"Altitude five zero. Tension one two five percent. Hard to keep on course. Some buffeting."

It was inconceivable that, with a mere fifty kilometers to go, the little probe would not complete its thirty-six-thousand-kilometer journey. But how many aircraft, and spacecraft, had come to grief in the last few *meters?*

"Altitude four five. Strong shear wind. Going off course again. Three-second impulse."

"Lost it," said Morgan in disgust. "Cloud in the way."

"Altitude four zero. Buffeting bad. Tension peaking at one five zero percent. I repeat, one five zero percent."

That was bad. Duval knew that the breaking strain was two hundred percent. One bad jerk, and the experiment would be over.

"Altitude three five. Wind getting worse. One-second impulse. Propellent reserve almost gone. Tension still peaking. Up to one seven zero percent."

Another thirty percent, thought Duval, and even that incredible fiber would snap, like any other material when its tensile strength had been exceeded.

"Range three zero. Turbulence getting worse. Drifting badly to the left. Impossible to calculate correction. Movements too erratic."

"I've got it!" Morgan cried. "It's through the clouds!"

"Range two five. Not enough propellent to get back on course. Estimate we'll miss by three kilometers."

"It doesn't matter," shouted Morgan. "Crash where you can!"

"Will do soonest. Range two zero. Wind force increasing. Losing stabilization. Payload starting to spin."

"Release the brake. Let the wire run out!"

"Already done," said that maddeningly calm voice. Duval could have imagined that a machine was speaking, if she had not known that Morgan had borrowed a top space-station traffic controller for the job.

"Dispenser malfunction. Payload spin now five revs per second. Wire probably entangled. Tension one eight zero percent. One nine zero. Two zero zero. Range one five. Tension two one zero. Two two zero. Two three zero . . ."

It can't last much longer, thought Duval. Only a dozen kilometers to go, and the damned wire has got tangled up in the spinning probe . . .

"Tension zero. Repeat, *zero*."

That was it. The wire had snapped, and now must be slowly snaking back toward the stars. Doubtless the operators on Ashoka would wind it in again, but Duval had now glimpsed enough of the theory to realize that this would be a long and complicated task.

And the little payload would crash somewhere down there in the fields and jungles of Taprobane. Yet,

as Morgan had said, it had been more than ninety-
five percent successful. Next time, when there was no
wind . . .

"There it is!" someone shouted.

A brilliant star had ignited, between two of the
cloud galleons sailing across the sky. It looked like a
daylight meteor, falling down to earth. Ironically, as if
mocking its builders, the flare installed on the probe to
assist terminal guidance had automatically triggered.
Well, it could still serve some useful purpose: it would
help in locating the wreckage.

Duval's Rem slowly pivoted so that she could watch
the blazing day-star sail past the mountain and disappear into the east. She estimated that it would land
less than five kilometers away. "Take me back to Dr.
Morgan," she said. "I'd like a word with him."

She had intended to make a few cheerful remarks—
loud enough for the Martian banker to hear—express-
ing her confidence that next time the lowering would
be a complete success. Duval was still composing her
little speech of reassurance when it was swept out of
her mind. . . .

She was to play back the events of the next thirty
seconds until she knew them by heart. But she was
never quite sure if she fully understood them.

30

THE LEGIONS OF THE KING

Vannevar Morgan was used to setbacks—even disasters—and this was, he hoped, a minor one. His real worry, as he watched the flare vanish over the shoulder of the mountain, was that Narodny Mars would consider its money wasted. The hard-eyed observer in his elaborate wheelchair had been extremely uncommunicative; earth's gravity seemed to have immobilized his tongue as effectively as his limbs. But now he addressed Morgan before the engineer could speak to him.

"Just one question, Dr. Morgan. I know that this gale is unprecedented—yet it happened. So it may happen again. What if it does *after the Tower is built?*"

Morgan thought quickly. It was impossible to give an accurate answer at such short notice, and he could still scarcely believe what had happened.

"At the very worst, we might have to suspend operations briefly: there could be some track distortion. No wind forces that *ever* occur at this altitude could endanger the Tower structure itself. Even this experimental fiber would have been perfectly safe if we'd succeeded in anchoring it."

He hoped that this was a fair analysis; in a few minutes, Warren Kingsley would let him know whether it was true or not.

To his relief, the banker answered with apparent

162

satisfaction: "Thank you; that was all I wanted to know."

Morgan was determined, however, to drive the lesson home.

"And on Mount Pavonis, of course, such a problem couldn't possibly arise. The atmospheric density there is less than a hundredth—"

Not for decades had he heard the sound that now crashed upon his ears, but it was one that no man could ever forget. Its imperious summons, overpowering the roar of the gale, transported Morgan halfway around the world.

He was no longer standing on a wind-swept mountainside. He was beneath the dome of the Hagia Sophia, looking up in awe and admiration at the work of men who had died sixteen centuries ago. And in his ears sounded the tolling of the mighty bell that had once summoned the faithful to prayer.

The memory of Istanbul faded. He was back on the mountain, more puzzled and confused than ever.

What was it that the monk had told him? That Kalidasa's unwelcome gift had been silent for centuries, and was allowed to speak only in time of disaster? There had been no disaster here; as far as the monastery was concerned, precisely the opposite.

Just for a moment, the embarrassing possibility occurred to Morgan that the probe might have crashed into the temple precincts. No, that was out of the question. It had missed the peak with kilometers to spare. And, in any event, it was much too small an object to do any serious damage as it half fell, half glided out of the sky.

He stared up at the monastery, from which the voice of the great bell still challenged the gale. The orange robes had all vanished from the parapets; there was not a monk in sight.

Something brushed delicately against Morgan's cheek, and he automatically flicked it aside. It was hard even to think while that dolorous throbbing filled the air, and hammered at his brain. He supposed he had better walk up to the temple and politely ask the Mahanayake Thero what had happened. . . .

Once more, that soft, silken contact against his face, and this time he caught a glimpse of yellow out of the corner of his eye. His reactions had always been swift; he grabbed, and did not miss.

The insect lay crumpled in the palm of his hand, yielding up the last seconds of its ephemeral life even as Morgan watched—and the universe he had always known seemed to tremble and dissolve around him. His miraculous defeat had been converted into an even more inexplicable victory. Yet he felt no sense of triumph—only confusion and astonishment.

For he remembered now the legend of the golden butterflies. Driven by the gale, in their hundreds and thousands, they were being swept up the face of the mountain, to die upon its summit. Kalidasa's legions had at last achieved their goal—and their revenge.

31

EXODUS

"What happened?" asked Sheik Abdullah.

That's a question I'll never be able to answer, Morgan said to himself. But he repiled: "The mountain is ours, Mr. President. The monks have already started to leave. It's incredible. How could a two-thousand-year-old legend . . . ?" He shook his head in baffled wonder.

"If enough men believe in a legend, it becomes true."

"I suppose so. But there's much more to it than that. The whole chain of events seems impossible."

"That's always a risky word to use. Let me tell you a little story. A dear friend, a great scientist, now dead, used to tease me by saying that because politics is the art of the possible, it appeals only to second-rate minds. The *first*-raters, he claimed, were only interested in the *impossible*. And do you know what I answered?"

"No," said Morgan, politely and predictably.

"It's lucky there are so many of us—because *someone* has to run the world. . . . Anyway, if the impossible has happened, you should accept it thankfully."

I accept it, thought Morgan—*reluctantly*. There is something very strange about a universe where a few dead butterflies can balance a billion-ton tower.

And there was the ironic role of the Venerable Parakarma, who must surely now feel that he was the pawn of some malicious gods. The Monsoon Control Administrator had been most contrite, and Morgan had accepted his apologies with unusual graciousness. He could well believe that the brilliant Dr. Choam Goldberg had revolutionized micrometeorology, that no one had really understood all that he was doing, and that he had finally had some kind of nervous breakdown while conducting his experiments. It would never happen again. . . . Morgan had expressed his, quite sincere, hopes for the scientist's recovery, and had retained enough of his bureaucrat's instincts to hint that, in due course, he might expect future considerations from Monsoon Control. The Administrator had signed off with grateful thanks, doubtless wondering at Morgan's surprising magnanimity.

"As a matter of interest," asked the Sheik, "where are the monks going? I might offer them hospitality here. Our culture has always welcomed other faiths."

"I don't know; nor does Ambassador Rajasinghe. But when I asked him he said they'll be all right. An order that's lived frugally for three thousand years is not exactly destitute."

"Hmm. Perhaps we could use some of their wealth. This little project of yours gets more expensive each time you see me."

"Not really, Mr. President. That last estimate includes a purely bookkeeping figure for deep-space operations, which Narodny Mars has now agreed to finance. They will locate a carbonaceous asteroid and navigate it to earth orbit. They've much more experience at this sort of work, and it solves one of our main problems."

"What about the carbon for their own tower?"

"They have unlimited amounts on Deimos—exactly where they need it. Narodny has already started a survey for suitable mining sites, though the actual processing will have to be off-moon."

"Dare I ask why?"

"Because of gravity. Even Deimos has a few centimeters per second squared. Hyperfilament can only be manufactured in completely zero-gee conditions. There's no other way of guaranteeing a perfect crystalline structure with sufficient long-range organization."

"Thank you, Van. Is it safe for me to ask why you've changed the basic design? I liked that original bundle of four tubes, two up and two down. A straightforward subway system was something I could understand— even if it *was* upended ninety degrees."

Not for the first time, and doubtless not for the last, Morgan was amazed by the old man's memory and his grasp of details. It was never safe to take anything for granted with him. Though his questions were sometimes inspired by pure curiosity—often the mischievous curiosity of a man so secure that he had no need to uphold his dignity—he never overlooked anything of the slightest importance.

"I'm afraid our first thoughts were too earth-oriented. We were rather like the early motorcar designers, who kept producing horseless carriages. . . .

"So now our design is a hollow square tower with a track up each face. Think of it as four vertical railroads. . . . Where it starts from orbit, it's forty meters on a side, and it tapers down to twenty when it reaches earth."

"Like a stalag . . . stalac . . ."

"*Stalactite.* Yes, I had to look it up! From the engineering point of view, a good analogy now would be the old Eiffel Tower—turned upside down and stretched out a hundred thousand times."

"As much as *that?*"

"Just about."

"Well, I suppose there's no law that says a tower can't hang downward."

"We do have one going *upward* as well, remember

—from the synchronous orbit out to the mass anchor that keeps the whole structure under tension."

"And Midway Station? I hope you haven't changed that."

"No. It's at the same place—twenty-five thousand kilometers."

"Good. I know I'll never get there, but I like to think about it. . . ." He muttered something in Arabic. "There's another legend, you know—Mahomet's coffin, suspended between heaven and earth. Just like Midway."

"We'll arrange a banquet for you there, Mr. President, when we inaugurate the service."

"Even if you keep to your schedule—and I admit you only slipped a year on the Bridge—I'll be ninety-eight then. No, I doubt if I'll make it."

But *I* will, said Vannevar Morgan to himself. Because now I know that the gods are on my side; whatever gods may be.

IV

THE
TOWER

32

SPACE EXPRESS

"Now don't *you* say," begged Warren Kingsley, "it'll never get off the ground."

"I was tempted." Morgan chuckled as he examined the full-scale mock-up. "It *does* look rather like an upended railroad coach."

"That's exactly the image we want to sell," Kingsley answered. "You buy your ticket at the station, check in your baggage, settle down in your swivel seat, and admire the view. Or you can go up to the lounge-cum-bar and devote the next five hours to serious drinking, until they carry you off at Midway. Incidentally, what do you think of the Design Section's idea—nineteenth-century Pullman decor?"

"Not much. Pullman cars didn't have five circular floors, one on top of the other."

"Better tell Design that. They've set their hearts on gaslighting."

"If they want an antique flavor that's a little more appropriate, I once saw an old space movie at the Sydney Art Museum that had a shuttle craft of some kind with a circular observation lounge. Just what we need."

"Do you remember its name?"

"Oh—let's think—something like *Space Wars 2000*. I'm sure you'll be able to trace it."

"I'll tell Design to look it up. Now let's go inside. Do you want a hard-hat?"

"No," answered Morgan brusquely. That was one of the few advantages of being ten centimeters shorter than average height.

As they stepped into the mock-up, he felt an almost boyish thrill of anticipation. He had checked the designs, watched the computers playing with graphics and layout—everything here would be perfectly familiar. But this was *real*—solid. True, it would never leave the ground, just as the old joke said. But one day, its identical brethren would be hurtling up through the clouds and climbing, in only five hours, to Midway Station, twenty-five thousand kilometers from earth. And all for about one dollar's worth of electricity per passenger. . . .

Even now, it was impossible to realize the full meaning of the coming revolution. For the first time, space itself would become as accessible as any point on the surface of the familiar earth. In a few more decades, if the average man wanted to spend a weekend on the moon, he could afford to do so. Even Mars would not be out of the question. There were no limitations to what might now be possible.

Morgan came back to earth with a bump as he almost tripped over a piece of badly laid carpet.

"Sorry," said his guide. "Another of Design's ideas —that green is supposed to remind people of earth. The ceilings are going to be blue, getting deeper and deeper on the upper floors. And they want to use indirect lighting everywhere, so that the stars will be visible."

Morgan shook his head.

"That's a nice idea, but it won't work. If the lighting's good enough for comfortable reading, the glare will wipe out the stars. You'll need a section of the lounge that can be completely blacked-out."

"That's already planned for part of the bar. You can order your drink and retire behind curtains."

They were now standing on the lowest floor of the

capsule, a circular room eight meters in diameter, three meters high. All around were miscellaneous boxes, cylinders, and control panels bearing such labels as OXYGEN RESERVE, BATTERY, CO_2 CRACKER, MEDICAL, TEMPERATURE CONTROL. Everything was clearly of a provisional, temporary nature, liable to be rearranged at a moment's notice.

"Anyone would think we were building a spaceship," Morgan commented. "Incidentally, what's the latest estimate of survival time?"

"As long as power's available, at least a week, even for a full load of fifty passengers. Which is really absurd, since a rescue team could always reach them in three hours, either from earth or from Midway."

"Barring a major catastrophe, like damage to the Tower or tracks."

"If *that* ever happens, I don't think there will be anyone to rescue. But if a capsule gets stuck for some reason, and the passengers don't go mad and gobble up all our delicious emergency compressed food tablets at once, their biggest problem will be boredom."

The second floor was completely empty, devoid even of temporary fittings. Someone had chalked a large rectangle on the curved plastic panel of the wall and printed inside it: AIR LOCK HERE?

"This will be the baggage room—though we're not sure if we'll need so much space. If not, it can be used for extra passengers. . . . Now, this floor's much more interesting."

The third level contained a dozen aircraft-type chairs, each of a different design. Two of them were occupied by realistic dummies, male and female, who looked very bored with the whole proceedings.

"We've practically decided on this model," said Kingsley, pointing to a luxurious tilting swivel chair with attached small table. "But we'll run the usual survey first."

Morgan punched his fist into the seat cushion.

"Has anyone actually *sat* in it for five hours?" he asked.

"Yes—a hundred-kilo volunteer. No bedsores. If people complain, we'll remind them of the pioneering days of aviation, when it took five hours merely to cross the Pacific. And of course we're offering low-gee comfort almost all the way. . . ."

The floor above was identical, though empty of chairs. They passed through it quickly, and reached the next level, to which the designers had obviously devoted most attention.

The bar looked almost functional, and the coffee dispenser was actually working. Above it, in an elaborate gilded frame, was an old engraving of such uncanny relevance that it took Morgan's breath away.

A huge full moon dominated the upper left quadrant, and racing toward it was a bullet-shaped train towing four carriages. In the windows of the compartment labeled "First Class," top-hatted Victorian personages could be seen admiring the view.

"Where *did* you get hold of that?" Morgan asked in astonished admiration.

"Looks as if the caption's fallen off again," Kingsley said apologetically, hunting around behind the bar. "Ah, here it is. . . ."

He handed Morgan a piece of card, upon which was printed, in an old-fashioned type face:

PROJECTILE TRAINS FOR THE MOON
Engraving from 1881 Edition of
From the Earth to the Moon
Direct
In 97 Hours and 20 Minutes
And a Trip Around It
By Jules Verne

"I'm sorry to say I've never read it," Morgan commented when he had absorbed this information. "It might have saved me a lot of trouble. But I'd like to know how he managed without any rails."

"We shouldn't give Jules too much credit—or blame. This picture was never meant to be taken seriously. It was a joke of the artist."

"Well—give Design my compliments. It's one of their better ideas."

Turning away from the dreams of the past, Morgan and Kingsley walked toward the reality of the future. Through the wide observation window, a back-projection system gave a stunning view of earth. And not just *any* view, Morgan was pleased to note, but the correct one. Taprobane itself was hidden, of course, being directly below; but there was the whole subcontinent of Hindustan, right out to the dazzling snows of the Himalayas.

"You know," Morgan said, "it will be exactly like the Bridge, all over again. People will take the trip just for the view. Midway Station could be the biggest tourist attraction ever." He glanced up at the azure-blue ceiling. "Anything worth looking at on the last floor?"

"Not really—the upper air lock is planned, but we haven't decided where to put the life-support backup gear and the electronics for the track-centering controls."

"Any problems there?"

"Not with the new magnets. Powered or coasting, we can guarantee safe clearance up to eight thousand kilometers an hour—fifty percent above maximum design speed."

Morgan permitted himself a mental sigh of relief. This was one area in which he was quite unable to make any judgments, and had to rely completely on the advice of others. From the beginning, it had been obvious that only some form of magnetic propulsion could operate at such speeds; the slightest *physical* contact—at more than a kilometer a second —would result in disaster. And yet the four pairs of guidance slots running up the faces of the Tower had only centimeters of clearance around the magnets. They had to be designed so that enormous restoring forces came instantly into play to correct any movement of the capsule away from the center line.

As Morgan followed Kingsley down the spiral stairway that extended the full height of the mock-up, he was struck by a somber thought. I'm getting old, he said to himself. Oh, I *could* have climbed to the sixth level without any trouble; but I'm glad we decided not to.

Yet I'm only fifty-nine—and it will be at least five years, even if all goes well, before the first passenger car rides up to Midway Station. Then another three years of tests, calibration, system tune-ups. Make it ten years, to be on the safe side . . .

Though it was warm, he felt a sudden chill. For the first time, it occurred to Vannevar Morgan that the triumph upon which he had set his soul might come too late for him. And quite unconsciously he pressed his hand against the slim metal disk concealed inside his shirt.

33

CORA

"*Why* did you leave it until now?" Dr. Sen had asked, in a tone appropriate for a retarded child.

"The usual reason," Morgan answered as he ran his good thumb along the seal of his shirt. "I was too busy—and whenever I felt short of breath, I blamed it on the height."

"Altitude was partly to blame, of course. You'd better check all your people on the mountain. How could you have overlooked anything so obvious?"

How indeed? thought Morgan, with some embarrassment.

"All those monks—some of them were over eighty! They seemed so healthy that it never occurred to me . . ."

"The monks have lived up there for years. They're completely adapted. But *you've* been hopping up and down several times a day—"

"Twice, at the most."

"—going from sea level to half an atomosphere in a few minutes. Well, there's no great harm done—if you follow instructions from now on. Mine, and CORA'S."

"CORA'S?"

"Coronary alarm."

"Oh—one of those things."

"Yes—one of *those* things. They save about ten million lives a year. Mostly top civil servants, senior administrators, distinguished scientists, leading engineers, and similar nitwits. I often wonder if it's worth the trouble. Nature may be trying to tell us something, and we're not listening."

"Remember your Hippocratic Oath, Bill," retorted Morgan with a grin. "And you must admit that I've always done just what you told me. Why, my weight hasn't changed a kilo in the last ten years."

"Um—well, you're not the worst of my patients," said the slightly mollified doctor. He fumbled around in his desk, and produced a large holopad. "Take your choice—here are the standard models. Any color you like as long as it's medic red."

Morgan triggered the images, and regarded them with distaste.

"Where do I have to carry the thing?" he asked. "Or do you want to implant it?"

"That isn't necessary, at least for the present. In five years, maybe, but perhaps not even then. I suggest you start with *this* model. It's worn just under the breastbone, so doesn't need remote sensors. After a while, you won't notice it's there. And it won't bother you unless it's needed."

"And then?"

"Listen."

The doctor threw one of the numerous switches on his desk console, and a sweet mezzo-soprano voice remarked in a conversational tone: "I think you should sit down and rest for about ten minutes." After a brief pause, it continued: "It would be a good idea to lie down for half an hour." Another pause. "As soon as convenient, make an appointment with Dr. Smith." Then:

"Please take one of the red pills immediately."

"I have called the ambulance. Just lie down and relax. Everything will be all right."

Morgan almost clapped his hands over his ears to cut out the piercing whistle.

"THIS IS A CORA EMERGENCY! WILL ANYONE WITHIN
RANGE OF MY VOICE PLEASE COME IMMEDIATELY.
THIS IS A CORA EMERGENCY! WILL—"

"I think you get the general idea," said the doctor,
restoring silence to his office. "Of course, the programs and responses are individually tailored to the
subject. And there's a wide range of voices, including
some quite famous ones."

"That will do nicely. When will my unit be
ready?"

"I'll call you in about three days. Oh yes—there's
an advantage of the chest-worn units I should mention."

"What's that?"

"One of my patients is a keen tennis player. He
tells me that when he opens his shirt, the sight of that
little red disk has an absolutely devastating effect on
his opponent's game. . . ."

34

VERTIGO

There had once been a time when a minor, and often major, chore of every civilized man had been the regular updating of his address book. The universal code had made that unnecessary, since once a person's lifetime identity number was known, he could be located within seconds. And even if his number was *not* known, the standard search program could usually find it fairly quickly, given the approximate date of birth, his profession, and a few other details. (There were, however, problems if the name was Smith, or Singh, or Mohammed.)

The development of global information systems had also rendered obsolete another annoying task. It was necessary only to make a special notation against the names of those friends one wished to greet on their birthdays or other anniversaries, and the household computer would do the rest. On the appropriate day (unless, as was frequently the case, there had been some stupid mistake in programing) the right message would be automatically flashed to its destination. And even though the recipient might shrewdly suspect that the warm words on his screen were entirely due to electronics—the nominal sender not having thought of him for years—the gesture was nevertheless welcome.

But the same technology that had eliminated one set of tasks had created even more demanding successors. Of these, perhaps the most important was the design of the Personal Interest Profile.

Most men updated their PIP on New Year's Day or their birthday. Morgan's list contained fifty items; he had heard of people with hundreds. They must spend all their waking hours battling with the flood of information, unless they were like those notorious pranksters who enjoyed setting up news alerts on their consoles for such classic improbabilities as:

Eggs, Dinosaur, hatching of
Circle, squaring of
Atlantis, re-emergence of
Christ, Second Coming of
Loch Ness monster, capture of

or, finally

World, end of.

Usually, of course, egotism and professional requirements insured that the subscriber's own name was the first item on every list. Morgan was no exception, but the entries that followed were slightly unusual:

Tower, orbital
Tower, space
Tower, (geo)synchronous
Elevator, space
Elevator, orbital
Elevator, (geo)synchronous

These words covered most of the variations used by the media, and ensured that he saw at least ninety percent of the news items concerning the project. The vast majority were trivial, and sometimes he wondered if it was worth searching for them. The

ones that really mattered would reach him quickly
enough.

Morgan was still rubbing his eyes, and the bed had
scarcely retracted itself into the wall of his modest
apartment, when he noticed that the ALERT was flashing on his console. Punching the COFFEE and READ-
OUT buttons simultaneously, he awaited the latest
overnight sensation.

ORBITAL TOWER SHOT DOWN

said the headline.

"Follow up?" asked the console.

"You bet," replied Morgan, now instantly awake.
During the next few seconds, as he read the text
display, his mood changed from incredulity to indignation, and then to concern. He switched the whole
news package to Warren Kingsley with a "Please call
me back as soon as possible" tag, and settled down to
breakfast, fuming.

Less than five minutes later, Kingsley appeared on
the screen.

"Well, Van," he said with humorous resignation,
"we should consider ourselves lucky. It's taken him
five years to get around to us."

"It's the most ridiculous thing I ever heard of!
Should we ignore it? If we answer, that will only give
him publicity. Which is just what he wants."

Kingsley nodded.

"That would be the best policy—for the present.
We shouldn't overreact. At the same time, he *may*
have a point."

"What do you mean?"

Kingsley had become serious, and even looked a
little uncomfortable.

"There *are* psychological problems as well as engineering ones," he said. "Think it over. I'll see you at
the office."

The image faded from the screen, leaving Morgan in a somewhat subdued frame of mind. He was used to criticism, and knew how to handle it; indeed, he thoroughly enjoyed the give-and-take of technical arguments with his peers, and was seldom upset on those rare occasions when he lost. It was not so easy to cope with Donald Duck.

That, of course, was not his real name; but Dr. Donald Bickerstaff's peculiar brand of indignant negativism often recalled that mythological twentieth-century character. His degree (adequate, but not brilliant) was in pure mathematics; his assets were an impressive appearance, a mellifluous voice, and an unshakable belief in his ability to deliver judgments on *any* scientific subject. In his own field, he was quite good. Morgan remembered with pleasure an old-style public lecture by the doctor that he had once attended at the Royal Institution. For about a week afterward, he had almost understood the peculiar properties of transfinite numbers.

Unfortunately, Bickerstaff did not know his limitations. Though he had a devoted coterie of fans who subscribed to his information service—in an earlier age, he would have been called a pop scientist—he had an even larger circle of critics. The kinder ones considered that he had been educated beyond his intelligence. The others labeled him a self-employed idiot.

It was a pity, thought Morgan, that Bickerstaff couldn't be locked in a room with Dr. Goldberg/Parakarma. They might annihilate each other like electron and positron—the genius of one canceling out the fundamental stupidity of the other. That unshakable stupidity against which, as Goethe lamented, the gods themselves contend in vain.

No gods being currently available, Morgan knew that he would have to undertake the task himself. Though he had much better things to do with his time, it might provide some comic relief; and he had an inspiring precedent.

There were few pictures in the hotel room that had been one of Morgan's four "temporary" homes for almost a decade. Most visitors could not believe that its components were all perfectly genuine.

It was dominated by the graceful, beautifully restored steamship, ancestor of every vessel that could thereafter call itself modern. By her side, standing on the dock to which she had been miraculously returned a century and a quarter after her launch, was Dr. Vannevar Morgan. He was looking up at the scrollwork of the painted prow; and a few meters away, looking quizzically at *him*, was Isambard Kingdom Brunel, hands thrust in pockets, cigar clenched firmly in his mouth, and wearing a very rumpled, mud-spattered suit.

Everything in the photo was quite real. Morgan had indeed been standing beside the *Great Britain,* on a sunny day in Bristol the year after the Gibraltar' Bridge was completed. But Brunel was back in 1857, still awaiting the launch of his later and more famous leviathan, whose misfortunes were to break his body and spirit.

The photograph had been presented to Morgan on his fiftieth birthday, and it was one of his most cherished possessions. His colleagues had intended it as a sympathic joke, Morgan's admiration for the greatest engineer of the nineteenth century being well known. There were times, however, when he wondered if their choice was more appropriate than they realized. The *Great Eastern* had devoured her creator. The Tower might yet do the same to him.

Brunel had been surrounded by Donald Ducks. The most persistent was one Dr. Dionysius Lardner, who had proved beyond all doubt that no steamship could ever cross the Atlantic.

An engineer could refute criticisms based on errors of fact or simple miscalculations. But the point that Donald Duck had raised was more subtle and not so easy to answer. Morgan recalled that his hero had to face something very similar, three centuries ago.

He reached toward his small but priceless collection of genuine books, and pulled out the one he had read more often, perhaps, than any other: Rolt's classic biography *Isambard Kingdom Brunel*. Leafing through the well-thumbed pages, he quickly found the item that had stirred his memory.

Brunel had planned a railway tunnel almost three kilometers long—a "monstrous and extraordinary, most dangerous and impracticable" concept. It was inconceivable, said the critics, that human beings could tolerate the ordeal of hurtling though its Stygian depths. "No person would desire to be shut out from daylight with a consciousness that he had a superincumbent weight of earth sufficient to crush him in case of accident . . . the noise of two trains passing would shake the nerves . . . no passenger would be induced to go twice. . . ."

It was all so familiar. The motto of the Lardners and the Bickerstaffs seemed to be: "Nothing shall be done for the first time."

And yet—*sometimes they were right,* if only through the operation of the laws of chance. Donald Duck made it sound so reasonable.

He had begun by saying, in a display of modesty as unusual as it was spurious, that he would not presume to criticize the *engineering* aspects of the Space Elevator. He wanted to talk only about the psychological problems it would pose. They could be summed up in one word: vertigo.

The normal human being, he had pointed out, had a well-justified fear of high places. Only acrobats and tightrope artistes were immune to this natural reaction. The tallest structure on earth was less than five kilo-

meters high—and there were not many people who
would care to be hauled vertically up the piers of the
Gibraltar Bridge.

Yet that was *nothing* compared to the appalling
prospect of the Orbital Tower. "Who has not stood,"
Bickerstaff declaimed, "at the foot of some immense
building, staring up at its sheer precipitous face, until
it seemed about to topple and fall? Now imagine
such a building soaring on and on through the clouds,
up into the blackness of space, through the ionosphere,
past the orbits of all the great space stations—up and
up until it reaches a large fraction of the way to the
moon! An engineering triumph, no doubt, but a psychological nightmare. I suggest that some people will
go mad at its mere contemplation. And how many
could face the vertiginous ordeal of the ride—*straight
upward,* hanging over the empty space, for twenty-
five thousand kilometers, to the first stop, at the Midway Station.

"It is no answer to say that perfectly ordinary in-
dividuals can fly in spacecraft to the same altitude,
and far beyond. The situation then is completely different, as indeed it is in ordinary atmospheric flight.
The normal man does not feel vertigo even in the
open gondola of a balloon floating through the air a
few kilometers above the ground. But put him at the
edge of a cliff at the same altitude, and study his reactions *then!*

"The reason for this difference is quite simple. In
an aircraft, there is no *physical* connection linking
the observer and the ground. Psychologically, therefore, he is completely detached from the hard, solid
earth far below. Falling no longer has terrors for him.
He can look down upon remote and tiny landscapes
that he would never dare to contemplate from any
high elevation.

"That saving physical detachment is precisely what
the Space Elevator will lack. The hapless passenger,

whisked up the sheer face of the gigantic Tower, will be all too conscious of his link with earth. What guarantee can there possibly be that anyone not drugged or anesthetized could survive such an experience? I challenge Dr. Morgan to answer."

Dr. Morgan was still thinking of answers, few of them polite, when the screen lit up again with an incoming call. When he pressed the ACCEPT button he was not in the least surprised to see Maxine Duval.

"Well, Van," she said, without any preamble, "what are you going to do?"

"I'm sorely tempted, but I don't think I should argue with that idiot. Incidentally, do you suppose that some aerospace organization has put him up to it?"

"My men are already digging. I'll let you know if they find anything. Personally, I feel it's all his own work. I recognize the hallmarks of the genuine article. But you haven't answered my question."

"I haven't decided. I'm still trying to digest my breakfast. What do *you* think I should do?"

"Simple. Arrange a demonstration. When can you fix it?"

"In five years, if all goes well."

"That's ridiculous. You've got your first cable in position. . . ."

"Not cable—*tape*."

"Don't quibble. What load can it carry?"

"Oh—at the earth end, a mere five hundred tons."

"There you are. Offer Donald Duck a ride."

"I wouldn't guarantee his safety."

"Would you guarantee *mine*?"

"You're not serious!"

"I'm always serious, at this hour of the morning. It's time I did another story on the Tower, anyway. That capsule mock-up is very pretty, but it doesn't *do* anything. My viewers like action, and so do I. The last time we met, you showed me drawings of those little cars the engineers will use to run up and down the cables—I mean tapes. What did you call them?"

"Spiders."

"Ugh—that's right. I was fascinated by the idea. Here's something that has *never* been possible before, by any technology. For the first time you could sit still in the sky, even above the atmosphere, and watch the earth beneath. Something that no spacecraft can ever do. I'd like to be the first to describe the sensation. *And* clip Donald Duck's wings at the same time."

Morgan waited for a full five seconds, staring Duval straight in the eyes, before he decided that she was perfectly serious.

"I can understand," he said rather wearily, "just how a poor struggling young media girl, trying desperately to make a name for herself, would jump at such an opportunity. I don't want to blight a promising career, but the answer is definitely no."

The doyen of media people emitted several unladylike, and even ungentlemanly, words, not commonly transmitted over public circuits.

"Before I strangle you in your own hyperfilament, Van," she said, "why not?"

"Well, if anything went wrong, I'd never forgive myself."

"Spare the crocodile tears. Of course my untimely demise would be a major tragedy—for *your* project. But I wouldn't dream of going until you'd made all the tests necessary and were sure it was one hundred percent safe."

"It would look too much like a stunt."

"As the Victorians—or was it the Elizabethans?—used to say, so what?"

"Look, Maxine, there's a flash that New Zealand has just sunk; they'll need you in the studio. But thanks for the generous offer."

"Dr. Vannevar Morgan, I know exactly why you're turning me down. *You* want to be the first."

"As the Victorians used to say, so what?"

"*Touché*. But I'm warning you, Van—just as soon as you have one of those spiders working, you'll be hearing from me again."

Morgan shook his head.

"Sorry, Maxine," he answered. "Not a chance."

35

STARGLIDER PLUS EIGHTY

Extract from **God and Starholme**, Mandala Press, Moscow, 2149

"Exactly eighty years ago, the robot interstellar probe now known as Starglider entered the solar system, and conducted its brief but historic dialogue with the human race. For the first time, we knew what we had always suspected: that ours was not the only intelligence in the universe, and that out among the stars were far older, and perhaps far wiser, civilizations.

"After that encounter, nothing would ever be the same again. And yet, paradoxically, in many ways little has changed. Mankind still goes about its business much as it has always done. How often do we stop to think that the Starholmers, back on their own planet, have already known of our existence for twenty-eight years, or that, almost certainly, we will be receiving their first direct messages only twenty-four years from now; And what if, as some have suggested, they themselves **are already on the way?**

"Men have an extraordinary, and perhaps fortunate, ability to tune out of their consciousness the most awesome future possibilities. The Roman farmer, plowing the slopes of Vesuvius, gave no thought to the mountains smoking overhead. Half the twentieth century lived with the hydrogen bomb; half the twenty-first, with the Golgotha virus. We have learned to live with the threat, or the promise, of Starholme. . . .

"Starglider showed us many strange worlds and races, but it revealed almost no advanced technology, and so had minimal impact upon the technically orientated aspects of our culture. Was this accidental, or the result of some deliberate policy? There are many questions one would like to ask Starglider, now that it is too late—or too early.

"On the other hand, it did discuss many matters of philosophy and religion, and in these fields its influence was profound. Although the phrase nowhere occurs in the transcripts, Starglider is generally credited with the famous aphorism 'Belief in God is apparently a psychological artifact of mammalian reproduction.'

"But what if this is true? It is totally irrelevant to the question of God's **actual** existence, as I shall now proceed to demonstrate. . . ."

Swami Krisnamurthi (Dr. Choam Goldberg)

36

THE CRUEL SKY

The eye could follow the tape much farther by night than by day. At sunset, when the warning lights were switched on, it became a thin band of incandescence, slowly dwindling away until, at some indefinite point, it was lost against the background of stars.

Already, it was the greatest wonder of the world. Until Morgan put his foot down and restricted the site to essential engineering staff, there was a continual flood of visitors—pilgrims, someone had ironically called them—paying homage to the sacred mountain's last miracle.

They would all behave in exactly the same way. First they would reach out and gently touch the five-centimeter-wide band, running their finger tips along it with something approaching reverence. Then they would listen, an ear pressed against the smooth cold material of the ribbon, as if they hoped to catch the music of the spheres. There were some who claimed to have heard a deep bass note at the uttermost threshold of audibility, but they were deluding themselves. Even the highest harmonics of the tape's natural frequency were far below the range of human hearing.

And some would go away shaking their heads, saying, "You'll never get *me* to ride up *that* thing!" But they were the type who had made similar remarks about the fusion rocket, the space shuttle, the airplane, the automobile—even the steam locomotive.

To these skeptics, the usual answer was: "Don't worry—this is merely part of the scaffolding, one of the four tapes that will guide the Tower down to earth. Riding up the final structure will be exactly like taking an elevator in any high building. Except that the trip will be longer, and much more comfortable."

Maxine Duval's trip, on the other hand, would be very short, and not particularly comfortable. But once Morgan had capitulated, he had done his best to make sure that it would be uneventful.

The flimsy spider—a prototype test vehicle that looked like a motorized bo'sun's chair—had already made a dozen ascents to twenty kilometers, with twice the load it would be carrying now. There had been the usual minor teething problems, but nothing serious; the last five runs had been completely trouble-free. And what *could* go wrong? If there was a power failure—almost unthinkable in such a simple battery-operated system—gravity would bring Duval safely home, the automatic brakes limiting the speed of descent. The only real risk was that the drive mechanism might jam, trapping the spider and its passenger in the upper atmosphere. And Morgan had an answer even for this.

"Only fifteen kilometers?" Duval had protested. "A *glider* can do better than that!"

"But *you* can't, with nothing more than an oxygen mask. Of course, if you'd like to wait a year, until we have the operational unit with its life-support system. . . ."

"What's wrong with a spacesuit?'

Morgan had refused to budge, for his own good reasons. Though he hoped it would not be needed, a small jet crane was standing by at the foot of Sri Kanda. Its highly skilled operators were used to odd assignments; they would have no difficulty in rescuing a stranded Duval, even at an altitude of twenty kilometers.

But there was no vehicle in existence that could reach her at twice that height. Above forty kilometers was no man's land—too low for rockets, too high for balloons.

In theory, a rocket *could* hover beside the tape, for a very few minutes, before it burned up all its propellent. But the problems of navigation and actual contact with the spider were so horrendous that Morgan had not even bothered to think about them. It could never happen in real life, and he hoped that no producer of video drama would decide that there was good material here for a cliff-hanger. That was the sort of publicity he could do without.

Duval looked rather like a typical Antarctic tourist as, glittering in her metal-foil thermosuit, she walked toward the waiting spider and the group of technicians around it. She had chosen the time carefully. The sun had risen only an hour ago, and its slanting rays would show the Taprobanean landscape to best advantage. Her remote, even younger and huskier than the one used on the last memorable occasion, recorded the sequence of events for her systemwide audience.

She had, as always, been thoroughly rehearsed. There was no fumbling or hesitation as she strapped herself in, pressed the BATTERY CHARGE button, took a deep draught of oxygen from her face mask, and checked the monitors on all her video and sound channels. Then, like a fighter pilot in some old historical movie, she signaled "thumbs up" and gently eased the speed control forward.

There was a small burst of ironic clapping from the assembled engineers, most of whom had already taken joy rides up to heights of a few kilometers. Someone shouted, "Ignition! We have lift-off!" Moving about as swiftly as a brass birdcage elevator in the reign of Victoria I, the spider began its stately ascent.

This must be like ballooning, Duval told herself. Smooth, effortless, silent. No—not completely silent. She could hear the gentle whirr of the motors powering the multiple drive wheels that gripped the flat face of the tape.

There was none of the sway or vibration that she had half expected. Despite its slimness, the incredible band she was climbing was as rigid as a bar of steel, and the vehicle's gyros were holding it rock steady. If she closed her eyes, she could easily imagine that she was already ascending the final Tower.

But she would not close her eyes. There was so much to see and absorb. There was even a good deal to hear. It was amazing how well sound carried; the conversations below were still quite audible.

She waved to Morgan, and looked for Kingsley. To her surprise, she was unable to find him. Though he had helped her aboard the spider, he had now vanished. Then she remembered his frank admission— sometimes he made it sound almost like a wry boast— that the best structural engineer in the world couldn't stand heights.

Everyone had some secret, or perhaps not-so-secret, fear. Duval did not appreciate spiders, and wished that the vehicle she was riding in had some other name. Yet she could handle one if it was really necessary.

The creature she could *never* bear to touch—though she had met it often enough on her diving expeditions —was the shy and harmless octopus.

The whole mountain was now visible, though from directly above it was impossible to appreciate its true height. The two ancient stairways winding up its face might have been oddly twisting level roads. Along their entire length, as far as she could observe, there was no sign of life. One section had been blocked by a fallen tree, as if Nature had given advance notice, after three thousand years, that she was about to reclaim her own.

Leaving camera one pointed downward, Duval started to pan with number two. Fields and forests drifted across the monitor screen, then the distant white domes of Ranapura, then the dark waters of the inland sea. And, presently, there was Yakkagala. . . .

She zoomed onto the Rock, and could just make out the faint pattern of the ruins covering the entire upper surface. The Mirror Wall was still in shadow, as was the Gallery of the Princesses—not that there was any hope of making them out from such a distance. But the layout of the pleasure gardens, with their ponds and walkways and massive surrounding moat, was clearly visible.

The line of tiny white plumes puzzled her for a moment, until she realized that she was looking down upon another symbol of Kalidasa's challenge to the gods—his so-called Fountains of Paradise. She wondered what the King would have thought could he have seen her rising so effortlessly toward the heaven of his envious dreams.

It was almost a year since she had spoken to Ambassador Rajasinghe. On a sudden impulse, she called the villa.

"Hello, Johan," she greeted him. "How do you like *this* view of Yakkagala?"

"So you've talked Morgan into it. How does it feel?"

"Exhilarating—that's the only word for it. And unique. I've flown and traveled in everything you can mention, but this feels quite different. . . ."

" 'To ride secure the cruel sky . . .' "

"What was that?"

"An English poet, early twentieth century: 'I care not if you bridge the seas, / Or ride secure the cruel sky. . . .' "

"Well *I* care, and I'm feeling secure. Now I can see the whole island—even the Hindustan coast. How high am I ,Van?"

"Coming up to twelve kilometers, Maxine. Is your oxygen mask on tight?"

"Confirmed. I hope it's not muffling my voice."

"Don't worry—you're still unmistakable. Three kilometers to go."

"How much gas is left in the tank?"

"Sufficient. And if you try to go above fifteen, I'll use the override to bring you home."

"I wouldn't dream of it. And congratulations, by the way. This is an excellent observation platform. You may have customers standing in line."

"We've thought of that. The comsat and metsat people are already making bids. We can give them relays and sensors at any height they like. It will all help to pay the rent."

"I can see you!" exclaimed Rajasinghe suddenly. "Just caught your reflection in the scope. . . . Now you're waving your arm. . . . Aren't you lonely up there?"

For a moment, there was an uncharacteristic silence. Then Duval answered quietly: "Not as lonely as Yuri Gagarin must have been, a hundred kilometers higher still. Van, you have brought something new into the world.

"The sky may still be cruel—but you have tamed it. There may be some people who could never face this ride: I feel very sorry for them."

37

THE BILLION-TON DIAMOND

In the last seven years, much had been done, yet there was so much to do. Mountains—or at least asteroids—had been moved. Earth now possessed a second natural moon, circling just above synchronous altitude. It was less than a kilometer across, and was rapidly becoming smaller as it was rifled of its carbon and other light elements. Whatever was left—the core of iron, tailings, and industrial slag—would form the counterweight that would keep the Tower in tension. It would be the stone in the forty-thousand-kilometer-long sling that now turned with the planet once every twenty-four hours.

Fifty kilometers eastward of Ashoka Station floated the huge industrial complex that processed the weightless, but not massless, megatons of raw material and converted them into hyperfilament. Because the final product was more than ninety percent carbon, with its atoms arranged in a precise crystalline lattice, the Tower had acquired the popular nickname "the Billion-Ton Diamond." The Jewelers' Association of Amsterdam had sourly pointed out that (a) hyperfilament wasn't diamond at all, and (b) if it *was,* then the Tower weighed five times ten to the fifteen carats.

Carats or tons, such enormous quantities of material had taxed to the utmost the resources of the space colonies and the skills of the orbital technicians. Into the automatic mines, production plants, and zero-gravity assembly systems had gone much of the engineering genius of the human race, painfully acquired during two hundred years of spacefaring. Soon all the components of the Tower—a few standardized units, manufactured by the million—would be gathered in huge floating stockpiles, waiting for the robot handlers.

Then the Tower would grow in two opposite directions—down to earth and simultaneously up to the orbital mass anchor, the whole process being adjusted so that it would always be in balance. Its cross section would decrease steadily from orbit, where it would be under the maximum stress, down to earth; it would also taper off toward the anchoring counterweight.

When its task was complete, the entire construction complex would be launched into a transfer orbit to Mars. This was a part of the contract that had caused some heartburning among terrestrial politicians and financial experts now that, belatedly, the Space Elevator's potential was being realized.

The Martians had driven a hard bargain. Though they would wait another five years before they had any return on their investment, they would then have a virtual construction monopoly for perhaps another decade. Morgan had a shrewd suspicion that the Pavonis tower would merely be the first of several. Mars might have been designed as a location for Space Elevator systems, and its energetic occupants were not likely to miss such an opportunity. If they make their world the center of interplanetary commerce in the years ahead, good luck to them; Morgan had other problems to worry about, and some of them were still unsolved.

The Tower, for all its overwhelming size, was merely the support for something much more complex. Along each of its four sides must run thirty-six-thousand kilometers of track capable of operation at speeds never before attempted. This had to be powered for its entire length by superconducting cables, linked to massive fusion generators, the whole system being controlled by an incredibly elaborate, fail-safe computer network.

The Upper Terminal, where passengers and freight would transfer between the Tower and the spacecraft docked to it, was a major project in itself. So was Midway Station. So was Earth Terminal, now being lasered into the heart of the sacred mountain. And in addition to all *this,* there was Operation Cleanup.

For two hundred years, satellites of all shapes and sizes, from loose nuts and bolts to entire space villages, had been accumulating in earth orbit. All that came below the extreme elevation of the Tower, at *any* time, now had to be accounted for, since they created a possible hazard. Three quarters of this material was abandoned junk, much of it long forgotten. Now it had to be located, and somehow disposed of.

Fortunately, the old orbital forts were superbly equipped for this task. Their radars—designed to locate oncoming missiles at extreme ranges with no advance warning—could easily pinpoint the debris of the early Space Age. Then their lasers vaporized the smaller satellites, while the larger ones were nudged into higher and harmless orbits.

Some, of historic interest, were recovered and brought back to earth. During this operation, there were quite a few surprises—for example, three Chinese astronauts who had perished on some secret mission, and several reconnaissance satellites constructed from such an ingenious mix of components that it was quite impossible to discover what country had launched them. Not that it now mattered a great deal, since they were at least a hundred years old.

The multitude of active satellites and space stations, forced for operational reasons to remain close to earth, all had to have their orbits carefully checked, and in some cases modified. But nothing could be done about the random and unpredictable visitors that might arrive at any time from the outer reaches of the solar system. Like all the creations of mankind, the Tower would be exposed to meteorites. Several times a day its network of seismometers would detect milligram impacts; and once or twice a year, minor structural damage could be expected.

Sooner or later, during the centuries to come, it might encounter a giant that could put one or more tracks out of action for a while. In the worst possible case, the Tower might even be severed somewhere along its length.

That was about as likely to happen as the impact of a large meteorite upon London or Tokyo, which presented roughly the same target area. The inhabitants of those cities did not lose much sleep worrying over this possibility.

Nor did Vannevar Morgan. Whatever problems might lie ahead, no one doubted now that the Orbital Tower was an idea whose time had come.

V

ASCENSION

38

A PLACE OF SILENT STORMS

Extract from Professor Martin Sessui's address, on receiving the Nobel Prize for Physics, Stockholm, 16 December 2154

"Between heaven and earth lies an invisible region of which the old philosophers never dreamed. Not until the dawn of the twentieth century—to be precise, on 12 December 1901—did it make its first impact upon human affairs.

"On that day, Guglielmo Marconi radioed the three dots of the Morse letter *s* across the Atlantic. Many experts had declared this to be impossible, because electromagnetic waves could travel only in straight lines, and would be unable to bend around the curve of the globe. Marconi's feat not only heralded the age of world-wide communications, but also proved that, high up in the atmosphere, there exists an electrified mirror capable of reflecting radio waves back to earth.

". . . The Kennelly-Heaviside layer, as it was originally named, was soon found to be a region of great complexity, containing at least three main layers, all subject to major variations in height and intensity. At their upper limit they merge into the Van Allen radiation belt, whose discovery was the first triumph of the early Space Age.

"This vast region, beginning at a height of approximately fifty kilometers and extending outward for several radii of the earth, is now known as the ionosphere. Its exploration by rockets, satellites, and radio waves has been a continuing process for more than two centuries. I would like to pay a tribute to my precursors in this enterprise—the Americans M. A. Tuve and G. Breit, the Englishman E. V. Appleton, the Norwegian F. C. M. Størmer, and, especially, the man who, in 1970, won the very award I am now so honored to accept, your countryman Hannes Alfvén. . . .

"The ionosphere is the wayward child of the sun; even now, its behavior is not always predictable. In the days when long-range radio depended upon its idiosyncrasies, it saved many lives—but more men than we shall ever know of were doomed when it swallowed their despairing signals without trace.

"For less than one century, before the communications satellites took over, it was our invaluable but erratic servant—a previously unsuspected natural phenomenon, worth countless billions of dollars to the three generations who exploited it.

"Only for a brief moment in history was it of direct concern to mankind. And yet, if it had never existed, we would not be here! In one sense, therefore, it was of vital importance even to pretechnological humanity, right back to the first ape man—indeed, right back to the first living creatures on this planet. For the ionosphere is part of the shield that protects us from the sun's deadly X-ray and ultraviolet radiations. If they had penetrated to sea level, perhaps some kind of life might still have arisen on earth; but it would never have evolved into anything remotely resembling us.

". . . Because the ionosphere, like the atmosphere below it, is ultimately controlled by the sun, it, too, has its weather. During times of solar disturbance, it is blasted by planet-wide gales of charged particles, and twisted into loops and whirls by the earth's magnetic field. On such occasions, it is no longer invisible. It reveals itself in the glowing curtains of the aurora—one of Nature's most awesome spectacles, illuminating the cold polar nights with its eerie radiance. . . .

"Even now, we do not understand all the processes occurring in the ionosphere. One reason why it has proved difficult to study is that all our rocket and satellite-borne instruments race through it at thousands of kilometers an hour. We have never been able to stand still to make observations. Now, for the first time, the construction of the proposed Orbital Tower gives us a chance of establishing *fixed* observatories in the ionosphere. It is also possible that the Tower may itself modify the characteristics of the ionosphere—though it will certainly not, as Dr. Bickerstaff has suggested, short-circuit it!

"Why should we study this region, now that it is no longer important to the communications engineers? Well, apart from its beauty, its strangeness, and its scientific interest, its behavior is closely linked with that of the sun—the master of our destiny. We know now that the sun is *not* the steady, well-behaved star that our ancestors believed. It undergoes both long- and short-period fluctuations. At the present time it is still emerging from the so-called Maunder Minimum of 1645 to 1715. As a result, the climate now is milder than at any time since the early Middle Ages. But how long will this upswing last? Even more important, when will the inevitable downturn begin, and what effect will this have upon climate, weather, and every aspect of human civilization—not only on this planet, but on the others as well? For they are all children of the sun. . . .

"Some very speculative theories suggest that the sun is now entering a period of instability, which may produce a new Ice Age, more universal than any in the past. If this is true, we need every scrap of information we can get to prepare for it. Even a century's warning might not be long enough. . . .

"The ionosphere helped to create us; it launched the communications revolution; it may yet determine much of our future. That is why we must continue the study of this vast, turbulent arena of solar and electric forces—this mysterious place of silent storms."

39

THE WOUNDED SUN

The last time that Morgan had seen Dev, his nephew had been a child. Now he was a boy in his early teens; and at their next meeting, at this rate, he would be a man.

The engineer felt only a mild sense of guilt. Family ties had been weakening for the last two centuries. He and his sister had little in common except the accident of genetics. Though they exchanged greetings and small talk perhaps half a dozen times a year, and were on the best of terms, he was not even sure when and where they had last met.

Yet when he greeted the eager, intelligent boy (not in the least overawed, it seemed, by his famous uncle), Morgan was aware of a certain bittersweet wistfulness. He had no son to continue the family name. Long ago, he had made that choice between work and life that can seldom be avoided at the highest levels of human endeavor. On three occasions—*not* including the liaison with Ingrid—he might have taken a different path, but accident or ambition had deflected him.

He knew the terms of the bargain he had made, and he accepted them; it was too late now to grumble about the small print. Any fool could shuffle genes, and most did. But whether or not history gave him credit, few men could have achieved what he had done—and was about to do.

In the last three hours, Dev had seen far more of
Earth Terminal than any of the usual run of VIPs.
He had entered the mountain at ground level, along
the almost completed approach to South Station, and
had been given the quick tour of the passenger and
baggage-handling facilities, the control center, and the
switching yard, where capsules would be routed
from the east and west Down tracks to the north and
south Up ones. He had stared up the five-kilometer-
long shaft—like a giant gun barrel aimed at the stars,
as several hundred reporters had already remarked in
hushed voices—along which the lines of traffic would
rise and descend. And his questions had exhausted
three guides before the last one had thankfully
handed him over to his uncle.

"Here he is, Van," said Warren Kingsley as they
arrived via the high-speed elevator at the truncated
summit of the mountain. "Take him away before he
grabs my job."

"I didn't know you were so keen on engineering,
Dev."

The boy looked hurt, and a little surprised.

"Don't you remember, Uncle, that Number 12
Meccamax set you gave me on my tenth birthday?"

"Of course, of course. I was only joking." And, to
tell the truth, he had not *really* forgotten the construction set; it had merely slipped his mind for the moment. . . . "You're not cold up here?" Unlike the
well-protected adults, the boy had disdained the usual
light thermocoat.

"No, I'm fine. What kind of jet is that? When are
you going to open the shaft? Can I touch the tapes?"

"See what I mean?" Kingsley chuckled.

"One: that's Sheik Abdullah's Special; his son Feisal
is visiting. Two: we'll keep this lid on until the Tower
reaches the mountain and enters the shaft. We need it
as a working platform, and it keeps out the rain.

Three: you can touch the tapes if you want to. *Don't
run*—it's bad for you at this altitude!"

"If you're thirteen, I doubt it," said Kingsley, looking at Dev's rapidly receding back. Taking their time,
they caught up with him at the East anchor.

The boy was staring, as so many thousands of others
had already done, at the narrow band of dull gray that
rose straight out of the ground and soared vertically
into the sky. Dev's gaze followed it up, up, up, until
his head was tilted as far back as it would go. Morgan
and Kingsley did not follow suit, though the temptation, after all these years, was still strong. Nor did they
warn him that some visitors got so giddy that they
collapsed and were unable to walk away without as-
sistance.

The boy was tough: he gazed intently at the zenith
for almost a minute, as if hoping to see the thousands
of men and millions of tons of material poised there
beyond the deep blue of the sky. Then he closed his
eyes with a grimace, shook his head, and looked down
at his feet for an instant, as if to reassure himself that
he was still on the solid, dependable earth.

He reached out a cautious hand and stroked the
narrow ribbon linking the planet with its new moon.

"What would happen," he asked, "if it broke?"

That was an old question. Most people were surprised at the answer.

"Very little. At this point, it's under practically no
tension. If you cut the tape, it would just hang there,
waving in the breeze."

Kingsley made an expression of distaste; both knew
that this was a considerable oversimplification. At the
moment, each of the four tapes was stressed at about a
hundred tons, but that was negligible compared to the
design loads they would be handling when the system
was in operation and they had been integrated into the
structure of the Tower. There was no point, however,
in confusing the boy with such details.

Dev thought this over. Then he gave the tape an experimental flick, as if he hoped to extract a musical note from it. But the only response was an unimpressive "click" that instantly died away.

"If you hit it with a sledge hammer," said Morgan, "and came back about ten hours later, you'd be just in time for the echo from Midway."

"Not any longer," said Kingsley. "Too much damping in the system."

"Don't be a spoilsport, Warren. Now come and see something really interesting."

They walked to the center of the circular metal disk that now capped the mountain and sealed the shaft like a giant saucepan lid. Here, equidistant from the four tapes down which the Tower was being guided earthward, was a small geodesic hut, looking even more temporary than the surface on which it had been erected. It housed an oddly designed telescope, which pointed straight upward and was apparently incapable of being aimed in any other direction.

"This is the best time for viewing, just before sunset. The base of the Tower is nicely lit up then."

"Talking of the sun," said Kingsley, "just look at it now. It's even clearer than yesterday." There was something approaching awe in his voice as he pointed at the brilliant flattened ellipse sinking down into the western haze. The horizon mists had dimmed its glare so much that one could stare at it in comfort.

Not for more than a century had such a group of spots appeared. They stretched across almost half the golden disk, making it seem as if the sun had been stricken by some malignant disease or pierced by falling worlds. Yet not even mighty Jupiter could have created such a wound in the solar atmosphere. The largest spot was a quarter of a million kilometers across, and could have swallowed a hundred earths.

"There's another big auroral display predicted for

tonight. Professor Sessui and his merry men certainly timed it well."

"Let's see how they're getting on," said Morgan as he made some adjustments to the eyepiece. "Have a look, Dev."

The boy peered intently for a moment. "I can see the four tapes, going inward—I mean upward—until they disappear."

"Nothing in the middle?"

Another pause.

"No—not a sign of the Tower."

"Correct. It's still six hundred kilometers up, and we're on the lowest power of the telescope. Now I'm going to zoom. Fasten your seat belt."

Dev gave a little laugh at the ancient cliché, familiar from dozens of historical dramas. At first he could see no alteration, except that the four lines pointing toward the center of the field were becoming a little less sharp. It took him a few seconds to realize that no change could be expected as his point of view hurtled upward along the axis of the system; the quartet of tapes would look exactly the same at any point along its length.

Then, quite suddenly, it was *there,* taking him by surprise even though he had been expecting it. A tiny bright spot had materialized in the exact center of the field. It was expanding as he watched it, and now for the first time he had a real sensation of speed.

A few seconds later, he could make out a small circle—no, now both brain and eye agreed that it was a square. He was looking directly up at the base of the Tower, crawling earthward along its guiding tapes at a couple of kilometers a day. The four tapes had now vanished, being far too small to be visible at this distance. But that square fixed magically in the sky continued to grow, though now it had become fuzzy under the extreme magnification.

"What do you see?" asked Morgan.

"A bright little square."

"Good. That's the underside of the Tower, still in full sunlight. When it's dark down here, you can see it with the naked eye for another hour before it enters the earth's shadow. Now, do you see anything else?"

"Nooo . . ." replied the boy, after a long pause.

"You should. There's a team of scientists visiting the lowest section to set up some research equipment. They've just come down from Midway. If you look carefully, you'll see their transporter. It's on the south track—that will be the right side of the picture. Look for a bright spot, about a quarter the size of the Tower."

"Sorry, Uncle, I can't find it. *You* have a look."

"Well, the seeing may have got worse. Sometimes the Tower disappears completely though the atmosphere may look—"

Before Morgan could take Dev's place at the eyepiece, his personal receiver gave two shrill double bleeps. A second later, Kingsley's alarm also erupted.

It was the first time the Tower had ever issued a four-star emergency alert.

40

THE END OF THE LINE

No wonder they called it the Trans-Siberian Railroad. Even on the easy downhill run, the journey from Midway Station to the base of the Tower lasted fifty hours.

One day it would take only five, but that lay two years in the future, when the tracks were energized and their magnetic fields activated. The inspection and maintenance vehicles that now ran up and down the faces of the Tower were propelled by old-fashioned tires gripping the interior of guidance slots. Even if the limited power of the batteries permitted, it was not safe to operate such a system at more than five hundred kilometers an hour.

Yet everyone had been far too busy to be bored. Professor Sessui and his three students had been observing, checking their instruments, and making sure that no time would be wasted when they transferred into the Tower. The capsule driver, his engineering assistant, and the one steward, who made up the entire cabin staff, were also fully occupied, because this was no routine trip. The "Basement," twenty-five thousand kilometers below Midway—and now only six hundred kilometers from earth—had never been visited since it was built. Until now, there had been no purpose in going there, since the handful of monitors had never reported anything amiss. Not that there was much to go wrong, because the Basement was merely

214

a fifteen-meter-square pressurized chamber—one of the scores of emergency refuges at intervals along the Tower.

Sessui had used all his considerable influence to borrow this unique site, now crawling down through the ionosphere at two kilometers a day toward its rendezvous with earth. It was essential, he had argued forcibly, to get his equipment installed before the peak of the current sunspot maximum.

Already, solar activity had reached unprecedented levels, and Sessui's young assistants often found it hard to concentrate on their instruments; the magnificent auroral displays outside were too much of a distraction. For hours on end, both northern and southern hemispheres were filled with slowly moving curtains and streamers of greenish light, beautiful and awe-inspiring—yet only a pale ghost of the celestial firework displays taking place around the poles. It was rare for the aurora to wander so far from its normal domains; only once in generations did it invade the equatorial skies.

Sessui had driven his students back to work with the admonition that they would have plenty of time for sightseeing during the long climb back to Midway. Yet it was noticeable that even the Professor himself sometimes stood at the observation window for minutes at a time, entranced by the spectacle of the burning heavens.

Someone had christened the project Expedition to Earth—which, as far as distance was concerned, was ninety-eight percent accurate. As the capsule crawled down the face of the Tower at its miserable five hundred klicks, the increasing closeness of the planet beneath made itself obvious. Gravity was slowly increasing, from the delightful less-than-lunar buoyancy of Midway to almost its full terrestrial value. To any experienced space traveler, this was strange indeed: to feel *any* gravity before the moment of atmospheric entry seemed a reversal of the normal order of things.

Apart from complaints about the food, stoically endured by the overworked steward, the journey had been devoid of incident. A hundred kilometers from the Basement, the brakes had been gently applied and speed had been halved. It was halved again at fifty kilometers; as one of the students remarked: "Wouldn't it be embarrassing if we ran off the end of the track?"

The driver—who insisted on being called pilot—retorted that this was impossible, because the guidance slots down which the capsule was falling terminated several meters short of the Tower's end, and there was also an elaborate buffer system, just in case *all* four independent sets of brakes failed to work.

And everyone agreed that the joke, besides being perfectly ridiculous, was in extremely poor taste.

41

METEOR

The vast artificial lake known for two thousand years as the Sea of Paravana lay calm and peaceful beneath the stone gaze of its builder. Though few now visited the lonely statue of Kalidasa's father, his work, if not his fame, had outlasted that of his son; and it had served his country infinitely better, bringing food and drink to a hundred generations of men.

And to many more generations of birds, deer, buffalo, monkeys, and their predators, like the sleek and well-fed leopard now drinking at the water's edge. The big cats were becoming rather too common, and were inclined to be a nuisance now that they no longer had anything to fear from hunters. But they never attacked men unless they were cornered or molested.

Confident of his security, the leopard was leisurely drinking his fill as the shadows around the lake lengthened and twilight advanced from the east. Suddenly, he pricked up his ears, instantly alert; but no mere human senses could have detected any change in land, water, or sky. The evening was as tranquil as ever.

Then, directly out of the zenith, came a faint whistling that grew steadily to a rumbling roar, with tearing, ripping undertones, quite unlike that of a reentering spacecraft. Up in the sky, something metallic was sparkling in the last rays of the sun, growing larger and leaving a trail of smoke behind it.

As it expanded, it disintegrated. Pieces shot off in

all directions, some of them burning as they did so. For a few seconds, an eye as keen as the leopard's might have glimpsed a roughly cylindrical object, before it exploded into a myriad fragments. But the leopard did not wait for the final catastrophe; it had already disappeared into the jungle.

The Sea of Paravana erupted in thunder. A geyser of mud and spray shot a hundred meters into the air —a fountain far surpassing those of Yakkagala, and one almost as high as the Rock itself. It hung suspended for a moment in futile defiance of gravity before tumbling back into the shattered lake.

At once, the sky was full of waterfowl wheeling in startled flight. Almost as numerous, flapping among them like leathery pterodactyls who had somehow survived into the modern age, were the big fruit bats who normally took to the air only after dusk. Equally terrified, birds and bats shared the sky.

The last echoes of the crash died away into the encircling jungle, and silence swiftly returned to the lake. But long minutes passed before its mirror surface was restored and little waves ceased to scurry back and forth beneath the unseeing eyes of Paravana the Great.

42

DEATH IN ORBIT

Every large building, it is said, claims a life; fourteen names were engraved on the piers of the Gibraltar Bridge. But thanks to an almost fanatical safety campaign, casualties on the Tower had been remarkably low. There had even been one year without a single death.

And there had been one year with four—two of them particularly harrowing. A space-station assembly supervisor, accustomed to working under zero gravity, had forgotten that though he was in space he was not in orbit, and a lifetime's experience had betrayed him. He had plummeted more than fifteen thousand kilometers, to burn up like a meteor upon entry into the atmosphere. Unfortunately, his suit radio had remained switched on during those last few minutes. . . .

It was a bad year for the Tower; the second tragedy had been much more protracted, and equally public. An engineer on the counterweight, far beyond synchronous orbit, had failed to fasten her safety belt properly, and had been flicked off into space like a stone from a sling.

She was in no danger, at that altitude, of either falling back to earth or being launched on an escape trajectory. Unfortunately, her suit held less than two hours' air. There was no possibility of rescue at such short notice; and despite a public outcry, no attempt was made.

The victim had co-operated nobly. She had transmitted her farewell messages, and then, with thirty minutes of oxygen still unused, opened her suit to vacuum. The body was recovered a few days later, when the inexorable laws of celestial mechanics brought it back to the perigee of its long ellipse.

These tragedies flashed through Morgan's mind as he took the high-speed elevator down to the operations room, closely followed by a somber Kingsley and the now almost forgotten Dev. But this catastrophe was of an altogether different type, involving an explosion at or near the Basement of the Tower. That the transporter had fallen to earth was obvious, even before the garbled report was received of a "giant meteor shower" somewhere in central Taprobane.

It was useless to speculate, Morgan thought, until he had more facts; and in this case, where all the evidence had been destroyed, they might never be available. He knew that space accidents seldom had a single cause. They were usually the result of a chain of events, often quite harmless in themselves. All the foresight of the safety engineers could not guarantee absolute reliability, and sometimes their own overelaborate precautions contributed to disaster.

Morgan was not ashamed of the fact that the safety of the project now concerned him far more than any loss of life. Nothing could be done about the dead; one could only ensure that the same accident would never happen again. But that the almost completed Tower might be endangered was a prospect too appalling to contemplate.

The elevator floated to a halt, and he stepped out into the operations room—just in time for the evening's second stunning surprise.

43

FAIL-SAFE

Five kilometers from the terminus, driver-pilot Rupert Chang had reduced speed again. Now, for the first time, the passengers could see the face of the Tower as something more than a featureless blur dwindling away to infinity in both directions. Upward, it was true, the twin grooves along which they were riding still stretched forever—or at least for twenty-five thousand kilometers, which on the human scale was much the same. But downward, the end was already in sight. The truncated base of the Tower was clearly silhouetted against the verdant green background of Taprobane, which it would reach and unite with in little more than a year.

Across the display panel, the red ALARM symbols flashed again. Chang studied them with a frown of annoyance and pressed the RESET button. They flickered once, then vanished.

The first time this happened, two hundred kilometers higher, there had been a hasty consultation with Midway Control. A quick check of all systems had revealed nothing amiss; indeed, if all the warnings were to be believed, the transporter's passengers were already dead. *Everything* had gone outside the limits of tolerance.

It was obviously a fault in the alarm circuits themselves, and Professor Sessui's explanation was accepted with general relief. The vehicle was no longer in the pure vacuum environment for which it had been designed. The ionospheric turmoil it had now entered must be triggering the sensitive detectors of the warning systems.

"Someone should have thought of *that*," Chang had grumbled. But with less than an hour to go, he was not really worried. He would make constant manual checks of all the critical instrument readings. Midway approved, and in any case there was no alternative.

Battery condition was, perhaps, the item that concerned him most. The nearest charging point was two thousand kilometers higher, and if they couldn't climb back to that they would be in trouble. But he was quite happy on this score; during the braking process, the transporter's drive motors had been functioning as dynamos, and ninety percent of its gravitational energy had been pumped back into the batteries. Now that they were fully charged, the surplus hundreds of kilowatts still being generated should be diverted into space through the big cooling fins at the rear.

Those fins, as Chang's colleagues had often pointed out to him, made his unique vehicle look rather like an old-time aerial bomb. By this time, at the end of the braking process, they should have been glowing a dull red. Chang would have been very worried had he known that they were still comfortably cool. Energy can never be destroyed; it has to go *somewhere*. And often it goes to the wrong place.

When the FIRE—BATTERY COMPARTMENT sign came on for the third time, Chang did not hesitate to reset it. A real fire, he knew, would have triggered the extinguishers. In fact, one of his biggest worries was that these might operate unnecessarily.

There were several anomalies on the board now, especially in the battery-charging circuits. As soon as the journey was over and he'd powered down the transporter, Chang was going to climb into the motor room and give everything a good old-fashioned eye-ball inspection.

As it happened, his nose alerted him first, when there was barely more than a kilometer to go. Even as he stared incredulously at the thin wisp of smoke oozing out of the control board, the coldly analytical part of his mind was saying, "What a lucky coincidence that it waited until the end of the trip!"

Then he remembered all the energy being produced during the final braking, and had a pretty shrewd guess at the sequence of events. The protective circuits must have failed to operate, and the batteries had been over-charging. One fail-safe after another had let them down. Helped by the ionospheric storm, the sheer perversity of inanimate things struck again.

Chang punched the battery-compartment fire-extinguisher button. At least *that* worked, because he could hear the muffled roar of the nitrogen blasts on the other side of the bulkhead. Ten seconds later, he triggered the VACUUM DUMP, which would sweep the gas out into space, with, he hoped, most of the heat it had picked up from the fire. That, too, operated correctly. It was the first time that Chang had ever listened with relief to the unmistakable shriek of atmosphere escaping from a space vehicle; he hoped it would also be the last.

He dared not rely on the automatic-braking sequence as the vehicle finally crawled into the terminus. Fortunately, he had been well rehearsed and recognized all the visual signals, so that he was able to stop within a centimeter of the docking adapter. In frantic haste, the air locks were coupled together, and stores and equipment were hurled through the connecting tube.

And so was Professor Sessui, by the combined exertions of pilot, assistant engineer, and steward, when he tried to go back for his precious instruments. The air-lock doors were slammed shut just seconds before the engine compartment bulkhead finally gave way.

After that, the refugees could do nothing but wait in the bleak fifteen-meter-square chamber, with considerably fewer amenities than a well-furnished prison cell, and hope that the fire would burn itself out. Perhaps it was as well for the passengers' peace of mind that only Chang and his engineer appreciated one vital statistic: the fully charged batteries contained the energy of a large chemical bomb, now ticking away on the outside of the Tower.

Ten minutes after their hasty arrival, the bomb went off, causing slight vibrations of the Tower, followed by the sound of ripping and tearing metal. Though the breaking-up noises were not impressive, they chilled the hearts of the listeners. Their only means of transport was being destroyed, leaving them stranded twenty-five thousand kilometers from safety.

There was another, more protracted, explosion— then silence. The refugees guessed that the vehicle had fallen off the face of the Tower. Numbed, they started to survey their resources; and slowly they began to realize that their miraculous escape might have been wholly in vain.

44

A CAVE IN THE SKY

Deep inside the mountain, amid the display and communications equipment of the Earth Operations Center, Morgan and his engineering staff stood around the tenth-scale hologram of the Tower's lowest section. It was perfect in every detail, even to the four thin ribbons of the guiding tapes extending along each face. They vanished into thin air just above the floor, and it was hard to appreciate that, even on this diminished scale, they should continue downward for another sixty kilometers—completely through the crust of the earth.

"Give us the cutaway," said Morgan, "and lift the Basement up to eye level."

The Tower lost its apparent solidity and became a luminous ghost—a long, thin-walled square box, empty except for the superconducting cables of the power supply. The lowest section—"Basement" was indeed a good name for it, even if it was at a hundred times the elevation of this mountain—had been sealed off to form a single square chamber, fifteen meters on a side.

"Access?" queried Morgan.

Two sections of the image started to glow more brightly. Clearly defined on the north and south faces, between the slots of the guidance tracks, were the outer doors of the duplicate air locks—as far apart

225

as possible, according to the usual safety precautions for all space habitats.

"They went in through the south door, of course," explained the Duty Officer. "We don't know if it was damaged in the explosion."

Well, there were three other entrances, thought Morgan, and it was the lower pair that interested him. This had been one of those afterthoughts, incorporated at a late stage in the design. Actually, the whole Basement was an afterthought. At one time it had been considered unnecessary to build a refuge there, in the section of the Tower that would eventually become part of Earth Terminal itself.

"Tilt the underside toward me," Morgan ordered.

The Tower toppled, in a falling arc of light, and lay floating horizontally in mid-air, with its lower end toward Morgan. Now he could see all the details of the twenty-meter-square floor—or roof, if one looked at it from the point of view of its orbital builders.

Near the north and south edges, leading into the two independent air locks, were the hatches that allowed access from below. The only problem was to reach them—six hundred kilometers up in the sky.

"Life support?"

The air locks faded back into the structure. The visual emphasis moved to a small cabinet at the center of the chamber.

"*That's* the problem, Dr. Morgan," the Duty Officer answered somberly. "There's only a pressure-maintenance system. No purifiers, and of course no power. Now what they've lost the transporter, I don't see how they can survive the night. The temperature's already falling—down ten degrees since sunset."

Morgan felt as if the chill of space had entered his own soul. The euphoria of discovering that the lost transporter's occupants were still alive faded swiftly away. Even if there was enough oxygen in the Basement to last them for several days, that would be of no importance if they froze before dawn.

"I'd like to speak to Professor Sessui."

"We can't tell him directly. The Basement emergency phone goes only to Midway. No problem, though."

That turned out to be not completely true. When the connection was made, Driver-Pilot Chang came on the line.

"I'm sorry," he said, "the Professor is busy."

After a moment's incredulous silence, Morgan replied, pausing between each word and emphasizing his name: "Tell him that Dr. Vannevar Morgan wants to speak to him."

"I will, Dr. Morgan—but it won't make the slightest difference. He's working on some equipment with his students. It was the only thing they were able to save—a spectroscope of some kind. They're aiming it through one of the observation windows. . . ."

Morgan controlled himself with difficulty. He was about to retort "Are they crazy?" when Chang anticipated him.

"You don't know the Prof. *I've* spent the last week with him. He's—well—I guess you could say single-minded. It took three of us to stop him from going back into the cabin to get some more of his gear. And he's just told me that if we're all going to die anyway, he'll make damn sure that *one* piece of eqiupment is working properly."

Morgan could tell from Chang's voice that, for all his annoyance, he felt a considerable admiration for his distinguished and difficult passenger. And the Professor did have logic on his side. It made good sense to salvage what he could, out of the years of effort that had gone into this ill-fated expedition.

"Very well," said Morgan at length, co-operating with the inevitable. "Since I can't get an appointment,

I'd like *your* summary of the situation. So far, I've only had it secondhand."

It now occurred to him that, in any event, Chang could probably give a much more useful report than the Professor. Though the Driver-Pilot's insistence on the second half of his title often caused derision among genuine astrogators, he was a highly skilled technician with a good training in mechanical and electrical engineering.

"There's not much to say. We had such short notice that there was no time to save anything—except that damned spectroscope. Frankly, I never thought we'd make it through the air lock. . . .

"We have the clothes we're wearing—and that's about it. One of the students grabbed her travel bag. Guess what—it contained her draft thesis, written on *paper,* for heaven's sake. Not even flame-proofed, despite regulations. If we could afford the oxygen, we'd burn it to get some heat. . . ."

Listening to that voice from space, and looking at the transparent—yet apparently solid—hologram of the Tower, Morgan had a most curious illusion. He could imagine that there were tiny, tenth-scale human beings moving around there in the lowest compartment; it was only necessary to reach in his hand to carry them out to safety. . . .

"Next to the cold, the big problem is air. I don't know how long it will be before CO_2 build-up knocks us out. Perhaps someone will work out *that* as well. Whatever the answer, I'm afraid it will be too optimistic. . . ."

Chang's voice dropped several decibels and he began to speak in an almost conspiratorial tone, obviously to prevent being overheard.

"The Prof and his students don't know this, but the south air lock was damaged in the explosion. There's a leak—a steady hiss around the gaskets. How serious it is, I can't tell."

The speaker's voice rose to normal level again.

"Well, that's the situation. We'll be waiting to hear from you. . . ."

And just what the hell *can* we say, Morgan thought, except "Good-by"?

Crisis management was a skill Morgan admired, but did not envy. Janos Bartok, the Tower Safety Officer up at Midway, was now in charge of the situation. Those inside the mountain twenty-five thousand kilometers below, and a mere six hundred from the scene of the accident, could only listen to the reports, give helpful advice, and satisfy the curiosity of the news media as best they could.

Needless to say, Maxine Duval had been in touch within minutes of the disaster, and as usual her questions were much to the point.

"Can Midway Station reach them in time?"

Morgan hesitated. The answer to that was undoubtedly "No." Yet it was unwise, not to say cruel, to abandon hope as early as this. And there had been one stroke of good luck.

"I don't want to raise false hopes, but we may not need Midway. There's a crew working much closer, at 10K Station; that's ten thousand kilometers above them. Their transporter can reach the Basement in twenty hours."

"Then why isn't it on the way down?"

"Safety Officer Bartok will be making the decision shortly—but it could be a waste of effort. We think they have air for only half that time. And the temperature problem is even more serious."

"What do you mean?"

"It's night up there, and they have no source of heat. Don't put this out yet, Maxine, but it may be a race between freezing and anoxia."

There was a pause for several seconds. Then Duval said in an uncharacteristically diffident tone of voice:.

"Perhaps I'm being stupid, but surely the weather stations, with their big infrared lasers—"

"Thank you, Maxine. *I'm* the one who's being stupid. Just a minute while I speak to Midway."

Bartok was polite enough when Morgan called, but his brisk reply made his opinion of meddling amateurs abundantly clear.

"Sorry I bothered you," apologized Morgan, and switched back to Duval.

"Sometimes the expert does know his job," he told her with rueful pride. *"Our* man knows his. He called Monsoon Control ten minutes ago. They're computing the beam power now. They don't want to overdo it, of course, and burn everybody up."

"So I was right," said Duval sweetly. *"You* should have thought of that, Van. What else have you forgotten?"

No answer was possible, nor did Morgan attempt one. He could see Duval's computer mind racing ahead, and guessed what her next question would be. He was right.

"Can't you use the spiders?"

"Even the final models are altitude-limited. Their batteries can only take them up to three hundred kilometers. They were designed to inspect the Tower when it had already entered the atmosphere."

"Well, put in bigger batteries."

"In a couple of hours? But *that's* not the problem. The only unit under test at the moment can't carry passengers."

"You could send it up empty."

"Sorry—we've thought of that. There must be an operator aboard to manage the docking when the spider comes up to the Basement. And it would take days to get out seven people, one at a time. . . ."

"Surely you have *some* plan!"

"Several, but they're all crazy. If any make sense,

I'll let you know. Meanwhile, there's something you can do for us."

"What's that?" Duval asked suspiciously.

"Explain to your audience just why spacecraft can dock with each other six hundred kilometers up, but *not* with the Tower. By the time you've done that, we may have some news for you."

As Duval's slightly indignant image faded from the screen, and Morgan turned back once more to the well-orchestrated chaos of the operations room, he tried to let his mind roam as freely as possible over every aspect of the problem. Despite the polite rebuff of the Safety Officer, efficiently doing his duty up on Midway, he might be able to come up with some useful ideas. Although he did not imagine that there would be any magical solution, he understood the Tower better than any living man, with the possible exception of Warren Kingsley. Kingsley probably knew more of the fine details; but Morgan had the clearer overall picture.

Seven men and women were stranded in the sky, in a situation that was unique in the whole history of space technology.

There *must* be a way of getting them to safety before they were poisoned by CO_2, or the pressure dropped so low that the chamber became, in literal truth, a tomb like Mahomet's, suspended between heaven and earth.

45

THE MAN FOR THE JOB

"We can do it," said Kingsley with a broad smile. "Spider *can* reach the Basement."

"You've been able to add enough extra battery power?"

"Yes, but it's a very close thing. It will have to be a two-stage affair, like the early rockets. As soon as the battery is exhausted, it must be jettisoned to get rid of the dead weight. That will be around four hundred kilometers. Spider's internal battery will take it the rest of the way."

"And how much payload will *that* give?"

Kingsley's smile faded.

"Marginal. About fifty kilos, with the best batteries we have."

"Only fifty! What use will *that* be?"

"It should be enough. A couple of those new thousand-atmosphere tanks, each holding five kilos of oxygen. Molecular filter masks to keep out the CO_2. A little water and compressed food. Some medical supplies. We can bring it all in under forty-five kilos."

"Phew! And you're *sure* that's sufficient?"

"Yes—it will tide them over until the transporter arrives from 10K Station. And if necessary, Spider can make a second trip."

"What does Bartok think?"

"He approves. After all, no one has any better ideas."

Morgan felt that a great weight had been lifted from his shoulders. Plenty of things could still go wrong but at last there was a ray of hope; the feeling of utter helplessness had been dispelled.

"When will all this be ready?" he asked.

"If there are no holdups, within two hours. Three at the most. It's all standard equipment, luckily. Spider's being checked out right now. There's only one matter to be decided. . . ."

Vannevar Morgan shook his head.

"No, Warren," he answered slowly, in a calm, implacably determined voice that his friend had never heard before. "There's nothing more to decide."

"I'm not trying to pull the rank on you, Bartok," said Morgan. "It's a simple matter of logic. True, anyone can drive Spider—but only half a dozen men know *all* the technical details involved. There may be some operational problems when we reach the Tower, and I'm in the best position to solve them."

"May I remind you, Dr. Morgan," said the Safety Officer, "that you are sixty-five. It would be wiser to send a younger man."

"I'm *not* sixty-five; I'm sixty-six. And age has absolutely nothing to do with it. There's no danger, and certainly no requirement for physical strength."

And, he might have added, the psychological factors were far more important than the physical ones. Almost anybody could ride passively up and down in a capsule, as Maxine Duval had done and millions of others would be doing in the years ahead. It would be quite another matter to face some of the situations that could easily arise six hundred kilometers up in the empty sky.

"I still think," said Bartok, with gentle persistence, "that it would be best to send a younger man. Dr. Kingsley, for example."

Behind him, Morgan heard (or had he imagined?)

his colleague's suddenly indrawn breath. For years they had joked over the fact that Kingsley had such an aversion to heights that he never inspected the structures he designed. His fear fell short of genuine acrophobia, and he could overcome it when absolutely necessary. He had, after all, joined Morgan in stepping from Africa to Europe. But that was the only time that anyone had ever seen him drunk in public, and he was not seen at all for twenty-four hours afterward.

Kingsley was out of the question, even though Morgan knew that he would be prepared to go. There were times when technical ability and sheer courage were not enough. No man could fight against fears that had been implanted in him at his birth, or during his earliest childhood.

Fortunately, there was no need to explain this to the Safety Officer. There was a simpler and equally valid reason why Kingsley should not go. Only a few times in his life had Morgan been glad of his small size; this was one of them.

"I'm fifteen kilos lighter than Kingsley," he told Bartok. "In a marginal operation like this, that should settle the matter. So let's not waste any more precious time in argument."

He felt a slight twinge of conscience, knowing that this was unfair. Bartok was only doing his job, very efficiently, and it would be another hour before the capsule was ready. No one was wasting any time.

For long seconds, the two men stared into each other's eyes, as if the twenty-five thousand kilometers between them did not exist. If there was a direct trial of strength, the situation could be messy. Bartok was nominally in charge of all safety operations, and could theoretically overrule even the Chief Engineer and Project Manager. But he might find it difficult to enforce his authority. Both Morgan and Spider were far below him, on Sri Kanda, and possession was nine points of the law.

Bartok shrugged his shoulders, and Morgan relaxed. "You have a point. I'm still not too happy, but I'll go along with you. Good luck."

"Thank you," Morgan answered quietly as the image faded from the screen. Turning to the silent Kingsley, he said: "Let's go."

Only as they were leaving the operations room, on the way back to the summit, did Morgan automatically feel for the little pendant concealed beneath his shirt. CORA had not bothered him for months, and not even Kingsley knew of her existence. Was he gambling with other lives as well as his own just to satisfy his selfish pride? If Safety Officer Bartok had known about *this* . . .

It was too late now. Whatever his motives, he was committed.

46

SPIDER

How the mountain had changed, thought Morgan, since he had first seen it! The summit had been entirely sheared away, leaving a perfectly level plateau. At its center was the giant "saucepan lid," sealing the shaft that would soon carry the traffic of many worlds. Strange to think that the greatest spaceport in the solar system would be deep inside the heart of a mountain . . .

No one could have guessed that an ancient monastery had once stood here, focusing the hopes and fears of billions for at least three thousand years. The only token that remained was the ambiguous bequest of the Mahanayake Thero, now crated and waiting to be moved. But so far, neither the authorities at Yakkagala nor the director of the Ranapura Museum had shown much enthusiasm for Kalidasa's ill-omened bell.

The last time it had tolled, the peak had been swept by that brief but eventful gale—a wind of change indeed. Now the air was almost motionless, as Morgan and his aides walked slowly to the waiting capsule, glittering beneath the inspection lights. Someone had stenciled the name SPIDER MARK II on the lower part of the housing; and beneath that had been scrawled the promise: WE DELIVER THE GOODS. I hope so, thought Morgan.

Every time he came here, he found it more difficult

to breathe, and he looked forward to the flood of oxygen that would soon gush into his starved lungs. But CORA, to his surprised relief, had never issued even a preliminary admonition when he visited the summit. The regime that Dr. Sen had prescribed seemed to be working admirably.

Everything had been loaded aboard Spider, which had been jacked up so that the extra battery could be hung beneath it. Mechanics were making hasty last-minute adjustments and disconnecting power leads, since the tangle of cabling underfoot was a mild hazard to a man unused to walking in a spacesuit.

Morgan's Flexisuit had arrived from Gagarin only thirty minutes ago, and for a while he had seriously considered leaving without one. Spider Mark II was a far more sophisticated vehicle than the simple prototype that Duval had once ridden; indeed, it was a tiny spaceship with its own life-support system. If all went well, Morgan should be able to mate it with the air lock on the bottom of the Tower, designed years ago for this very purpose. But a suit would provide more than insurance in case of docking problems; it would give him enormously greater freedom of action.

Almost form-fitting, the Flexisuit bore little resemblance to the clumsy armor of the early astronauts, and, even when pressurized, would scarcely restrict his movements. He had once seen a demonstration by its manufacturers of some spacesuited acrobatics, culminating in a sword fight and a ballet. The last was hilarious—but it had proved the designer's claims.

Morgan climbed the short flight of steps and stood for a moment on the capsule's tiny metal porch before backing cautiously inside. As he settled down and fastened the safety belt, he was agreeably surprised at the amount of room. Although the Mark II was certainly a one-man vehicle, it was not as claustrophobic as he had feared—even with the extra equipment that had been packed into it.

The two oxygen cylinders had been stowed under the seat, and the CO_2 masks were in a small box behind the ladder that led to the overhead air lock. It seemed astonishing that such a small amount of equipment could mean the difference between life and death for so many people.

Morgan had taken one personal item—a memento of that first day, long ago, at Yakkagala, where in a sense all this had started. The spinnerette took up little room and weighed only a kilo. Over the years, it had become something like a talisman. It was, moreover, one of the most effective ways of demonstrating the properties of hyperfilament, and whenever he left it behind, he almost invariably found that he needed it. And on this, of all trips, it might well prove useful.

He plugged in the quick-release umbilical of his spacesuit, and tested the air flow on both the internal and the external supply. Outside, the power cables were disconnected. Spider was on its own.

Brilliant speeches were seldom forthcoming at such moments, and this, after all, was going to be a perfectly straightforward operation. Morgan grinned rather stiffly at Kingsley and said, "Mind the store, Warren, until I get back."

Then he noticed the small, lonely figure in the crowd around the capsule. My God, he thought, I'd almost forgotten the poor kid. . . .

"Dev," he called. "Sorry I haven't been able to look after you. I'll make up for it when I get back."

And I will, he told himself. When the Tower was finished, there would be time for everything—even the human relations he had so badly neglected. Dev would be worth watching; a boy who knew when to keep out of the way showed unusual promise.

The curved door of the capsule—the upper half of it

transparent plastic—thudded softly shut against its gaskets. Morgan pressed the CHECK-OUT button, and Spider's vital statistics appeared on the screen one by one. All were green; there was no need to note the actual figures. If any of the values had been outside nominal, they would have flashed red twice a second. Nevertheless, with his usual engineer's caution, Morgan observed that oxygen stood at one hundred two percent, main battery power at one hundred one percent, booster battery at one hundred five percent. . . .

The quiet, calm voice of the controller—the same unflappable expert who had watched over all operations since that first abortive lowering years ago—sounded in his ear.

"All systems nominal. You have control."

"I have control. I'll wait until the next minute comes up."

It was hard to think of a greater contrast to an old-time rocket launch, with its elaborate countdown, its split-second timing, its sound and fury. Morgan merely waited until the last two digits on the clock became zeroes, then switched on power at the lowest setting.

Smoothly, *silently*, the floodlit mountaintop fell away beneath him. Not even a balloon ascent could have been quieter. If he listened carefully, he could just hear the whirring of the twin motors as they drove the big friction drive wheels that gripped the tape above and below the capsule.

Rate of ascent, five meters a second, said the velocity indicator. In slow, regular steps Morgan increased the power until it read fifty—just under two hundred kilometers an hour. That gave maximum efficiency at Spider's present loading. When the auxiliary battery was dropped off, speed could be increased by twenty-five percent, to almost two-fifty klicks.

"Say *something*, Van!" called Kingsley's amused voice from the world below.

"Leave me alone," Morgan replied equably. "I intend to relax and enjoy the view for the next couple of hours. If you wanted a running commentary, you should have sent Maxine."

"She's been calling you for the last hour."

"Give her my love, and say I'm busy. Maybe when I reach the Tower . . . What's the latest from there?"

"Temperature's stabilized at twenty. Monsoon Control zaps them with a modest megawattage every ten minutes. But Professor Sessui is furious—complains that it upsets his instruments."

"What about the air?"

"Not so good. The pressure has definitely dropped, and of course the CO_2's building up. But they should be O.K. if you arrive on schedule. They're avoiding all unnecessary movement, to conserve oxygen."

All except Sessui, I'll bet, thought Morgan. It would be interesting to meet the man whose life he was trying to save. He had read several of the scientist's widely praised popular books, and considered them florid and overblown. He suspected that the man matched the style.

"And the status at 10K?"

"Another two hours before the transporter can leave. They're installing some special circuits to make quite sure that nothing catches fire on *this* trip."

"A good idea—Bartok's, I suppose."

"Probably. And they're coming down the north track, just in case the south one was damaged by the explosion. If all goes well, they'll arrive in—oh— twenty-one hours. Plenty of time, even if we don't send Spider up again with a second load."

Despite his only half-jesting remark to Kingsley, Morgan knew that it was far too early to start relaxing. Yet all did seem to be going as well as could be expected; and there was certainly nothing else that he could do for the next three hours except to admire the ever-expanding view.

He was already thirty kilometers up in the sky, rising swiftly and silently through the tropical night. There was no moon, but the land beneath was revealed by the twinkling constellations of its towns and villages. When he looked at the stars above and the stars below, Morgan found it easy to imagine that he was far from any world, lost in the depths of space.

Soon he could see the whole island of Taprobane, faintly outlined by the lights of the coastal settlements. Far to the north, a dull glowing patch was creeping up over the horizon like the herald of some displaced dawn. It puzzled him for a moment, until he realized that he was looking at one of the great cities of southern Hindustan.

He was higher now than any aircraft could climb, and what he had already done was unique in the history of transportation. Although Spider and its precursors had made innumerable trips up to twenty kilometers, no one had been allowed to go higher because of the impossibility of rescue. It had not been planned to begin serious operations until the base of the Tower was much closer, and until Spider had at least two companions who could spin themselves up and down the other tapes of the system. Morgan pushed aside the thought of what could happen if the drive mechanism jammed. That would doom the refugees in the Basement, as well as himself.

Fifty kilometers. He had reached what would, in normal times, have been the lowest level of the ionosphere. He did not, of course, expect to see anything; but he was wrong.

The first intimation was a faint crackling from the capsule speaker. Next, out of the corner of his eye, he saw a flicker of light. It was immediately below him, glimpsed in the downward-viewing mirror just outside Spider's little bay window.

He twisted the mirror around as far as it would

adjust, until it was aimed at a point a couple of meters below the capsule. For a moment, he stared with astonishment, and more than a twinge of fear. Then he called the mountain.

"I've got company," he said. "I think this is in Professor Sessui's department. There's a ball of light— oh—about twenty centimeters across, running along the tape just below me. It's keeping a constant distance, and I hope it stays there. But I must say it's quite beautiful—a lovely bluish glow, flickering every few seconds. And I can hear it on the radio link."

It was a full minute before Kingsley answered, in a reassuring tone of voice.

"Don't worry. It's only St. Elmo's fire. We've had similar displays along the tape during thunderstorms. They can make your hair stand on end aboard the Mark I. But *you* won't feel anything; you're too well shielded."

"I'd no idea it could happen at this altitude."

"Neither did we. You'd better take it up with the Professor."

"Oh—it's fading out—getting bigger and fainter. Now it's gone. I suppose the air's too thin for it. . . . I'm sorry to see it go—"

"*That's* only a curtain raiser," said Kingsley. "Look what's happening directly above you."

A rectangular section of the star field flashed by as Morgan tilted the mirror toward the zenith. At first he could see nothing unusual so he switched off all the indicators on his control panel and waited in total darkness.

Slowly, his eyes adapted, and in the depths of the mirror a faint red glow began to burn, and spread, and consume the stars. It grew brighter and brighter and flowed beyond the limits of the mirror. Now he could see it directly, for it extended halfway down the sky. A cage of light, with flickering, moving bars, was descending upon the earth. Seeing it, Morgan could understand how a man like Sessui could devote his life to unraveling its secrets.

On one of its rare visits to the equator, the aurora had come marching down from the poles.

47

BEYOND THE AURORA

Morgan doubted if even Professor Sessui, five hundred kilometers above, had so spectacular a view. The storm was developing rapidly. Short-wave radio, still used for many nonessential services, would by now have been disrupted all over the world. Morgan was not sure if he heard, or felt, a faint rustling, like the whisper of falling sand or the crackle of dry twigs. Unlike the static of the fireball, it certainly did not come from the speaker system, because it was still there when he switched off the circuit.

Curtains of pale-green fire, edged with crimson, were being drawn across the sky, and shaken slowly back and forth as if by an invisible hand. They were trembling before the gusts of the solar wind, the million-kilometer-an-hour gale blowing from sun to earth, and far beyond. Even above Mars, a feeble auroral ghost was flickering now; and sunward, the poisonous skies of Venus were ablaze.

Above the pleated curtains, long rays like the ribs of a half-opened fan were sweeping around the horizon. Sometimes they shone straight into Morgan's eyes like the beams of a giant searchlight, leaving him dazzled for minutes. There was no need, any longer, to turn off the capsule illumination to prevent it from blinding him; the celestial fireworks outside were brilliant enough to read by.

Two hundred kilometers. Spider was climbing

silently, effortlessly. It was hard to believe that he had left earth exactly an hour ago. Hard even to believe that earth still existed, for he was now rising between the walls of a canyon fire.

The illusion lasted only for seconds. Then the momentary unstable balance between magnetic fields and incoming electric clouds was destroyed. But for that brief instant, Morgan could truly believe that he was ascending out of a chasm that would dwarf even Valles Marineris, the Grand Canyon of Mars. Then the shining cliffs, at least a hundred kilometers high, became translucent and were pierced by stars. He could see them for what they really were—mere phantoms of fluorescence.

And now, like an airplane breaking through a ceiling of low-lying clouds, Spider was climbing above the display. Morgan was emerging from a fiery mist, which was twisting and turning beneath him. Many years ago he had been aboard a tourist liner cruising through the tropical night, and he remembered how he had joined the other passengers on the stern, entranced by the beauty and wonder of the bioluminescent wake. Some of the greens and blues flickering below him now matched the plankton-generated colors he had seen then, and he could easily imagine that he was again watching the by-products of life—the play of giant, invisible beasts, denizens of the upper atmosphere. . . .

He had almost forgotten his mission, and it was a distinct shock when he was recalled to duty.

"How's power holding up?" Kingsley asked. "You've only another twenty minutes on that battery."

Morgan glanced at his instrument panel.

"It's dropped to ninety-five percent—but my rate of climb has *increased* by five percent. I'm doing two hundred ten klicks."

"That's about right. Spider's feeling the lower gravity. It's aready down by ten percent at your altitude."

That was not enough to be noticeable, particularly

if one was strapped in a seat and wearing several kilos of spacesuit. Yet Morgan felt positively buoyant, and he wondered if he was getting too much oxygen.

No, the flow rate was normal. It must be the sheer exhilaration produced by that marvelous spectacle beneath him—though it was diminishing now, drawing back to north and south, as if retreating to its polar strongholds. That, and the satisfaction of a task well begun, using a technology that no man had ever before tested to such limits.

The explanation was perfectly reasonable, but he was not satisfied with it. It did not wholly account for his sense of happiness—even of joy. Kingsley, who was fond of diving, had often told him that he felt such an emotion in the weightless environment of the sea. Morgan had never shared it, but now he knew what it must be like. He seemed to have left all his cares down there on the planet hidden below the fading loops and traceries of the aurora.

The stars were coming back into their own, no longer challenged by the eerie intruder from the poles. Morgan began to search the zenith, not with any high expectations, wondering if the Tower was yet in sight. But he could make out only the first few meters, lit by the faint auroral glow, of the narrow ribbon up which Spider was swiftly and smoothly climbing.

That thin band upon which his own life, and the lives of seven others, now depended was so uniform and featureless that it gave no hint of the capsule's speed. Morgan found it difficult to believe that it was flashing through the drive mechanism at more than two hundred kilometers an hour. And with that thought, he was suddenly back in his childhood, and knew the source of his contentment.

He had quickly recovered from the loss of that first kite, and had graduated to larger and more elaborate models. Next, just before he had discovered

Meccamax and abandoned kites forever, he had experimented briefly with toy parachutes.

Morgan liked to think that he had invented the idea himself, though he might well have come across it somewhere in his reading or viewing. The technique was so simple that generations of boys must have rediscovered it.

First he had whittled a thin strip of wood about five centimeters long, and fastened a couple of paper clips to it. He had hooked these around the kite string, so that the little device could slide easily up and down.

He had next made a handkerchief-sized parachute of rice paper, with silk strings. A small square of cardboard served as payload. When he had fastened that square to the wooden strip by a rubber band—not too firmly—he was in business.

Blown by the wind, the little parachute would go sailing up the string, climbing the graceful catenary to the kite. Then Morgan would give a sharp tug, and the cardboard weight would slip out of the rubber band. The parachute would float away into the sky, while the wood-and-wire rider came swiftly back to his hand, in readiness for the next launch.

With what envy he had watched his flimsy creations drift effortlessly out to sea! Most of them fell into the water before they had traveled even one kilometer, but sometimes a little parachute would be bravely maintaining altitude when it vanished from sight. He liked to imagine that these lucky voyagers reached the enchanted islands of the Pacific; but though he had written his name and address on the cardboard squares, he never received any reply.

Morgan could not help smiling at these long-forgotten memories; yet they explained so much. The dreams of childhood had been far surpassed by the reality of adult life. He had earned the right to his contentment.

"Coming up to three eighty," said Kingsley. "How is the power level?"

"Beginning to drop—down to eighty-five percent. The battery's starting to fade."

"Well, if it holds out for another twenty kilometers, it will have done its job. How do you feel?"

Morgan was tempted to answer with superlatives, but his natural caution dissuaded him.

"I'm fine," he said. "If we could guarantee a display like this for all our passengers, we wouldn't be able to handle the crowds."

"Perhaps it could be arranged." Kingsley laughed. "We could ask Monsoon Control to dump a few barrels of electrons in the right places. Not their usual line of business, but they're good at improvising . . . aren't they?"

Morgan chuckled, but did not answer. His eyes were fixed on the instrument panel, where both power and rate of climb were now visibly dropping. But this was no cause for alarm. Spider had reached three hundred eight-five kilometers out of the expected four hundred, and the booster battery still had some life in it.

At three hundred ninety kilometers, Morgan started to cut back the rate of climb, until Spider crept more and more slowly upward. Finally, the capsule was barely moving, and it came to rest just short of four hundred five kilometers.

"I'm dropping the battery," Morgan reported. "Mind your heads."

A good deal of thought had been given to recovering that heavy and expensive battery, but there had been no time to improvise a braking system that would let it slide safely back, like one of Morgan's kite riders. And though a parachute had been available, it was feared that the shrouds might become entangled with the tape. Fortunately, the impact area, just ten kilometers east of Earth Terminal, lay in dense jungle. The wildlife of Taprobane would have to take its chances, and Morgan was prepared to argue with the Department of Conservation later.

He turned the safety key and pressed the red button that fired the explosive charges. Spider shook briefly as they detonated. Then he switched to the internal battery, slowly released the friction brakes, and again fed power into the drive motors.

The capsule started to climb on the last lap of its journey. But one glance at the instrument panel told Morgan that something was seriously wrong. Spider should have been rising at over two hundred klicks; it was doing less than one hundred, even at full power.

No tests or calculations were necessary. Morgan's diagnosis was instant, because the figures spoke for themselves. Sick with frustration, he reported back to earth.

"We're in trouble," he said. "The charges blew—but the battery never dropped. Something's holding it on."

It was unnecessary to add that the mission must now be aborted. Everyone knew perfectly well that Spider could not possibly reach the base of the Tower carrying several hundred kilos of dead weight.

48

NIGHT AT THE VILLA

Ambassador Rajasinghe needed little sleep these nights; it was as if a benevolent Nature was granting him the maximum use of his remaining years. And at a time like this, when the Taprobanean skies were blazing with their greatest wonder for centuries, who could have stayed abed?

How he wished that Paul Sarath were here to share the spectacle! He missed his old friend more than he would have thought possible. There was no one who could annoy and stimulate him in the way that Paul had done—no one with the same bond of shared experience stretching back to boyhood.

Rajasinghe had never thought that he would outlive Paul, or would see the fantastic billion-ton stalactite of the Tower almost span the gulf between its orbital foundation and Taprobane, thirty-six thousand kilometers below. To the end, Paul had been utterly opposed to the project. He had called it a Sword of Damocles, and had never ceased to predict its eventual plunge to earth. Yet even Paul had admitted that the Tower had already produced some benefits.

For perhaps the first time in history, the rest of the world actually knew that Taprobane existed, and was discovering its ancient culture. Yakkagala, with its brooding presence and its sinister legends, had attracted special attention. As a result, Paul had been

able to get support for some of his cherished projects.
The enigmatic personality of Yakkagala's creator had
already given rise to numerous books and video
dramas, and the *son-et-lumière* display at the foot of
the Rock was invariably sold out. Shortly before his
death, Paul had remarked wryly that a minor
Kalidasa industry was in the making, and it was becoming more and more difficult to distinguish fiction
from reality.

Soon after midnight, when it was obvious that the
auroral display had passed its climax, Rajasinghe had
been carried back into his bedroom. As he always
did when he had said good night to his household
staff, he relaxed with a glass of toddy and switched on
the late news summary. The only item that really
interested him was the progress that Morgan was
making. By this time, he should be approaching the
base of the Tower.

The news editor had already starred the latest
development. A line of continuously flashing type announced:

MORGAN STUCK 200 KM SHORT OF GOAL

Rajasinghe's finger tips requested the details, and
he was relieved to find that his first fears were
groundless. Morgan was *not* stuck; he was unable to
complete the journey. He could return to earth whenever he wished. But if he did, Professor Sessui and his
colleagues would certainly be doomed.

Directly above his head, the silent drama was being
played out at this very moment. Rajasinghe switched
from text to video, but there was nothing new. The
item now being screened in the news recap was
Maxine Duval's ascent, years ago, in Spider's precur-
sor.

"*I* can do better than that," muttered Rajasinghe,
and switched to his beloved telescope.

For the first months after he had become bed-ridden, he had been unable to use it. Then Morgan had paid one of his brief courtesy calls, analyzed the situation, and swiftly prescribed the remedy. A week later, to Rajasinghe's surprise and pleasure, a small team of technicians had arrived at the Villa Yakka-gala, and had modified the instrument for remote operation. Now he could lie comfortably in bed, and still explore the starry skies and the looming face of the Rock. He was deeply grateful to Morgan for the gesture, which had shown a side of the engineer's personality he had not suspected.

He was not sure what he could see, in the darkness of the night, but he knew exactly where to look, since he had long been watching the slow descent of the Tower. When the sun was at the correct angle, he could even glimpse the four guiding tapes converging into the zenith, a quartet of shining hairlines scratched upon the sky.

He set the azimuth bearing on the telescope control and swung the instrument around until it pointed above Sri Kanda. As he began to track slowly upward, looking for any sign of the capsule, he wondered what Bodhidharma was thinking about this latest development.

Though Rajasinghe had not spoken to the Mahana-yake, now well into his nineties, since the order had moved to Lhasa, he gathered that the Potala had not provided the hoped-for accommodation. The huge palace was slowly falling into decay while the Dalai Lama's executors haggled with the Chinese federal government over the cost of maintenance. According to Rajasinghe's latest information, the Mahanayake Thero was now negotiating with the Vatican—also in chronic financial difficulties, but at least still master of its own house.

All things were indeed impermanent, and it was not easy to discern any cyclic pattern. Perhaps the mathematical genius of Parakarma-Goldberg might be able to do so. The last time Rajasinghe had seen *him*, he was receiving a major scientific award for his contributions to meteorology. Rajasinghe would never have recognized him; he was clean-shaven and wearing a suit cut in the latest neo-Napoleonic fashion. But now, it seemed, he had switched religions again. . . .

The stars slid slowly down the big monitor screen at the end of the bed as the telescope tilted up toward the Tower. But there was no sign of the capsule, though Rajasinghe was sure that it must now be in the field of view.

He was about to switch back to the regular news channel when, like an erupting nova, a star flashed out near the lower edge of the picture. Rajasinghe wondered if the capsule had exploded, but then he saw that it was shining with a perfectly steady light. He centered the image and zoomed to maximum power.

Long ago, he had seen a two-century-old video documentary of the first aerial wars, and he remembered a sequence showing a night attack upon London. An enemy bomber had been caught in a cone of search-lights, and had hung like an incandescent mote in the sky. He was seeing the same phenomenon now, on a hundredfold greater scale; but this time, all the resources on the ground were combined to help, not to destroy, the determined invader of the night.

49

A BUMPY RIDE

Warren Kingsley's voice had regained its control. Now it was merely dull and despairing.

"We're trying to stop that mechanic from shooting himself," he said. "But it's hard to blame him. He was interrupted by *another* rush job on the capsule, and simply forgot to remove the safety strap."

So, as usual, it was human error. While the explosive links were being attached, the battery had been held in place by two metal bands. And only *one* of them had been removed.

Such things happened with monotonous regularity. Sometimes they were merely annoying; sometimes they were disastrous, and the man responsible had to carry the guilt for the rest of his days. In any event, recrimination was pointless. The only thing that mattered now was what to do next.

Morgan adjusted the external viewing mirror to its maximum downward tilt, but it was impossible to see the cause of the trouble. Now that the auroral display had faded, the lower part of the capsule was in total darkness, and he had no means of illuminating it. But that problem, at least, could be readily solved. If Monsoon Control could dump kilowatts of infrared into the Basement of the Tower, it could easily spare him a few visible photons.

"We can use our own searchlights," said Kingsley, when Morgan passed on his request.

"No good. They'll shine straight into my eyes, and I won't be able to see a thing. I want a light behind and *above* me—there must be somebody in the right position."

"I'll check," Kingsley answered, obviously glad to make some useful gesture. It seemed a long time before he called again, but looking at his timer, Morgan was surprised to see that only three minutes had elapsed.

"Monsoon Control *could* manage it, but they'd have to retune and defocus—I think they're scared of frying you. But Kinte can light up immediately. They have a psuedo-white laser—*and* they're in the right position. Shall I tell them to go ahead?"

Morgan checked his bearings. Let's see, Kinte would be very high in the west—that would be fine.

"I'm ready," he answered, and closed his eyes. Almost instantly, the capsule exploded with light.

Cautiously, Morgan opened his eyes again. The beam was coming from high in the west, dazzlingly brilliant despite its journey of almost forty thousand kilometers. It appeared to be pure white, but he knew that it was actually a blend of three sharply tuned lines in the red, green, and blue parts of the spectrum.

After a few seconds' adjustment of the mirror, he managed to get a clear view of the offending strap, half a meter beneath his feet. The end that he could see was secured to the base of Spider by a large butterfly nut. All that he had to do was to unscrew *that,* and the battery would drop off. . . .

Morgan sat silently analyzing the situation for so many minutes that Kingsley called him again. For the first time, there was a trace of hope in his deputy's voice.

"We've been doing some calculations, Van. . . . What do you think of this idea?"

Morgan heard him out, then whistled softly.

"You're certain of the safety margin?" he asked.

"Of course," answered Kingsley, sounding some-what aggrieved. Morgan hardly blamed him, but *he* was not the one who would be risking his neck.

"Well—I'll give it a try. But only for one second, the first time."

"That won't be enough. Still, it's a good idea—you'll get the feel of it."

Gently, Morgan released the friction brakes that were holding Spider motionless on the tape. Instantly, he seemed to rise out of the seat, as weight vanished. He counted, "One, TWO!" and engaged the brakes again.

Spider gave a jerk, and for a fraction of a second Morgan was pressed uncomfortably down into the seat. There was an ominous squeal from the braking mechanism, then the capsule was at rest again, apart from a slight torsional vibration that quickly died away.

"That was a bumpy ride," said Morgan. "But I'm still here—and so is that infernal battery."

"So I warned you. You'll have to try harder. Two seconds at least."

Morgan knew that he could not outguess Kingsley, with all the figures and computing power at his com-mand, but he felt the need for some reassuring mental arithmetic. Two seconds of free fall—say half a sec-ond to put on the brakes—allowing one ton for the mass of Spider . . .

The question was: which would go first—the strap retaining the battery, or the tape that was holding him here four hundred kilometers up in the sky? In the usual way, it would be no contest in a trial between hyperfilament and ordinary steel. But if he applied the brakes too suddenly—or they seized owing to this maltreatment—*both* might snap. And then he and the battery would reach the earth at very nearly the same time.

"Two seconds it is," he told Kingsley. "Here we go."

This time, the jerk was nerve-racking in its violence, and the torsional oscillations took much longer to die out. Morgan was certain that he would have felt—or heard—the breaking of the strap. He was not surprised when a glance in the mirror confirmed that the battery was still there.

Kingsley did not seem too worried.

"It may take three or four times," he said.

Morgan was tempted to retort, "Are you after my job?" but thought better of it. Kingsley would be amused; unknown listeners might not.

After the third fall—he felt he had dropped kilometers, but it was only about a hundred meters—even Kingsley's optimism started to fade. It was obvious that the trick was not going to work.

"I'd like to send my compliments to the people who made that safety strap," said Morgan wryly. "Now what do you suggest? A *three*-second drop before I slam on the brakes?"

He could almost see Kingsley shake his head.

"Too big a risk. I'm not so much worried about the tape as the braking mechanism. It wasn't designed for this sort of thing."

"Well, it was a good try," Morgan answered. "But I'm not giving up yet. I'm damned if I'll be beaten by a simple butterfly nut, fifty centimeters in front of my nose. I'm going outside to get at it."

50

THE FALLING FIREFLIES

"01 15 24 This is Friendship Seven. I'll try to describe what I'm in here. I am in a big mass of some very small particles that are brilliantly lit up like they're luminescent. . . . They're coming by the capsule, and they look like little stars. A whole shower of them coming by . . .

"01 16 10 They're very slow; they're not going away from me more than maybe three or four miles an hour. . . .

"01 19 38 Sunrise has just come up behind in the periscope . . . as I looked back out of the window, I had literally thousands of small, luminous particles swirling round the capsule. . . ."

Commander John Glenn
Mercury **Friendship Seven,**
20 Feb. 1962

With the old-style spacesuits, reaching that butterfly nut would have been completely out of the question. Even with the Flexisuit that Morgan was now wearing, it might be difficult, but at least he could make the attempt.

Very carefully, because more lives than his own depended upon it, he rehearsed the sequence of events. He must check the suit, depressurize the capsule, and open the hatch—which, luckily, was almost full-length. Then he must release the safety belt, get down on his knees—if he could!—and reach for that butterfly nut. Everything depended upon its tightness. There were no tools of any kind aboard Spider, but Morgan was prepared to match his fingers—even in space gloves—against the average small wrench.

He was just about to describe his plan of operations, in case anyone on the ground could find a flaw, when he became aware of a certain mild discomfort. He could readily tolerate it for much longer, if necessary, but there was no point in taking chances. If he used the capsule's own plumbing, he would not have to bother with the awkward diver's friend incorporated in the suit. . . .

When he had finished, he turned the key of the urine dump—and was startled by a tiny explosion near the base of the capsule. Almost instantly, to his astonishment, a cloud of twinkling stars winked into existence, as if a microscopic galaxy had been suddenly created. He had the illusion that, just for a fraction of a second, it hovered motionless outside the capsule before it started to fall straight down, as swiftly as any stone dropped on earth. Within seconds, it had dwindled to a point, and was gone.

Nothing could have brought home more clearly the fact that he was still wholly a captive of the earth's gravitational field. He remembered how, in the early days of orbital flight, the first astronauts had been puzzled and then amused by the haloes of ice crystals that accompanied them around the planet; there had been some feeble jokes about "Constellation Urion." That could not happen here; anything he dropped, however fragile it might be, would crash straight back into the atmosphere. He must never forget that, despite his altitude, he was not an astronaut, reveling in the freedom of weightlessness.

He was a man inside a building four hundred kilometers high, preparing to open the window and go out on the ledge.

51

ON THE PORCH

Though it was cold and uncomfortable on the summit, the crowd continued to grow. There was something hypnotic about that brilliant little star in the zenith, upon which the thoughts of the world, as well as the laser beam from Kinte, were now focused.

As they arrived, all the visitors headed for the north tape, and stroked it in a shy, half-defiant manner, as if to say, "I know this is silly, but it makes me feel I'm in contact with Morgan." Then they would gather around the coffee dispenser and listen to the reports coming over the speaker system.

There was nothing new from the refugees in the Tower. They were all sleeping, or trying to sleep, in an attempt to conserve oxygen. Since Morgan was not yet overdue, they had not been informed of the holdup; but within the next hour they would undoubtedly be calling Midway to find out what had happened.

Maxine Duval had arrived at Sri Kanda just ten minutes too late to see Morgan. There was a time when such a near-miss would have made her very angry. Now she merely shrugged her shoulders and reassured herself with the thought that she would be the first to grab the engineer on his return. Kingsley had not allowed her to speak to him, and she had even accepted this ruling with good grace. Yes, she was growing old. . . .

For the last five minutes, the only sound that had come from the capsule was a series of "Check"'s as Morgan went through the suit routine with an expert up in Midway. When that was completed, everyone waited tensely for the crucial next step.

"Valving the air," said Morgan, his voice overlaid with a slight echo now that he had closed the visor of his helmet. "Capsule pressure zero. No problem with breathing."

A thirty-second pause.

"Opening the front door—there it goes. Now releasing the seat belt."

There was an unconscious stirring and murmuring among the watchers. In imagination, every one of them was up there in the capsule, aware of the void that had opened before Morgan.

"Quick-release buckle operated. I'm stretching my legs. Not much headroom . . .

"Just getting the feel of the suit. Quite flexible. Now I'm going out on the porch. Don't worry! I've got the seat belt wrapped around my left arm. . . .

"Phew. Hard work, bending as much as this. But I can see that butterfly nut, underneath the porch grille. I'm working out how to reach it. . . .

"On my knees now—not very comfortable . . .

"I've got it! Now to see if it will turn . . ."

The listeners became rigid, silent—then, in unison, relaxed with virtually simultaneous sighs of relief.

"No problem! I can turn it easily. Two revs already. Any moment now. Just a bit more. I can feel it coming off—LOOK OUT DOWN BELOW!"

There was a burst of clapping and cheering. Some people put their hands over their heads and cowered in mock terror. One or two, not fully understanding that the falling nut would not arrive for five minutes and would descend ten kilometers to the east, looked genuinely alarmed.

Only Kingsley failed to share the rejoicing.

"Don't cheer too soon," he said to Duval. "We're not out of the woods yet."

The seconds dragged by. One minute . . . two minutes . . .

"It's no use," said Morgan at last, his voice thick with rage and frustration. "I can't budge the strap. The weight of the battery is holding it jammed in the threads. Those jolts we gave must have welded it to the bolt."

"Come back as quickly as you can," said Kingsley. "There's a new power cell on the way, and we can manage a turnaround in less than an hour. So we can still get up to the Tower in . . . oh, say, six hours. Barring any further accidents, of course."

Precisely, thought Morgan; and he would not care to take Spider up again without a thorough check of the much-abused braking mechanism. Nor would he trust himself to make a second trip. He was already feeling the strain of the last few hours, and fatigue would soon be slowing down his mind and his body, just when he needed maximum efficiency from both.

He was back in the seat now, but the capsule was still open to space and he had not yet refastened the safety belt. To do so would be to admit defeat, and that had never been easy for Morgan.

The unwinking glare of the Kinte laser, coming from almost immediately above, transfixed him with its pitiless light. He tried to focus his mind on the problem as sharply as that beam was focused upon him.

All that he needed was a metal cutter—a hacksaw or a pair of shears—he could sever the retaining strap. Once again he cursed the fact that there was no tool kit aboard Spider. Even so, it would hardly have contained what he needed.

There were megawatt-hours of energy stored in Spider's own battery. Could he use them in any way? He had a brief fantasy of establishing an arc and burning through the strap. But even if suitable heavy conductors were available—and of course they weren't—the main power supply was inaccessible from the control cab.

Kingsley and all the skilled brains gathered around him had failed to find any solution. He was on his own, physically and intellectually. It was, actually, the situation he had always preferred. . . .

And then, just as he was about to reach out and close the capsule door, Morgan knew what he had to do. All the time, the answer had been right by his finger tips.

52

THE OTHER PASSENGER

To Morgan, it seemed that a huge weight had lifted from his shoulders. He felt completely, irrationally confident. This time, surely, it *had* to work.

Nevertheless, he did not move from his seat until he had planned his actions in minute detail. And when Kingsley, sounding a little anxious, once again urged him to hurry back, he gave an evasive answer. He did not wish to raise any false hopes—on earth or in the Tower.

"I'm trying an experiment," he said. "Leave me alone for a few minutes."

He picked up the fiber dispenser that he had used for so many demonstrations—the little spinnerette that, years ago, had allowed him to descend the face of Yakkagala. One change had been made for reasons of safety: the first meter of filament had been coated with a layer of plastic, so that it was no longer quite invisible, and could be handled cautiously, even with bare fingers.

As Morgan looked at the little box in his hand, he realized how much he had come to regard it as a talisman, almost a good-luck charm. Of course, he did not *really* believe in such things; he always had a perfectly logical reason for carrying the spinnerette around with him. On this ascent, it had occurred to him that it might be useful because of its strength and unique lifting power. He had almost forgotten that it had other abilities as well. . . .

Once more he clambered out of the seat, and knelt down on the metal grille of Spider's tiny porch to examine the cause of all the trouble. The offending bolt was only ten centimeters on the other side of the grid, and although its bars were too close together for him to put his hand through them, he had already proved that he could reach around it without too much difficulty.

He released the first meter of coated fiber, and, using the ring at the end as a plumb bob, lowered it down through the grille. Tucking the dispenser itself firmly in a corner of the capsule, so that he could not accidentally knock it overboard, he reached around the grille until he could grab the swinging weight. This was not as easy as he had expected, because even this remarkable spacesuit would not allow his arm to bend quite freely, and the ring eluded his grasp as it pendulumed back and forth.

After half a dozen attempts—tiring, rather than annoying, because he knew that he would succeed sooner or later—he had looped the fiber around the shank of the bolt, just behind the strap it was holding in place. Now for the really tricky part . . .

He released just enough filament from the spinnerette for the naked fiber to reach the bolt, and to pass around it. Then he drew both ends tight—until he felt the loop catch in the thread.

Morgan had never attempted this trick with a rod of tempered steel more than a centimeter thick, and had no idea how long it would take. Bracing himself against the porch, he began to operate his invisible saw.

After five minutes, he was sweating badly, and could not tell if he had made any progress at all. He was afraid to slacken the tension, lest the fiber escape from the equally invisible slot it was, he hoped, slicing through the bolt. Several times Kingsley had called him, sounding more and more alarmed, and he had given a brief reassurance. Soon he would rest for a while, recover his breath—and explain what he was trying to do. This was the least that he owed to his anxious friends.

"Van," said Kingsley, "just what *are* you up to? The people in the Tower have been calling. What shall I say to them?"

"Give me another few minutes. I'm trying to cut the bolt—"

The calm but authoritative woman's voice that interrupted Morgan gave him such a shock that he almost let go of the precious fiber. The words were muffled by his suit, but that did not matter. He knew them all too well, though it had been months since he had last heard them.

"Dr. Morgan," said CORA, "please lie down and relax for the next ten minutes."

"Would you settle for five?" he pleaded. "I'm rather busy at the moment."

CORA did not deign to reply. Although there were units that could conduct simple conversations, his model was not among them.

Morgan kept his promise, breathing deeply and steadily for a full five minutes. Then he started sawing again.

Back and forth, back and forth, he worked the filament as he crouched over the grille and the four-hundred-kilometer-distant earth. He could feel considerable resistance, so he must be making some progress through that stubborn steel. But just how much, there was no way of telling.

"Dr. Morgan," said CORA, "you really must lie down for half an hour."

Morgan swore softly to himself.

"You're making a mistake, young lady," he retorted. "I'm feeling fine." But he was lying; CORA knew about the ache in his chest. . . .

"Who the hell are you talking to, Van?" asked Kingsley.

"Just a passing angel," answered Morgan. "Sorry I forgot to switch off the mike. I'm going to take another rest."

"What progress are you making?"

"Can't say. But I'm sure the cut's pretty deep by this time. It *must* be. . . ."

He wished that he could switch CORA off, but that, of course, was impossible, even if she had not been out of reach between his breastbone and the fabric of his spacesuit. A heart monitor that could be silenced was worse than useless—it was dangerous.

"Dr. Morgan," said CORA, now distinctly annoyed, "I really *must* insist. At least half an hour's *complete* rest."

This time, Morgan did not feel like answering. He knew that CORA was right; but she could not be expected to understand that his was not the only life involved. And he was also sure that she had, like one of his bridges, a built-in safety factor. Her diagnosis would be pessimistic; his condition would not be as serious as she was pretending. Or so he devoutly hoped. . . .

The pain in his chest certainly seemed to be getting no worse. He decided to ignore both it and CORA, and started to saw away, slowly but steadily, with the loop of fiber. He would keep going, he told himself grimly, just as long as was necessary.

The warning he had relied upon never came. Spider lurched violently as a quarter ton of dead weight ripped away, and Morgan was almost pitched out into the abyss. He dropped the spinerette and grabbed for the safety belt.

Everything seemed to happen in dreamlike slow motion. He had no sense of fear, only an utter determination not to surrender to gravity without a fight.

But he could not find the safety belt. It must have swung back into the cabin. . . .

He was not conscious of using his left hand, but suddenly he realized that it was clamped around the hinges of the open door. Yet still he did not pull himself back into the cabin. He was hypnotized by the sight of the falling battery, slowly rotating like some strange celestial body as it dwindled from sight. It took a long tome to vanish completely; and not until then did Morgan drag himself to safety, and collapse into his seat.

For a long time he sat there, his heart hammering, awaiting CORA'S next indignant protest. To his surprise, she was silent, almost as if she, too, had been startled. Well, he would give her no further cause for complaint. From now on, he would sit quietly at the controls, trying to relax his jangled nerves.

When he was himself again, he called the mountain.

"I've got rid of the battery," he said, and heard the cheers float up from earth. "As soon as I've closed the hatch, I'll be on my way again. Tell Sessui and Company to expect me in just over an hour. And thank Kinte for the light—I don't need it now."

He repressurized the cabin, opened the helmet of his suit, and treated himself to a long, cold sip of fortified orange juice. Then he engaged the drive, released the brakes, and lay back with a sense of overwhelming relief as Spider came up to full speed.

He had been climbing for several minutes before he realized what was missing. In anxious hope, he peered out at the metal grille of the porch. No, it was not there.

Well, he could always get another spinnerette, to replace the one now following the discarded battery back to earth. It was a small sacrifice for such an achievement. Strange, therefore, that he was so upset, and unable fully to enjoy his triumph.

He felt that he had lost an old and faithful friend.

53

FADE-OUT

The fact that he was only thirty minutes behind schedule seemed too good to be true; Morgan would have been prepared to swear that the capsule had halted for at least an hour. Up there in the Tower, now much less than two hundred kilometers away, the reception committee would be preparing to welcome him. He refused even to consider the possibility of any further problems.

When he passed the five-hundred kilometer mark, going strong, there was a message of congratulation from the ground. "By the way," added Kingsley, "the Game Warden in the Ruhana Sanctuary's reported an aircraft crashing. We were able to reassure him. If we can find the hole, we may have a souvenir for you."

Morgan had no difficulty in restraining his enthusiasm; he was glad to see the last of that battery. Now, if they could find the spinnerette—but *that* would be a hopeless task. . . .

The first sign of trouble came at five hundred fifty kilometers. By now, the rate of ascent should have been over two hundred klicks; it was only one nine eight. Slight though the discrepancy was—and it would make no appreciable difference to his arrival time—it worried Morgan.

By the time he was thirty kilometers from the Tower, he had diagnosed the problem, and he knew that this time there was absolutely nothing he could do about it. Although there should have been ample reserve, the battery was beginning to fade.

Perhaps those sudden jolts and restarts had brought on the malaise; possibly there was even some physical damage to the delicate components. Whatever the explanation, the current was slowly dropping, and with it the capsule's speed.

There was consternation when Morgan reported the indicator readings back to the ground.

"I'm afraid you're right," Kingsley lamented, sounding almost in tears. "We suggest you cut speed back to one hundred klicks. We'll try to calculate battery life—though it can be only an educated guess."

Twenty-five kilometers to go—a mere fifteen minutes, even at this reduced speed! If Morgan had been able to pray, he would have done so.

"We estimate you have between ten and twenty mintutes, judging by the rate the current is dropping. It will be a close thing, I'm afraid."

"Shall I reduce speed again?"

"Not for the moment. We're trying to optimize your discharge rate, and this seems about right."

"Well, you can switch on your beam now. If I can't get to the Tower, at least I want to see it."

Neither Kinte nor the other orbiting stations could help him, now that he wished to look up at the underside of the Tower. This was a task for the searchlight on Sri Kanda itself, pointing vertically toward the zenith.

A moment later, the capsule was impaled by a dazzling beam from the heart of Taprobane. Only a few meters away—so close that he felt he could touch them—the other three guiding tapes were ribbons of light, converging toward the Tower. He followed their dwindling perspective—and there it was. . . .

Just twenty kilometers away! He should be there in a dozen minutes, coming up through the floor of that tiny square building he could see glittering in the sky, bearing presents like some troglodytic Father Christmas. Despite his determination to relax, and obey CORA'S orders, it was quite impossible to do so. He found himself tensing his muscles, as if by his own physical exertions he could help Spider along the last fraction of its journey.

At ten kilometers, there was a distinct change of pitch from the drive motor. Morgan had been expecting this, and reacted to it at once. Without waiting for advice from the ground, he cut speed back to fifty klicks. At this rate, he *still* had twelve minutes to go, and he began to wonder despairingly if he was involved in an asymptotic approach. This was a variant of the race between Achilles and the tortoise. If he halved his speed every time he halved the distance, would he reach the Tower in a finite time? Once, he would have known the answer instantly; now, he felt too tired to work it out.

At five kilometers, he could see the constructional details of the Tower—the catwalk and protective rails, the futile safety net provided as a sop to public opinion. Although he strained his eyes, he could not yet make out the air lock toward which he was now crawling with such agonizing slowness.

And then it no longer mattered. Two kilometers short of the goal, Spider's motors stalled completely. The capsule even slid downward a few meters before Morgan was able to apply the brakes.

Yet this time, to Morgan's surprise, Kingsley did not seem utterly downcast.

"You can still make it," he said. "Give the battery ten minutes to recuperate. There's enough energy there for that last couple of kilometers."

It was one of the longest ten minutes that Morgan had ever known. Though he could have made it pass more swiftly by responding to Duval's increasingly desperate pleas, he was too emotionally exhausted to talk. He was genuinely sorry about this, and hoped that Maxine would understand and forgive him.

He did have one brief exchange with Driver-Pilot Chang, who reported that the refugees in the Basement were in fairly good shape and much encouraged by his nearness. They were taking turns to peer at him through the one small porthole of the air lock's outer door, and simply could not believe that he might never be able to bridge the trifling space between them.

Morgan gave the battery an extra minute for luck. To his relief, the motors responded strongly, with an encouraging surge of power. Spider got within half a kilometer of the Tower before stalling again.

"Next time does it," said Kingsley, though it seemed to Morgan that his friend's confidence sounded somewhat forced. "Sorry for all these delays . . ."

"Another ten minutes?" Morgan asked with resignation.

"I'm afraid so. And this time, use thirty-second bursts, with a minute between them. That way, you'll get the last erg out of the battery."

And out of me, thought Morgan. Strange that CORA had been quiet for so long. But this time he had not exerted himself physically; it only *felt* that way.

In this preoccupation with Spider, he had been neglecting himself. For the last hour he had quite forgotten his zero-residue glucose-based energy tablets and the little plastic bulb of fruit juice. After he had sampled both, he felt much better, and only wished that he could transfer some of the surplus calories to the dying battery.

Now for the moment of truth—the final exertion. Failure was unthinkable, when he was so close to the goal. The fates could not possibly be so malevolent, now that he had only a few hundred meters to go.

He was whistling in the dark, of course. How many aircraft had crashed at the very edge of the runway after safely crossing an ocean? How many times had machines or muscles failed when there were only millimeters to go? Every possible piece of luck, bad as well as good, happened to somebody, somewhere. He had no right to expect any special treatment.

The capsule heaved itself upward in fits and starts, like a dying animal seeking its last haven. When the battery finally expired, the base of the Tower seemed to fill half the sky.

But it was still twenty meters above him.

54

THEORY OF RELATIVITY

It was to Morgan's credit that he felt his own fate was sealed, in the desolating moment when the last dregs of power were exhausted and the lights on Spider's display panel finally faded out. Not for several seconds did he remember that he had only to release the brakes and he would slide back to earth. In three hours, he could be safely back in bed. No one would blame him for the failure of his mission; he had done all that was humanly possibly.

For a brief while, he stared in a kind of dull fury at that inaccessible square, with the shadow of Spider projected upon it. His mind revolved a host of crazy schemes, and rejected them all. If he still had his faithful little spinnerette—but there would have been no way of getting it to the Tower. If the refugees had possessed a spacesuit, someone could lower a rope to him—but there had been no time to collect a suit from the burning transporter.

Of course, if this was a video drama, and not a real-life problem some heroic volunteer could sacrifice himself—better still, herself—by going into the lock and tossing down a rope using the fifteen seconds of vacuum consciousness to save the others. It was some measure of Morgan's desperation that, for a fleeting moment, he even considered this idea before common sense reasserted itself.

From the time that Spider had given up the battle

with gravity until Morgan finally accepted that there was nothing more that he could do, probably less than a minute elapsed. Then Kingsley asked a question which, at such a time, seemed an annoying irrelevance.

"Give us your distance again, Van. Exactly *how* far are you from the Tower?"

"What the hell does it matter? It could be a light-year."

There was a brief silence before Kingsley spoke again, in the sort of tone one used to address a small child or a difficult invalid.

"It makes all the difference in the world. Did you say *twenty* meters?"

"Yes—that's about it."

Incredibly, unmistakably, Kingsley gave a clearly audible sigh of relief. There was even joy in his voice when he answered:

"And all these years, Van, I thought that *you* were the chief engineer on this project. Suppose it *is* twenty meters exactly—"

Morgan's explosive shout prevented him from finishing the sentence.

"What an idiot! Tell Sessui I'll dock in—oh—fifteen minutes."

"Fourteen point five, if you've guessed the distance right. And nothing on earth can stop you now."

That was a risky statement, and Morgan wished that Kingsley hadn't made it. Docking adapters sometimes failed to latch together properly, because of minute errors in manufacturing tolerances. And, of course, there had never been a chance of testing this particular system.

He felt only a slight embarrassment at his mental blackout. After all, under extreme stress a man could forget his own telephone number, even his own date of birth. And until this very moment, the now dominant factor in the situation had been so unimportant that it could be completely ignored.

It was all a matter of relativity. He could not reach the Tower; but the Tower would reach him—at its inexorable two kilometers a day.

55

HARD DOCK

The record for one day's construction had been thirty kilometers, when the slimmest and lightest section of the Tower was being assembled. Now that the most massive portion—the very root of the structure—was nearing completion in orbit, the rate was down to two kilometers. That was quite fast enough. It would give Morgan time to check the adapter line-up, and to rehearse mentally the rather tricky few seconds between confirming hard dock and releasing Spider's brakes. If he left them on for too long, there would be a very unequal trial of strength between the capsule and the moving megatons of the Tower.

It was a long but relaxed fifteen minutes—time enough, Morgan hoped, to pacify CORA. Toward the end, everything seemed to happen quickly, and at the last moment he felt like an ant about to be crushed in a stamping press, as the solid roof of the sky descended upon him. One second, the base of the Tower was meters away; an instant later, he felt and heard the impact of the docking mechanism.

Many lives depended now upon the skill and care with which the engineers and mechanics, years ago, had done their work. *If* the couplings did not line up within the allowed tolerances; *if* the latching mechanism did not operate correctly; *if* the seal was not airtight . . . Morgan tried to interpret the medley of sounds reaching his ears, but he was not skilled enough to read the messages.

Then, like a signal of victory, the DOCKING COMPLETED sign flashed on the indicator board. There would be ten seconds while the telescopic elements absorbed the movement of the advancing Tower. Morgan waited half of them before he cautiously released the brakes.

He was prepared to jam them on again instantly if Spider started to drop, but the sensors were telling the truth. Tower and capsule were now firmly mated together. Morgan had only to climb a few rungs of ladder, and he would have reached his goal.

After he had reported to the jubilant listeners on earth and Midway, he sat for a moment recovering his breath. Strange to think that this was his second visit, but he could remember little of that first one, years ago and thirty-six thousand kilometers higher. During what had, for want of a better term, been called the foundation-laying, there had been a small party in the Basement, and numerous zero-gee toasts had been squirted. This was not only the first section of the Tower to be built; it would also be the first to make contact with earth, at the end of its long descent from orbit. Some kind of ceremony had therefore seemed in order, and Morgan now recalled that even his old enemy Senator Collins had been gracious enough to attend and to wish him luck with a barbed but good-humored speech. There was even better cause for celebration now. . . .

Already, Morgan could hear a faint tattoo of welcoming raps from the far side of the air lock. He undid his safety belt, climbed awkwardly onto the seat, and started to ascend the ladder. The overhead hatch gave a token resistance, as if the powers marshaled against him were making one last feeble gesture, and air hissed briefly while pressure was equalized. Then the circular plate swung open and downward, and eager hands helped him up into the Tower. As Morgan took his first breath of the fetid air, he wondered how anyone could have survived here. If his mission had been aborted, he felt quite certain that a second attempt would have been too late.

The bare, bleak cell was lit only by solar-fluorescent panels, which had been patiently trapping and releasing sunlight for more than a decade, against the emergency that had arrived at last. Their illumination revealed a scene that might have come from some old war. Here were homeless and disheveled refugees from a devastated city, huddling in a bomb shelter with the few possessions they had been able to save.

Not many such refugees, however, would have carried bags labeled PROJECT ION, LUNAR HOTEL CORPORATION, PROPERTY OF THE FEDERAL REPUBLIC OF MARS, or the ubiquitous MAY/ NOT/ BE STOWED IN VACUUM. Nor would they have been so cheerful; even those who were lying down to conserve oxygen managed a smile and a languid wave. Morgan had just returned the salute when his legs buckled beneath him, and everything blacked out.

Never before in his life had he fainted, and when the blast of cold oxygen revived him, his first emotion was one of acute embarrassment. His eyes came slowly into focus, and he saw masked shapes hovering over him. For a moment he wondered if he was in a hospital; then brain and vision returned to normal. While he was unconscious, his precious cargo must have been unloaded.

Those masks were the molecular sieves he had carried up to the Tower. Worn over nose and mouth, they would block the CO_2 but allow oxygen to pass. Simple yet technologically sophisticated, they would enable men to survive in an atmosphere that would otherwise cause instant suffocation. It required a little extra effort to breathe through them, but Nature never gave something for nothing—and this was a small price to pay for life itself.

Rather groggily, but refusing any help, Morgan got to his feet and was belatedly introduced to the men and women he had saved. One matter still worried him: while he was unconscious, had CORA delivered any of her set speeches? He did not wish to raise the subject, but he wondered. . . .

"On behalf of all of us," said Professor Sessui, with sincerity yet with the obvious awkwardness of a man who was seldom polite to anyone, "I want to thank you for what you've done. We owe our lives to you."

Any logical or coherent reply to this would have smacked of false modesty, so Morgan used the excuse of adjusting his mask to mumble something unintelligible.

He was about to start checking that all the equipment had been unloaded when Sessui added, rather anxiously: "I'm sorry we can't offer you a chair—this is the best we can do." He pointed to a couple of instrument boxes, one on top of the other. "You really should take it easy."

The phrase was familiar; so CORA *had* spoken. There was a slightly embarrassed pause while Morgan registered this fact, and the others admitted that they knew, and he showed that he knew *they* knew—all without a word being uttered, in the kind of psychological infinite regress that occurs when a group of people shares completely a secret that nobody will ever mention again.

He took a few deep breaths—it was amazing how quickly one got used to the mask—and sat down on the proffered seat. I'm not going to faint again, he told himself with grim determination. I must deliver the goods and get out of here quickly—if possible, before there are any more pronouncements from CORA.

"That can of sealant," he said, pointing to the

smallest of the containers he had brought, "should take care of your leak. Spray it around the gasket of the air lock. It sets hard in a few seconds.

"Use the oxygen only when you have to. You may need it to sleep. There's a CO_2 mask for everyone, and a couple of spares.

"And here's food and water for three days. That should be plenty. The transporter from 10K should be here tomorrow. As for the Medikit—I hope you won't need *that* at all."

He paused for breath. It was not easy to talk while wearing a CO_2 filter, and he felt an increasing need to conserve his strength. Sessui's people could now take care of themselves, but he had one further job to do—and the sooner the better.

Morgan turned to Chang and said quietly: "Please help me to suit up again. I want to inspect the track."

"That's only a thirty-minute suit you're wearing!"

"I'll need ten minutes—fifteen at the most."

"Dr. Morgan—*I'm* a space-qualified operator; *you're* not. No one's allowed to go out in a thirty-minute suit without a spare pack, or an umbilical. Except in an emergency, of course."

Morgan gave a tired smile. Chang was right, and the excuse of immediate danger no longer applied. But an emergency was whatever the Chief Engineer said it was.

"I want to look at the damage," he answered, "and examine the tracks. It would be a pity if the people from 10K can't reach you because they weren't warned of some obstacle."

Chang was clearly not too happy about the situation (what *had* that gossiping CORA jabbered while he was unconscious) but raised no further arguments as he followed Morgan into the north lock.

Just before he closed the visor, Morgan asked: "Any more trouble with the Professor?"

Chang shook his head.

"I think the CO_2 has slowed him down. And if he starts up again—well, we outnumber him six to one, though I'm not sure if we can count on his students. Some of them are just as crazy as he is. Look at that girl who spends all her time scribbling in the corner. She's convinced that the sun's going out, or blowing up—I'm not sure which—and wants to warn the world before she dies. Much good *that* would do. I'd prefer not to know."

Though Morgan could not help smiling, he felt quite sure that none of the Professor's students were crazy. Eccentric, perhaps—but also brilliant. They would not be working with Sessui otherwise. One day he must find out more about the men and women whose lives he had saved. But that would have to wait until they had all returned to earth, by their separate ways.

"I'm going to take a quick walk around the Tower," said Morgan, "and I'll describe any damage, so you can report to Midway. It won't take more than ten minutes. And if it does—well, don't try to get me back."

Chang's reply, as he closed the inner door of the air lock, was practical and brief.

"How the hell *could* I?" he asked.

56

VIEW FROM THE BALCONY

The outer door of the north air lock opened without difficulty, framing a rectangle of complete darkness. Running horizontally across that darkness was a line of fire—the protective handrail of the catwalk, blazing in the beam of the searchlight pointed straight up from the mountain so far below.

Morgan took a deep breath and flexed the suit. He felt perfectly comfortable. Waving to Chang, who was peering at him through the window of the inner door, he stepped out of the Tower.

The catwalk that surrounded the Basement was a metal grille about two meters wide. Beyond it the safety net had been streched out for another thirty meters. The portion that Morgan could see had caught nothing whatsoever during its years of patient waiting.

He started his circumnavigation of the Tower, shielding his eyes against the glare blasting up from underfoot. The oblique lighting showed up every least bump and imperfection in the surface that stretched above him like a roadway to the stars—which, in a sense, it was.

As he had hoped and expected, the explosion on the far side of the Tower had caused no damage here. *That* would have required an atomic bomb, not a mere electrochemical one. The twin grooves of the track, now awaiting their first arrival, stretched endlessly upward in their pristine perfection. And fifty meters below the balcony—though it was hard to look in that direction because of the glare—he could just make out the terminal buffers, ready for a task they should never have to perform.

Taking his time, and keeping close to the sheer face of the Tower, Morgan walked slowly westward until he came to the first corner. As he turned, he looked back at the open door of the air lock, and the—relative, indeed!—safety that it represented, before continuing boldly along the blank wall of the west face.

He felt a curious mixture of elation and fear, such as he had not known since he had learned to swim and found himself, for the first time, in water out of his depth. Although he was certain that there was no real danger, there *could* be. He was acutely aware of CORA, biding her time. But he had always hated to leave any job undone, and his mission was not yet complete.

The west face was exactly like the north one, except for the absence of an air lock. Again, there was no sign of damage, even though it was closer to the scene of the explosion.

Checking the impulse to hurry—after all, he had been outside for only three minutes—Morgan strolled on to the next corner. Even before he turned it, he could see that he was not going to complete his planned circuit of the Tower. The catwalk had been ripped off, and was dangling out into space, a twisted tongue of metal. The safety net had vanished altogether, doubtless torn away by the falling transporter.

Don't press your luck, Morgan told himself. But he could not resist peering around the corner, holding on to the section of the guardrail that remained.

There was a good deal of debris stuck in the track, and the face of the Tower had been discolored by the explosion. But as far as he could see, even here there was nothing that could not be put right in a couple of hours by a few men with cutting torches. He gave a careful description to Chang, who expressed relief and urged Morgan to get back into the Tower as soon as possible.

"Don't worry," said Morgan. "I've still got ten minutes and all of thirty meters to go. I could manage on the air I have in my lungs now."

But he did not intend to put this to the test. He had already had quite enough excitement for one night. More than enough, if CORA was to be believed. From now on, he would obey her orders implicitly.

When he had walked back to the open door of the air lock, he stood for a few final moments beside the guardrail, drenched by the fountain of light leaping up from the summit of Sri Kanda far below. It threw his own immensely elongated shadow directly along the Tower, vertically upward toward the stars. That shadow must stretch for thousands of kilometers, and it occured to Morgan that it might even reach the transporter now dropping swiftly down from 10K Station. If he waved his arms, the rescuers might be able to see his signals; he could talk to them in Morse code.

This amusing fantasy inspired a more serious thought. Would it be best for him to wait here, with the others, and not risk the return to earth in Spider? But the journey up to Midway, where he could get good medical attention, would take a week. That was not a sensible alternative, since he could be back on Sri Kanda in less than three hours.

Time to go inside—his air must be getting low, and there was nothing more to see. That was a disappointing irony, considering the spectacular view one would normally have here, by day or by night. Now, however, the planet below and the heavens above were both banished by the blinding glare from Sri Kanda. He was floating in the tiny universe of light, surrounded by utter darkness on every side. It was almost impossible to believe that he was in space, if only because of his sense of weight. He felt as secure as if he were standing on the mountain itself, instead of six hundred kilometers above it. *That* was a thought to savor, and to carry back to earth.

He patted the smooth, unyielding surface of the Tower, more enormous in comparison to him than an elephant to an amoeba. But no amoeba could ever conceive of an elephant, still less create one.

"See you on earth in a year's time," Morgan whispered, and slowly closed the air-lock door behind him.

57

THE LAST DAWN

Morgan was back in the Basement for only five minutes. This was no time for social amenities, and he did not wish to consume any of the precious oxygen he had brought here with such difficulty. He shook hands all around and scrambled back into Spider.

It was good to breathe again without a mask, better still to know that his mission had been a complete success, and that in less than three hours he would be safely back on earth. Yet after all the effort that had gone into reaching the Tower, he was reluctant to cast off again, and to surrender once more to the pull of gravity—even though it would now be taking him home. But presently he released the docking latches, and started to fall downward, becoming weightless for several seconds.

When the speed indicator reached three hundred klicks, the automatic braking system came on, and weight returned. The brutally depleted battery would be recharging now, but it must have been damaged beyond repair and would have to be taken out of service.

There was an ominous parallel here. Morgan could not help thinking of his own overstrained body, but a stubborn pride kept him from asking for a doctor on stand-by. He had made a little bet with himself: he would do so only if CORA spoke again.

She was silent now as he dropped swiftly through

the night. Morgan felt totally relaxed, and left Spider to look after itself while he admired the heavens. Few spacecraft provided so panoramic a view, and not many men could ever have seen the stars under such superb conditions. The aurora had vanished completely, the searchlight had been extinguished, and there was nothing left to challenge the constellations.

Except, of course, the stars that man himself had made. Almost directly overhead was the dazzling beacon of Ashoka, poised forever above Hindustan, and only a few hundred kilometers from the Tower complex. Halfway down in the east was Confucius, much lower still Kamehameha, while high up from the west shone Kinte and Imhotep. These were merely the brightest signposts along the equator. There were literally scores of others, all of them far more brilliant than Sirius. How astonished one of the old astronomers would have been to see this necklace around the sky! And how bewildered he would have become when, after an hour or so's observation, he discovered that they were quite immobile, neither rising nor setting while the familiar stars drifted past in their ancient courses.

As he stared at the diamond necklace stretched across the sky, Morgan's sleepy mind slowly transformed it into something far more impressive. With only a slight effort of the imagination, those man-made stars became the lights of a titanic bridge.

He drifted into wilder fantasies. What was the name of the bridge into Valhalla, across which the heroes of the Norse legends passed from this world to the next? He could not remember, but it was a glorious dream.

And had other creatures, long before man, tried in vain to span the skies of their own worlds? He thought of the splendid rings encircling Saturn, the ghostly arches of Uranus and Neptune. Although he knew perfectly well that none of these worlds have ever felt the touch of life, it amused him to think that here were the shattered fragments of bridges that had failed.

He wanted to sleep, but, against his will, imagination had seized upon the idea. Like a dog that had just discovered a new bone, it would not let go.

The concept was not absurd; it was not even original. Many of the synchronous stations were already kilometers in extent, or linked by cables that stretched along appreciable fractions of their orbit. To join them together, thus forming a ring completely around the world, would be an engineering task much simpler than the building of the Tower, and would involve much less material.

No—not a ring—a *wheel*. This tower was only the first spoke. There would be others (four? six? a score?) spaced along the equator. When they were all connected rigidly up there in orbit, the problems of stability that plagued a single tower would vanish. Africa, South America, the Gilbert Islands, Indonesia —they could *all* provide locations for earth terminals, if desired.

For someday, as materials improved and knowledge advanced, the towers could be made invulnerable even to the worst hurricanes, and mountain sites would no longer be necessary. If he had waited another hundred years, perhaps he need not have disturbed the Mahanayake Thero. . . .

While he was dreaming, the thin crescent of the waning moon had lifted unobtrusively above the eastern horizon, already aglow with the first hint of dawn. Earthshine lit the entire lunar disk so brilliantly that Morgan could see much of the night-land detail. He strained his eyes in the hope of glimpsing that loveliest of sights, never seen by earlier ages, a star within the arms of the crescent moon. But none of the cities of man's second home was visible tonight.

Only two hundred kilometers—less than an hour to go. There was no point in trying to keep awake.

Spider had automatic terminal programing and would touch gently down without disturbing his sleep. . . .

The pain woke him first. CORA was a fraction of a second later.

"Don't try to move," she said soothingly. "I've radioed for help. The ambulance is on the way."

That was funny. But don't laugh, Morgan ordered himself; she's only doing her best. He felt no fear. Though the pain beneath his breastbone was intense, it was not incapacitating. He tried to focus his mind upon it, and the very act of concentration relieved the symptoms. Long ago, he had discovered that the best way of handling pain was to study it objectively.

Warren Kingsley was calling him, but the words were far away and had little meaning. He could recognize the anxiety in his friend's voice, and wished that he could do something to alleviate it, but he had no strength left to deal with this problem—or with any other.

Now he could not even hear the words. A faint but steady roar had obliterated all other sounds. Though he knew that it existed only in his mind—or the labyrinthine channels of his ears—it seemed completely real. He could believe that he was standing at the foot of some great waterfall.

It was growing fainter, softer, *more musical*. And suddenly he recognized it. How pleasant to hear once more, on the silent frontier of space, the sound he remembered from his very first visit to Yakkagala!

Gravity was drawing him home again, as through the centuries its invisible hand had shaped the trajectory of the Fountains of Paradise. But he had created something that gravity could never recapture, as long as men possessed the wisdom and the will to preserve it.

How cold his legs were! What had happened to

Spider's life-support system? But soon it would be dawn; then there would be warmth enough.

The stars were fading, far more swiftly than they had any right to do. That was strange; though the day was almost here, everything around him was growing dark. And the fountains were sinking back into the earth, their voices becoming fainter . . . fainter . . . fainter . . .

And now there was another voice, but Vannevar Morgan did not hear it. Between brief, piercing bleeps, CORA cried to the approaching dawn:

HELP! WILL ANYONE WHO HEARS ME PLEASE COME AT ONCE! THIS IS A CORA EMERGENCY!

HELP! WILL ANYONE WHO HEARS ME PLEASE COME AT ONCE!

She was still calling when the sun came up, and its first rays caressed the summit of the mountain that had once been sacred. Far below, the shadow of Sri Kanda leaped forth upon the clouds, its perfect cone still unblemished despite all that man had done.

There were no pilgrims now to watch that symbol of eternity lie across the face of the awakening land. But millions would see it, in the centuries ahead, as they rode in comfort and safety to the stars.

EPILOGUE: KALIDASA'S TRIUMPH

In the last days of that last brief summer, before the jaws of ice clenched shut around the equator, one of the Starholme envoys came to Yakkagala.

A Master of the Swarms, It had recently conjugated Itself into human form. Apart from one minor detail, the likeness was excellent; but the dozen children who had accompanied the Holmer in the autocopter were in a constant state of mild hysteria, the younger ones frequently dissolving into giggles.

"What's so funny?" It had asked in perfect solar. "Or is this a private joke?"

But they would not explain to the Starholmer, whose normal color vision lay entirely in the infrared, that the human skin was not a random mosaic of greens and reds and blues. Even when It had threatened to turn into a Tyrannosaurus Rex and eat them all up, they refused to satisfy Its curiosity. Indeed, they quickly pointed out—to an entity that had crossed scores of light-years and collected knowledge for thirty centuries!—that a mass of only a hundred kilograms would scarcely make an impressive dinosaur.

The Holmer did not mind. It was patient, and the children of earth were endlessly fascinating, in both their biology and their psychology. So were the young of all creatures—all, of course, that *did* have young. Having studied nine such species, the Holmer could now almost imagine what it must be like to grow up, mature, and die—almost, but not quite.

Spread out before the dozen humans and one non-human lay the empty land, its once luxuriant fields and forests blasted by the cold breaths from north and south. The graceful coconut palms had long since vanished, and even the gloomy pines that had succeeded them were naked skeletons, their roots destroyed by the spreading permafrost. No life was left upon the surface of the earth. Only in the oceanic abyss, where the planet's internal heat still kept the ice at bay, did a few blind, starveling creatures crawl and swim and devour each other.

Yet to a being whose home had circled a faint red star, the sun that blazed down from the cloudless sky seemed intolerably bright. Though all its warmth had gone, drained away by the sickness that had attacked its core a thousand years ago, its fierce, cold light revealed every detail of the stricken land, and flashed in splendor from the approaching glaciers.

For the children, still reveling in the powers of their awakening minds, the sub-zero temperatures were an exciting challenge. As they danced naked through the snowdrifts, bare feet kicking up clouds of powder-dry, shining crystals, their symbiotes often had to warn them: "Don't override your frostbite signals!" For they were not yet old enough to replace new limbs, without the help of their elders.

The oldest of the boys was showing off. He had launched a deliberate assault on the cold, announcing proudly that he was a fire-elemental. (The Star-holmer noted the term for future research, which would later cause It much perplexity.) All that could be seen of the small exhibitionist was a column of flame and steam, dancing to and fro along the ancient brickwork. The other children pointedly ignored this rather crude display.

To the Starholmer, however, it presented an interesting paradox. Just *why* had these people retreated to the inner planets, when they could have fought back the cold with the powers that they now possessed—as, indeed, their cousins were doing on Mars?

That was a question to which It had not received a satisfactory answer. It considered again the enigmatic reply given by ARISTOTLE, the entity with which It most easily communicated.

"For everything there is a season," the earth brain had replied. "There is a time to battle against Nature, and a time to obey her. True wisdom lies in making the right choice. When the long winter is over, man will return to an earth renewed and refreshed."

And so, during the past few centuries, the whole terrestrial population had streamed up the equatorial towers and flowed sunward toward the young oceans of Venus, the fertile plains of Mercury's temperate zone. Five hundred years hence, when the sun had recovered, the exiles would return. Mercury would be abandoned, except for the polar regions; but Venus would be a permanent second home. The quenching of the sun had given the incentive, and the opportunity, for the taming of that hellish world.

Important though they were, these matters concerned the Starholmer only indirectly. Its interest was focused upon more subtle aspects of human culture and society. Every species was unique, with its own surprises, its own idiosyncrasies. This one had introduced the Starholmer to the baffling concept of negative information—or, in the local terminology, humor, fantasy, myth.

As It grappled with these strange phenomena, the Starholmer had sometimes said despairingly to Itself: We will *never* understand human beings. On occasion, It had been so frustrated that It had feared an involuntary conjugation, with all the risks that entailed. But now It had made real progress. It could still re-

member Its satisfaction the first time It had made a
joke, and the children had all laughed.

Working with children had been the clue, again
provided by ARISTOTLE.

"There is an old saying: the child is father of the
man. Although the biological concept of 'father' is
alien to us both, in this context the word has a double
meaning—"

So here It was, hoping that the children would enable It to understand the adults into which they would
eventually metamorphize. Sometimes they told the
truth; but even when they were being playful (another
difficult concept) and dispensed negative information,
the Starholmer could now recognize the signs. . . .

Yet there were times when neither the children nor
the adults, nor even ARISTOTLE, knew the truth. There
seemed to be a continuous spectrum between absolute
fantasy and hard historical facts, with every possible
gradation between. At one end were such figures as
Columbus and Leonardo and Einstein and Lenin and
Newton and Washington, whose very voices and images had sometimes been preserved. At the other
extreme were Zeus and Alice and King Kong and Gul-
liver and Siegfried and Merlin, who could not *possibly*
have existed in the real world. But what was one to
make of Robin Hood and Tarzan and Christ and
Sherlock Holmes and Odysseus and Frankenstein? Allowing for a certain amount of exaggeration, they
might well have been actual historic personages. . . .

The Elephant Throne had changed little in three
and a half thousand years, but never before had it
supported the weight of so alien a visitor. As the
Starholmer stared into the south, It compared the half-
kilometer-wide column soaring from the mountain
peak with the feats of engineering It had seen on
other worlds. For such a young race, this was truly
impressive. Though it seemed always on the point of

toppling from the sky, it had stood now for fifteen centuries.

Not, of course, in its present form. The first hundred kilometers were now a vertical city—still occupied at some widely spaced levels—through which the sixteen sets of tracks had often carried a million passengers a day. Only two of those tracks were operating now; in a few hours, the Starholmer and Its escorts would be racing up that huge, fluted column, on the way back to the Ring City that encircled the globe.

The Holmer everted Its eyes to give telescopic vision, and slowly scanned the zenith. Yes, there it was —hard to see by day, but easy by night when the sunlight streaming past the shadow of earth still blazed upon it. The thin, shining band that split the sky into two hemispheres was a whole world in itself, where half a billion humans had opted for permanent zero-gravity life.

And up there beside Ring City was the starship that had carried the envoy and all the other Companions of the Hive across the interstellar gulfs. Even now it was being readied for departure—not with any sense of urgency, but several years ahead of schedule, in preparation for the next six-hundred-year lap of its journey.

That would represent no time at all to the Starholmer, of course, for It would not reconjugate until the end of the voyage. But then It might well face the greatest challenge of Its long career. For the first time, a Starprobe had been destroyed—or at least silenced —soon after it had entered a solar system. Perhaps it had at last made contact with the mysterious Hunters of the Dawn, who had left their marks upon so many worlds, so inexplicably close to the Beginning itself. If the Starholmer had been capable of awe, or of fear, It would have known both, as It contemplated Its future, six hundred years hence.

But now It was on the snow-dusted summit of Yakkagala, facing mankind's pathway to the stars. It summoned the children to Its side (they always understood when It *really* wished to be obeyed) and pointed to the mountain in the south.

"You know perfectly well," It said, with exasperation that was only partly feigned, "that Earthport One was built two thousand years *later* than this ruined palace."

The children all nodded in solemn agreement.

"Then why," asked the Starholmer, tracing the line from the zenith down to the summit of the mountain, *"why* do you call that column the Tower of Kalidasa?"

SOURCES AND ACKNOWLEDGMENTS

The writer of historical fiction has a peculiar responsibility to his readers, especially when he is dealing with unfamiliar times and places. He should not distort facts or events when they are known; and when he invents them, as he is often compelled to do, it is his duty to indicate the dividing line between imagination and reality.

The writer of science fiction has the same responsibility, squared. I hope that these notes will not only discharge that obligation well but also add to the reader's enjoyment.

TAPROBANE AND CEYLON

For dramatic reasons, I have made three trifling changes in the geography of Ceylon, now Sri Lanka. I have moved the island eight hundred kilometers south, so that it straddles the equator—as indeed it did twenty million years ago, and may someday do again. At the moment, it lies between six and ten degrees north.

In addition, I have doubled the height of the Sacred Mountain, and moved it closer to "Yakkagala." For both places exist, very much as I have described them.

Sri Pada, or Adam's Peak, is a striking cone-shaped mountain sacred to the Buddhists, the Muslims, the

Hindus, and the Christians, and bears a small temple on its summit. Inside the temple is a stone slab with a depression which, though two meters long, is reputed to be the footprint of the Buddha.

Every year, for many centuries, thousands of pilgrims have made the long climb to the 2,240-meter-high summit. The ascent is no longer dangerous, for there are two stairways (which must surely be the longest in the world) to the very top. I have climbed once, at the instigation of the *New Yorker's* Jeremy Bernstein (see his *Experiencing Science*), and my legs were paralyzed for several days afterward. But it was worth the effort, because we were lucky enough to see the beautiful and awe-inspiring spectacle of the peak's shadow at dawn—a perfectly symmetrical cone visible only for the few minutes after sunrise, and stretching almost to the horizon on the clouds far below.

I have since explored the mountain with much less effort in a Sri Lanka Air Force helicopter, getting close enough to the temple to observe the resigned expressions on the faces of the monks, now accustomed to such noisy intrusions.

The rock fortress of Yakkagala is actually Sigiriya (or Sigiri, "Lion Rock"), the reality of which is so astonishing that I have had no need to change it in any way. The only liberties I have taken are chronological. The palace on the summit was (according to the Sinhalese Chronicle the *Culavamsa*) built during the reign of the parricide King Kasyapa 1 (A.D. 478-495). However, it seems incredible that so vast an undertaking could have been carried out in a mere eighteen years by a usurper expecting to be challenged at any moment, and the real history of Sigiriya may well go back for many centuries before these dates.

The character, motivation, and actual fate of Kasyapa have been the subject of much controversy, recently fueled by the posthumously published *The*

Story of Sigiri (Lake House, Colombo, 1972), by the Sinhalese scholar Professor Senerat Paranavitana. I am also indebted to his monumental two-volume study of the inscriptions on the Mirror Wall, *Sigiri Graffiti* (Oxford University Press, 1956). Some of the verses I have quoted are genuine; others I have only slightly invented.

The frescoes which are Sigiriya's greatest glory have been handsomely reproduced in *Ceylon: Paintings from Temple, Shrine and Rock* (New York Graphic Society/UNESCO, 1957). Plate V shows the most interesting—and the one, alas, destroyed in the 1960's by unknown vandals. The attendant is clearly *listening* to the mysterious hinged box she is holding in her right hand. It remains unidentified, the local archaeologists refusing to take seriously my suggestion that it is an early Sinhalese transistor radio.

The legend of Sigiriya has recently been brought to the screen by Dimitri de Grunwald, in his production *The God King,* with Leigh Lawson as a very impressive Kasyapa.

THE SPACE ELEVATOR

This apparently outrageous concept was first presented to the West in a letter in the issue of *Science* for 11 February 1966, "Satellite Elongation into a True 'Sky-Hook,' " by John D. Isaacs, Hugh Bradner, and George E. Backus, of Scripps Institution of Oceanography, and Allyn C. Vine of Woods Hole Oceanographic Institution. Though it may seem odd that oceanographers should get involved with such an idea, this is not surprising when one realizes that they are about the only people (since the great days of barrage balloons) who concern themselves with very long cables hanging under their own weight. (Dr. Allyn

Vine's name, incidentally, is now immortalized in that of the famous research submersible *Alvin*.)

It was later discovered that the concept had already been developed, six years earlier, and on a much more ambitious scale, by a Leningrad engineer, Y. N. Artsutanov (*Komsomolskaya Pravda,* 31 July 1960). Artsutanov considered a "heavenly funicular," to use his engaging name for the device, lifting no less than twelve thousand tons a day to synchronous orbit. It seems surprising that this daring idea received so little publicity; the only mention I have ever seen of it is in the handsome volume of paintings by Alexei A. Leonov and Andrei K. Sokolov, *The Stars Are Awaiting Us* (Moscow, 1967). One color plate (page 25) shows the "Space Elevator" in action. The caption reads: ". . . the satellite will, so to say, stay fixed in a certain point in the sky. If a cable is lowered from the satellite to the earth you will have a ready cable-road. An 'Earth-Sputnik-Earth' elevator for freight and passengers can then be built, and it will operate without any rocket propulsion."

Although General Leonov gave me a copy of his book at the Vienna "Peaceful Uses of Space" conference in 1968, the idea simply failed to register on me —despite the fact that the elevator is shown hovering exactly over Sri Lanka! I probably thought that Cosmonaut Leonov, a noted humorist, was just having a little joke. (He is also a superb diplomat. After the Vienna screening, he made quite the nicest comment on 2001 I've ever heard: "Now I feel I've been in space *twice*." Presumably after the Apollo-Soyuz mission he would say *"three* times.")

The space elevator is quite clearly an idea whose time has come, as is demonstrated by the fact that within a decade of the 1966 Isaacs *et al*. letter it was independently reinvented at least three times. A detailed treatment, containing many new ideas, "The

Orbital Tower: A Spacecraft Launcher Using the Earth's Rotational Energy," was published by Jerome Pearson, of Wright-Patterson Air Force Base, in *Acta Astronautica* for September–October 1975. Dr. Pearson was astonished to hear of the earlier studies, which his computer survey had failed to locate. He discovered them through reading my own testimony to the House of Representatives Committee on Space Science and Applications in July 1975. (*See* "The View from Serendip.")

Six years earlier A. R. Collar and J. W. Flower had come to essentially the same conclusions in their paper "A (Relatively) Low Altitude 24-hour Satellite" in the *Journal of the British Interplanetary Society,* Vol. 22, pp. 442–457, 1969. They were looking into the possibility of suspending a synchronous communications satellite far below the natural thirty-six-thousand-kilometer altitude, and did not discuss taking the cable all the way down to the surface of the earth, but this is an obvious extension of their treatment.

And now for a modest cough. Back in 1963, in an essay commissioned by UNESCO and published in *Astronautics* for February 1964, "The World of the Communications Satellite" (now available in *Voices from the Sky*), I wrote: "As a much longer term possibility, it might be mentioned that there are a number of theoretical ways of achieving a *low-altitude, twenty-four-hour satellite;* but they depend upon technical developments unlikely to occur in this century. I leave their contemplation as an exercise for the student."

The first of these "theoretical ways" was, of course, the suspended satellite discussed by Collar and Flower. My crude back-of-an-envelope calculations, based on the strength of existing materials, made me so skeptical of the whole idea that I did not bother to spell it out in detail. If I had been a little less conservative—

or if a larger envelope had been available—I might have been ahead of everyone except Artsutanov himself.

As this book is, I hope, more a novel than an engineering treatise, those who wish to go into technical details are referred to the now rapidly expanding literature on the subject. Recent examples include Jerome Pearson's "Using the Orbital Tower to Launch Earth-Escape Payloads Daily" (*Proceedings* of the 27th International Astronautical Federation Congress, October 1976) and a remarkable paper by Hans Moravec, "A Non-Synchronous Orbital Skyhook" (American Astronautical Society Annual Meeting, San Francisco, 18–20 October 1977).

I am much indebted to my friends the late A. V. Cleaver, of Rolls-Royce, Dr. Ing. Harry O. Ruppe, Professor of Astronautics at the Technical University of Munich's Lehrstuhl für Raumfahrttechnic, and Dr. Alan Bond, of the Culham Laboratories, for their valuable comments on the Orbital Tower. They are not responsible for my modifications.

Walter L. Morgan (no relation to Vannevar Morgan, as far as I know) and Gary Gordon, of the COMSAT Laboratories, as well as L. Perek, of the United Nations Outer Space Affairs Division, have provided most useful information on the stable regions of the synchronous orbit. They have pointed out that natural forces, particularly sun-moon effects, would cause major oscillations, especially in the north-south directions. Thus "Taprobane" might not be as advantageous as I have suggested; but it would still be better than anywhere else.

The importance of a high-altitude site is also debatable, and I am indebted to Sam Brand, of the U.S. Naval Environmental Prediction Research Facility, Monterey, California, for information on equatorial winds. If it turns out that the tower *could* be safely taken down to sea level, then the Maldive island of Gan (recently evacuated by the Royal Air Force) may be the twenty-second century's most valuable piece of real estate.

Finally, it seems a very strange—and even scary— coincidence that, years before I ever thought of the subject of this novel, I myself should have unconsciously gravitated (*sic*) toward its locale. The house I acquired a decade ago on my favorite Sri Lankan beach (see *The Treasure of the Great Reef* and *The View from Serendip*) is at *precisely* the closest spot on any large body of land to the point of maximum geosynchronous stability.

So, in my retirement I hope to watch the other superannuated relics of the early Space Age, milling around in the orbital Sargasso Sea immediately above my head.

Colombo
1969–1978

And now, one of those extraordinary coincidences I have learned to take for granted . . .

While correcting the proofs of this novel, I received from Dr. Jerome Pearson a copy of NASA Technical Memorandum TM-75174, "A Space 'Necklace' About the Earth," by G. Polyakov. This is a translation of "Kosmicheskoye 'Ozhere'ye' Zemli," published in *Teknika Molodezhi,* No. 4, 1977, pp. 41-43.

In this brief but stimulating paper, Dr. Polyakov, of the Astrakhan Teaching Institute, describes in precise engineering detail Morgan's final vision of a continuous ring around the world. He sees this as a natural extension of the space elevator, whose construction and operation he also discusses in a manner virtually identical with my own treatment.

I salute *Tovarich* Polyakov, and am beginning to

wonder if, yet again, I have been too conservative. Perhaps the Orbital Tower may be an achievement of the twenty-first century, not the twenty-second.

Our own grandchildren may demonstrate that—sometimes—Gigantic is Beautiful.

Colombo
18 *September* 1978